Master Wycliffe's Summons

The chronicles of Hugh de Singleton, surgeon

Master Wycliffe's Summons

The fourteenth chronicle of Hugh de Singleton, surgeon

MEL STARR

LION FICTION

Published by **Lion Fiction**
www.lionhudson.com
Part of the SPCK Group
SPCK, 36 Causton Street, London, SW1P 4ST

ISBN 978 1 78264 347 0
e-ISBN 978 1 78264 348 7

First edition 2021

Acknowledgments
Extracts from The Authorized (King James) Version. Rights in the Authorized Version are vested in the Crown. Reproduced by permission of the Crown's patentee, Cambridge University Press.

A catalogue record for this book is available from the British Library

For
Kevin Kwilinski
and
Jeremy Reivitt

Acknowledgments

Several years ago, when Dr Dan Runyon, Professor of English at Spring Arbor University, learned that I had written an as-yet unpublished medieval mystery, he invited me to speak to his fiction-writing class about the trials of a rookie writer seeking a publisher. He sent chapters of Hugh de Singleton's first chronicle, *The Unquiet Bones*, to his friend Tony Collins at Lion Hudson. Thanks, Dan.

Tony has since retired, but many thanks to him and all those at Lion Hudson who saw Hugh de Singleton's potential. Thanks also to my editors: first, Jan Greenough, then Penelope Wilcock, and now Fiona Veitch Smith, who know Hugh well and excel at asking questions like, "Do you really want to say it this way?" and "Wouldn't Hugh do it like this?"

Dr. John Blair of Queen's College, Oxford, has written several papers about Bampton history. These have been valuable in helping me create an accurate time and place for Hugh.

In the summer of 1990 Susan and I found a delightful B&B in Mavesyn Ridware, a village north of Lichfield. Proprietors Tony and Lis Page became friends, and when they moved to Bampton some years later invited us to visit them there. Tony and Lis introduced me to Bampton and became a great source of information about the village. Tony died in March 2015, only a few months after being diagnosed with cancer. He is greatly missed.

Glossary

Ambler: an easy-riding horse, because it moved both right legs together, then both left legs.

Angelus: a devotional celebrated three times each day – dawn, noon, and dusk. Announced by the ringing of the church bell.

Beans eyffred: a dish of beans, onions, and garlic. The ingredients were boiled, then fried in oil or lard. Served with sugar and cinnamon if available.

Beating the bounds: a Rogation Day procession around the parish boundaries. Small boys were encouraged to swat boundary trees and rocks as an aid to memory.

Braes: medieval underpants.

Buboe: the inflammatory swelling of a lymph gland.

Burgher: a town merchant or tradesman.

Capon: a castrated male chicken. They could grow quite large and fat.

Chauces: tight-fitting trousers, sometimes of different colors for each leg.

Coppice: to cut back a tree to stimulate growth of young shoots from the roots. These were used for anything from arrows to rafters, depending on how much they were permitted to grow.

Cotehardie: the primary medieval outer garment. Women's were floor-length, men's ranged from thigh to ankle.

Couch: to treat a cataract by displacing the clouded lens of the eye into the vitreous humor.

Cresset: a bowl of oil with a floating wick used as a lamp.

Daub: a clay-and-plaster mix, reinforced with straw and/or horsehair, used to plaster the exterior of a house or create interior walls.

Farthing: one-fourth of a penny. The smallest silver coin.

Fewterer: the keeper of a lord's hunting dogs.

Galantyne: a sauce made with cinnamon, ginger, vinegar, and breadcrumbs.

Gentleman: a nobleman. The term had nothing to do with character or behavior.

Gongfermour: a laborer who cleaned cesspits.

Hanoney: an omelette with chopped fried onions.

Kirtle: the basic medieval undershirt.

Lammastide: August 1, when thanks was given for a successful wheat harvest. From Old English "Loaf Mass".

Lauds: the first canonical office of the day, celebrated at dawn.

Liripipe: a fashionably long tail to a man's cap, usually wound about the head rather than allowed to hang loose.

Lychgate: a roofed gate in a churchyard wall under which the corpse rested during the initial part of a funeral.

Marshalsea: the stables and their assorted accoutrements.

Martinmas: November 11. The traditional date to slaughter animals for winter food.

Maslin: bread made from a mixture of grains, commonly wheat and rye, or barley and rye.

Nine men's morris: a board game similar to tic-tac-toe but much more complicated.

Nones: the fifth canonical office, sung at the ninth hour – about 3 p.m.

Palfrey: a riding horse with a comfortable gait.

Pannage: to turn hogs loose in an autumn forest to fatten on roots and acorns.

Passing bell: ringing of the parish church bell to indicate the death of a resident of the parish.

Paternoster: literally, "Our Father", the Lord's Prayer.

Porre of peas: peas simmered until they burst, then in cold water the hulls are rubbed off. Returned to stock with chopped onions, salt, sugar, and saffron. Served hot.

Pottage: anything cooked in one pot, from soup and stews to simple porridge.

Pottage of whelks: whelks boiled, cleaned, and removed from shells. Then chopped finely, returned to stock with breadcrumbs, almond milk, saffron, pepper, and ground cumin. Served hot.

Ravioles: pastries filled with cheese, beaten eggs, occasionally minced pork or poultry, and spices.

Refectory: the dining room.

Remove: a course at dinner.

Runcie: a common horse of a lower grade than a palfrey.

Sackbut: an early form of trombone or trumpet.

St. Beornwald's Church: today the church of St. Mary the Virgin. In the fourteenth century it was dedicated to an obscure Saxon saint enshrined in the church.

Screens passage: a narrow corridor which "screened" the hall from the kitchen and from which the buttery and pantry were accessed.

Set books: the standard texts used by medieval university students.

Sexton: a church officer who cares for church property and related duties, such as bell ringing and grave digging.

Shilling: twelve pence. Twenty shillings made a pound, but there were no coins worth either a shilling or a pound.

Solar: a small private room in a castle, more easily heated than the great hall, where lords preferred to spend time, especially in winter.

Sophist: a teacher of rhetoric and philosophy in Ancient Greece. Associated with moral skepticism and specious reasoning, and an egotistic view of their own knowledge.

Squab: a young dove about four or five weeks old.

Statute of Laborers: following the plague of 1348–49, laborers realized their labor was in short supply and demanded higher wages. In 1351, parliament set wages at the 1347 level. The statute was generally a failure.

Stockfish: inexpensive fish, usually dried and salted cod or haddock, consumed on fast days.

Stone: fourteen pounds.

Tabula: a plank which, when struck, signaled time for dinner in a monastery.

Vespers: the sixth canonical office, celebrated at the approach of dusk.

Vigils: the night office, celebrated at midnight. When the service was completed Benedictines went back to bed, Cistercians stayed up for the new day.

Wattle: interlacing sticks used as a foundation and support for daub in building the wall of a house.

Yardland: about thirty acres. Also called a virgate, and in northern England an oxgang.

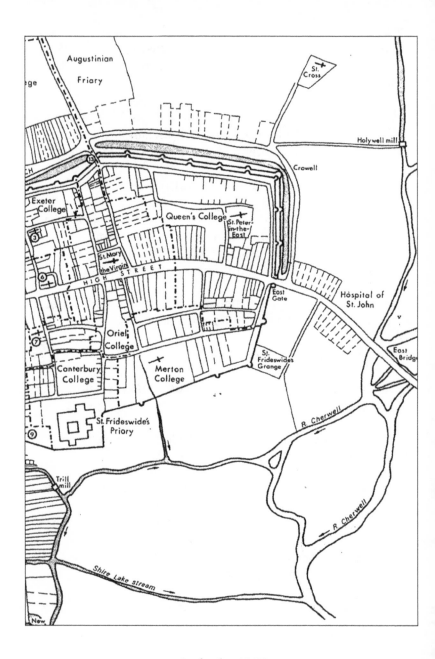

Oxford *c*.1375

Chapter 1

Bessie was perturbed that she could not join the lads of her acquaintance in wrenching new boughs from bushes and shrubs with which to beat the bounds of St. Beornwald's parish. 'Twas no use explaining to her that beating the bounds on Rogation Day was a thing boys did, not lasses. To all such assertions my daughter had one reply: "Why?"

"Because," I said, "'tis the way of things."

This reply was unsatisfactory. As Kate, Bessie, and John followed me to the procession I saw my daughter surreptitiously yank a tall weed from the roadside. She began to flick this stem at the trees, rocks, and stream that formed the parish boundaries, emulating the young males who were learning the boundaries of the parish. Their fathers and grandfathers had done the same for generations past, and their children and grandchildren would surely do likewise in years to come.

When the procession was completed, villagers gathered in the castle forecourt for the parish ale. Lord Gilbert provided the feast, and folk helped themselves to tables heaped with maslin loaves and stockfish from a barrel of salted cod. A few washed the meal down with too much of Lord Gilbert's ale and so, as night fell, wobbled unsteadily to their homes.

A golden sunset illuminated the spire of St. Beornwald's Church as Kate and I, with Bessie and John, made our way home to Galen House. The night before, a raging thunderstorm had battered the village, but clouds had cleared at dawn and the day had been bright and washed clean by the deluge.

My son dropped a sleepy head to my shoulder as I carried him up Church View Street to our home. And Bessie walked quietly, fatigued by the long walk circumscribing Bampton and the Weald. I and my family would sleep well this night.

Men wish to know the future, and seek those who claim to see it. The stars foretell what is to come, some say. But to know one's destiny would be to see sorrow as well as joy, and perhaps more of the first than the second. Holy Writ says that sufficient to the day is the evil thereof. So I rested my head upon my pillow that evening with no thought of what was in store. I am Sir Hugh de Singleton, surgeon, and bailiff to Lord Gilbert, Third Baron Talbot, at his manor of Bampton.

Thursday, at the third hour, I heard a rapping upon Galen House door and opened to two red-gowned youths. Scholars from Queen's College, Oxford, from their appearance. I soon learned that this surmise was accurate.

"I give you good day," one of the lads said. "We seek Sir Hugh de Singleton."

"You have found him," I replied. "How may I serve you?"

"I am William Sleyt. Here is Thomas Rous. Master John Wycliffe has sent us."

"Enter, and tell how I may be of service to Master Wycliffe."

"We are of Queen's College, and study with Wycliffe. Two days past one of Master Wycliffe's students perished."

I nodded, but did not reply. What was I to say of the death of a scholar I did not know? I felt sure I would soon learn more. I did.

"'Twas when a thunderstorm passed over Oxford," the lad continued. "We who lodge in chambers at Queen's heard a great crash, as if a bolt of lightning had struck the hall."

"The thunder was deafening," the other scholar agreed.

"When the storm had passed we emerged to see what damage was done. 'Twas then we found Richard."

"Dead, struck by lightning," the second youth said. "So we thought."

"What has this sorry event to do with me?" I asked.

"Master Wycliffe wishes you to attend him. He is not content that Richard was struck down by lightning and asks for you to investigate the matter."

"I serve Lord Gilbert Talbot. He does not pay me to inquire into matters at Queen's College."

"You will not come? Master Wycliffe has told us how you found his stolen books and unraveled other knotty incidents."

"Wycliffe suspects this scholar's death due to the act of a man rather than a storm?"

"Aye, he does, and asks for you to investigate the matter."

"What of the sheriff? Can he not inquire into the death?"

"Master Wycliffe asked Sir Roger, but could not convince him that the death was suspicious."

"What has caused him to believe a murder may have been done?"

"He has not confided in us. We know only that he is troubled and sent us to you, begging you to come to Oxford and sort out the matter."

My Kate had heard the conversation from the kitchen, where she and Adela – her servant – were preparing our dinner. She appeared in the doorway and her words surprised me.

"'Tis an honor that Master Wycliffe seeks your aid," she said. "Mayhap Lord Gilbert will release you from your duties here."

"You wish to be rid of me?" I said.

"Nay. But I know the regard you have for Master Wycliffe. If you refuse this request you will fret about the decision for weeks to come. Especially if it is so that murder has been done. With Adela's aid I can keep Galen House in good order... I have done so in the past when you were called away."

"When do you return to Oxford?" I asked the scholars.

"As soon as we have your answer."

"You may tell Master John that I will come to him tomorrow, so long as Lord Gilbert is agreeable. If you depart Bampton now and make haste, you may cross Bookbinders Bridge before nightfall."

After a hurried dinner of porre of peas with bacon, shared with the scholars, I sought the castle and my employer. Lord Gilbert, his household knights, his guests and servants, had but moments earlier finished their dinner. From the skeletal remains I saw that several roasted geese had been a feature of the last remove.

Lord Gilbert was about to depart the hall when he saw me approach. I lifted a hand to indicate a desire to speak and he waited at the screens passage.

"I give you good day, Hugh. Have you a matter for my consideration?"

"Aye."

"Then come. We will discuss it in the solar."

The day was sunny and warm so no fire burned upon the hearth. Lord Gilbert's solar has windows of glass, both clear and stained. Tapestries cunningly embroidered with hunting scenes cover two walls. Lady Petronilla and her maids did the work, before her untimely death, and I suspect that when Lord Gilbert looks at them he thinks of his lost wife. The lady has been deceased for several years, but he has not chosen another bride, although suitable candidates are plentiful. The solar is Lord Gilbert's favorite room, and especially does he seek it in winter, when, being smaller, 'tis more easily warmed than the hall.

My employer bade me be seated, and dropped into a thickly padded chair. Lord Gilbert enjoys a good meal, and this delight has increased his girth since I first came to his service more than a decade past. He still sits a horse well, but the beast does not enjoy the experience.

"What matter do you bring to me?" he said.

"Master John Wycliffe has requested that I attend him in Oxford."

"Why so?"

"You remember the thunderstorm that shattered our repose two days past? The same storm struck Oxford, and when it had passed a scholar of Queen's College was found dead in his chamber. Struck by lightning, men said."

"So what has this death to do with Master Wycliffe – or you?"

"Wycliffe is not satisfied that the lad's death came because of a lightning bolt. Your friend, Sheriff Elmerugg, disagrees and will not be bothered by sending a serjeant to inquire into the matter. So Master John asks me to seek the truth of the business."

"You wish my permission to leave your duties here?"

"Aye."

"You have it. Crops are planted, the harvest is yet months away, and, so far as I know, you have no local miscreants to deal with."

"Can you also spare Arthur Wagge?" I asked.

"Ah…your assistant in times past, when apprehending felons required some brawn. His son is now full grown, you know, and is the image of the father."

Arthur's son serves Lord Gilbert at Goodrich Castle. I've not seen the lad, but have heard that he is as sturdy as his father.

"Arthur has a brain to go with his brawn," I said. "Little escapes his notice."

"Aye, he does. I'll leave the matter to him, but I suspect he will be eager to assist you. And I'll inform the marshalsea to have beasts made ready. When? Will you leave tomorrow?"

"Aye."

Arthur was pleased to accompany me. Service as a groom to a great lord often requires onerous duties – mucking out the stables, for example – so a few days in Oxford appealed.

As Lord Gilbert said, Arthur is a sturdy fellow. His form resembles a wine cask set upon two coppiced stumps. He is not constructed so as to be able to chase down and catch a fleeing felon, but the miscreant who chases and catches Arthur will regret his success.

My Kate was pleased to learn that I would not travel to Oxford alone. King Edward is in his dotage, it is said, and cares for little but pleasing Alice Perrers. Prince Edward is ill, and not capable of governing in his father's place. So those who would do evil feel themselves unrestrained. Good and evil are always at war, and good men must decide what they will do about this conflict. Many seek the safety of home and hearth, for to oppose villains may be dangerous. I bear scars from Lord Gilbert's service to prove it so. I pray that I will never be found wanting when it is my duty to oppose miscreants.

The clear sky of Thursday gave way to clouds and mist on Friday. I kissed my Kate farewell at the second hour, hugged Bessie and John, and extracted from my daughter a promise to be helpful to her mother whilst I was away. Bessie may have trouble keeping this pledge. She can be an energetic child. I would not have her be otherwise, although at some future time her husband might wish her less obstreperous.

The morning mist gave way to broken clouds and sun by the time we crossed Bookbinders Bridge. The city glowed, its spires tracing the scudding clouds, reflected in the puddled streets. I knew of a stable just off High Street where we might leave Lord Gilbert's palfreys, and from thence we sought an inn where we might consume a belated dinner. The Green Dragon served a pottage of whelks that day, which met with my approval, but Arthur seemed to find the meal unappealing, unlike his usual robust appetite.

Master Wycliffe's dinner was not so toothsome. We found him in his chamber at Queen's College, munching upon a maslin loaf whilst he bent over a book open upon a table. His door was open, and when my shadow interrupted the light he looked up. I was surprised to see how grey his beard had become.

"Ah, Master Hugh… nay, 'tis Sir Hugh now. I forgot. William told me you had agreed to come. He told you why I have asked for your aid, did he not?"

"Aye. A scholar of the college is dead of a lightning bolt, but mayhap not."

"No 'mayhap' about his death, but I suspect a bolt of lightning had nothing to do with Richard's demise."

"Why do you think this?" I asked.

Wycliffe pushed the remainder of his loaf aside, took a quick draft from a cup of ale, then said, "Come with me and I will show you."

For a decade and more after its founding, Queen's was but a hall, with no building of its own. Its scholars, most poor lads from Cumberland, met with fellows in whatever chambers they could find. But now Queen's has a stone structure – two stories high, with a sturdy slate roof – where its students and their masters may reside and study and dispute.

Wycliffe led us to a stairway, thence to the upper floor. A narrow corridor divided the chambers, each of these no more than five paces long by three paces wide. Near to the end of this passage Wycliffe stopped and pointed into a chamber. The door to this chamber stood open, and I saw that it was askew upon its hinges and likely could not be closed completely.

"'Twas here Richard lived... and died," Wycliffe said. "The chamber is as it was when Richard was found. I asked that it remain unmolested when I saw things which troubled me."

"What things?" I asked.

"I'll not say. To do so might influence your opinion. Examine the chamber for yourself and decide if it has the appearance of a place damaged by a lightning bolt."

I did so. As the damaged door was at hand, I first inspected that. 'Twas not fashioned of oaken planks, but beech. The strength of oak was not required. The nails which held the upper hinge to the jamb had pulled loose, and one of the beech planks was split from top to bottom. Only a crossbuck held the plank together.

Straw from the scholar's mattress, and feathers from his pillow, littered the chamber. The wooden frame which had supported the mattress was splintered, and the desk upon which the lad had studied was tilted. One leg had been cracked away. The skin window above the desk was tattered and allowed the summer breeze to enter the room. Even so, the fresh air could not dispel the scent of burning and sulfur which yet permeated the place.

The walls which separated the chamber from those adjoining were of wattle and daub and flimsy. They were not made to resist the blast of a lightning bolt, so were bowed out. The daub was cracked and some was scattered about the floor with the straw and feathers. The ceiling likewise was cracked, with chunks of daub fallen away from the wattles.

Sunlight penetrated the chamber through the shattered ceiling, and where roofing slates were missing I saw sky and clouds between the exposed rafters. Where were the missing slates? Was their absence from the chamber floor one of the things which troubled Wycliffe?

"I would like to see the lane outside this window," I said.

Arthur and Master Wycliffe followed me down the stairs and out into Queen's Lane. I looked up to the tattered window skin of the blasted chamber, then examined the ground. I saw there a few fragments of slate which had been dislodged from the roof. There had been no slate driven into the chamber – at least none which I could see. Why would a bolt of lightning send pieces of slate outward rather than in? Perhaps there may be a reason. I am not well versed in the behavior of lightning, preferring to be elsewhere when it strikes.

But one thing I do know of lightning bolts is that they tend to strike the highest point close by. The hole in Queen's College roof was nearer to the eave than the peak, and across the lane was the squat tower of St. Peter-in-the-East, which loomed above the scene.

Master John watched as I studied the fractured roof and the church tower, but held his tongue. Arthur was not so reticent.

"Seen a tree what was struck by lightning. Me uncle had a barn near, an' it was unmarred. Tree was taller, an' was split top to bottom. Blew the bark off ten paces. Wonder why that church tower didn't get the bolt."

I wondered the same.

"Strange, is it not," Wycliffe finally said, "that lightning would strike where it should not?"

"This is why you suspect that the scholar died due to some other cause?"

"Among other reasons. Did you notice the stink in Richard's chamber?"

"There was a hint of brimstone, I thought."

"Indeed. 'Twas stronger two days past, but persists."

"I've not heard of lightning producing sulfur," I said.

"Nor I," Master John agreed. "Come. Return with me to Richard's chamber. I will show you another troubling thing, which mayhap you did not notice."

We again ascended the stairs and I studied the chamber anew, curious as to what might have caught Wycliffe's eye that I had missed. 'Twas the mark upon the planks of the floor, under the remains of the scholar's shattered bed.

Master John saw me gaze at the blackened boards and said, "Bend low. The smell of sulfur there is yet great."

I did and it was. Upon the floorboards where the splintered bed would have rested was a circular black patch, with rays extending out from the center as far as my arm is long. Here was the place where the sulfurous odor originated, for the stink of rotten eggs was strong.

"Was the scholar burned upon his body," I asked, "where the lightning bolt would have passed through him to strike the floor?"

"Nay. Nor was there a hole burned through his blanket. See, here it is."

Master John went to a corner of the chamber and fetched the blanket. It was ragged, as might be expected of a poor scholar, but there was no blackened hole in it.

"What say you, Sir Hugh?" Wycliffe asked as I studied the threadbare blanket.

"I have read *Opus Majus*," I said.

"As have I," Master John replied. "Has Roger Bacon told us from the grave what has happened here?"

"It may be so," I agreed.

Chapter 2

Arthur peered quizzically at me. "Who's Roger Bacon, an' how can a man dead an' buried speak?"

"He was a great scholar of a century past," I said. "*Opus Majus* is his great work, a book which explains all of natural science."

"An' lightnin'?"

"Nay," I replied. "I remember nothing of lightning."

"Sir Hugh and I," Master John said, "believe this destruction due to another cause. One that Bacon knew of. Not lightning."

Arthur's brows furrowed. The man was clearly confused. I did my best to enlighten him.

"Bacon wrote of a substance which he considered a child's amusement, made of saltpeter, sulfur, and charcoal, a quantity of which no larger than your thumb will, when a flame is put to it, assault the ear with the roar of thunder and a flash as brilliant as lightning."

"Like what 'appened 'ere?"

"Indeed," I said. Then, to Master Wycliffe, "What of the scholars whose chambers adjoin this? The blast must have been deafening. Have they spoken of it? Of course they would have. What was their experience?"

"You should speak to them yourself. They will be at a disputation conducted by the provost, but should return shortly."

Arthur had been pulling his beard thoughtfully as I spoke. "Me father was with Lord Gilbert's father at Crecy.

Said King Edward 'ad some weapons what could send a stone ball to the enemy. Poured some black powdery stuff in first, then the ball, an' when a flame was put to it the ball got sent on its way with a great roar. This the same stuff, you think?"

"Aye," I replied. "As Bacon wrote, 'tis a mixture of saltpeter, sulfur, and charcoal. I do not remember the proportions, but it seems to me the compound was three-quarters saltpeter."

"This is my recollection also," Wycliffe said.

"What is saltpeter?" Arthur asked.

"'Tis a salt extracted from urine," I replied.

Arthur's eyes widened. "You mean my urine can explode?"

"It is not likely to without refinement. But yes, if dealt with properly, the element is present which can send a stone ball crashing into a castle wall."

"Men are always seeking advantage when looking at ways to slay one another," Master John said softly. "Holy Writ tells that God, after the Flood, said the next time he destroyed mankind 'twould be with fire. Mayhap men will destroy themselves with this new fire without God's aid."

We heard voices from below, and then footsteps upon the stairs. The disputation was ended and the scholars, some of them, were returning to their chambers. The first of these entered the passage and hesitated when he saw Master Wycliffe standing with two strangers.

"Ah, Martyn," Wycliffe greeted the lad. "You are well met. Come and greet Sir Hugh de Singleton and his man Arthur."

The scholar, a youth of ruddy complexion and perhaps seventeen or eighteen years, approached and bowed, as lads are taught to do when introduced to men whose names are preceded by "sir".

"Sir Hugh," Wycliffe continued, "is investigating Richard Sabyn's death. You know I am not satisfied that the storm caused his demise."

The lad looked from Master John to me, anticipating my questions. I did not disappoint him.

"I am told that upon the night Richard died lightning flashed and thunder roared. Surely, then, you were awakened. Which chamber is yours?"

"Just here... next to Richard's. Lay awake in my bed. The storm was dreadful."

"You were awake when the blast slew Richard? It must have been louder, even, than the thunder which preceded it."

"Oh, aye, it was."

"And the flash of lightning which preceded this great crash – was it brighter than others for being so near?"

The lad hesitated. "Nay. Don't recall any flash. Just the terrible noise. The thunder knocked plaster from the wall of my chamber. The wattles between Richard's chamber and my own held firm. Well, mostly. Bent a little. But my blanket was covered with dust and bits of plaster. Got in my mouth, too."

"But you do not remember the lightning flash as the destruction came?"

"Nay."

Master John listened to this conversation whilst chewing upon his lip.

"You told Master Wycliffe of this? That you saw no great flash of lightning?"

"Aye. Next morning. When Simon found Richard."

"Simon?"

"Simon Duby. Has the chamber the other side of Richard's."

"Where is Simon? Was he at the disputation?"

"Aye. Stayed behind to speak to Master Whitfield."

"The provost," Wycliffe explained.

25

At that moment more voices came from the ground floor, then footsteps clattered upon the stairs. Three scholars appeared in the passage, their youthful chatter suddenly stilled when they saw their friend, Master Wycliffe, and two strangers standing before the open door to Richard Sabyn's chamber.

"Ah," Wycliffe said. "Here is Simon. Come, lad. Meet Sir Hugh de Singleton, brought to Queen's to investigate Richard's death." Master John nodded in my direction as he spoke.

Two of the scholars stood rooted to the planks, but one hesitantly approached. Simon, I assumed. The lad was slender, all knees and elbows beneath his gown, and with an Adam's apple of memorable proportions. I wondered if his fellows made sport of the organ.

As Simon approached warily, the scholar gave the impression that everything he did was done cautiously. He did not look me in the eye, but gazed at his feet, which were shod in shoes as over-proportioned as his knees, elbows, and Adam's apple.

"Three days past," I began, "did you lay awake in the night whilst the storm raged over Oxford?"

"Aye, sir. No man could sleep through such a tempest."

"Martyn said 'twas you who discovered Richard Sabyn dead."

"Aye."

"Was this discovery later, after the storm had passed, or while it yet raged?"

"Later. Dawn."

"Did so great a blast as that which slew your neighbor not rouse you to discover what damage was done?"

"Aye, sir. It did. But 'twas dark but for the lightning flashes and when I opened my door I saw nothing amiss."

"There is a window at the end of the corridor," I said, and nodded toward it. "Did not a flash or two of lightning illuminate the passage enough that you could see Richard's damaged door?"

"Not so much that I could see harm done."

"Martyn said he saw no flash of lightning before the roar of thunder which brought plaster down upon his head. Did you?"

"See a lightning flash? Before the blast? Nay. 'Twas as Martyn said. But the night was so lit by lightning 'twas difficult to discern one strike from another. Constant, they were."

"'Twas much the same in Bampton," I said.

"Where Sir Hugh serves Lord Gilbert Talbot as bailiff," Master John explained in response to Simon's blank expression.

"How was it that you found Richard?" I said.

"When I left my bed at dawn I saw the wall betwixt his chamber and mine was bowed and the plaster cracked and fallen upon my floor and blanket. 'Twas a mess. I was curious as to the damage the lightning bolt might have done there."

"You did not know the damage to your chamber until dawn?"

"Nay. Knew only that bits of plaster had fallen upon me."

"What did you see when you approached Richard's door?"

"'Twas as you said. The door was askew upon its hinges, and split."

"Did you open it then to learn what had happened to Richard?"

Simon hesitated, then spoke. "Not then. Richard did not welcome visitors to his chamber."

"When did you discover that he was dead?"

"Stood before his door, wondering what I should do. Thought to seek the provost, or Master Wycliffe."

"But you did not?"

"Nay. Not then. Called out Richard's name."

"And there was no response?"

"None. Spoke his name again, louder. When I could not rouse him I put my eye to the crack in his door. 'Twas then I saw him splayed upon the floor."

"Did you then enter?"

"Aye. Had to put a shoulder to the door to force it open. I thought I might be of assistance to Richard."

"But you found him dead?"

"Aye. Cold and stiff, he was."

Rigor mortis will cause the dead to become rigid within four or five hours of death. Then, after a day or so, the corpse will become flexible again. This knowledge was of no use in discovering why Richard Sabyn had died, and I already knew when. Or thought I did.

"You went then to seek Master Wycliffe?"

"Aye," Wycliffe said. "Simon was white with dread and plaster dust. Stammered out that Richard was dead."

"And," I said, "all of Queen's thought his death due to lightning."

"Indeed. The provost still does. But then I saw things which troubled me and sent for you."

"Richard, you said, did not welcome callers. Was he a solitary lad, or did he have friends?"

Neither Martyn nor Simon replied. They looked to each other, then to Master Wycliffe, as if imploring him to answer. He did.

"Richard," Wycliffe said, "could be irascible." The scholar spoke slowly, as if he wished to choose words carefully and not speak ill of the dead. From the corner of my eye I saw Martyn roll his eyes. I suspected "could be" might mean "usually was".

"Show me," I said to Simon, "where Richard lay when you first saw the corpse."

Master John led the way into the chamber, Simon

followed, and when Wycliffe stepped aside Simon pointed to the chamber wall opposite the splintered bed. I could then see what I had not before. The shattered plaster and fragments of straw and feathers and splintered wood were not so thickly strewn where Richard's corpse had rested. The place was close to the wall separating the chamber from Simon's.

"All is as it was when Richard was found," Wycliffe said, "except, of course, that he is gone to St. Peter's churchyard, and we who removed him left our footprints in the dust here."

There was little more I could learn from Martyn or Simon, and if I thought of new questions I knew where to find them, so I dismissed the lads.

"What are you thinking?" Master John said when the youths were out of earshot.

"Murder has been done here, I believe. Your suspicion is valid. You said that Richard could be irascible. Were you being tactful? Was the lad troublesome?"

Wycliffe studied the floor where the corpse had lain. Arthur cleared his throat and coughed. In the silence the sound was as if a man had struck a gong. Arthur does nothing in a small way. If he stood on a riverbank and sneezed, the blast would propel a boat across the stream.

"Richard was a brilliant scholar," Wycliffe began, "but peevish. His father was a tenant with but half a yardland in a village in Cumberland, where the soil is thin and the climate nearly as objectionable as Scotland. Mayhap the weather made Richard as he was. The village priest saw that Richard had a keen mind, taught him what he knew of Latin and logic, and convinced the Bishop of Carlisle to send the lad to Queen's, where he has been now for two years. Of his intelligence there was no question. 'Twas his wisdom which was lacking. He had but to utter three words and could antagonize all within the sound of his voice. Of course, he was not unique in Oxford. The halls and colleges are filled to the brim with men of much learning and little understanding."

"There are many who are not sorry that he is dead?"

"Aye. I tried to moderate his disposition, as I saw his intellect and believed that with his rough edges smoothed the lad could go far."

"You were unsuccessful?" I suggested.

"'Tis difficult to convince a shrewd scholar that he should change his behavior when he can defeat all those who may challenge him in debate."

"And this skill earned him enemies?"

"It won him no friends. And, as Simon said, Richard was a solitary sort. He made no friends and seemed not to desire any... else he would have modified his conduct."

While Master Wycliffe spoke, my eyes wandered about the disordered chamber and I bent to pick up the fractured table leg which lay at my feet. I had no reason in mind to examine the splintered wood, but fortuitous discoveries may often occur to a man who simply keeps his eyes open.

The bottom of the leg, where it had rested upon the floor, was hollow. Some man had used an auger to bore a hole deep into the wood. This opening was wide enough that I could insert two fingers, and when I did I felt something akin to a fragment of parchment rolled and inserted into the cavity.

I managed to slip fingers about the rolled leaf and drew it from the hole. Wycliffe had ceased his account of Richard Sabyn and watched as I unrolled the parchment. Laid flat upon the unsteady table it was as long as my forearm and as wide as my hand is long. Both sides were filled with a tiny script, and I had but to read a few lines to realize what Richard had hidden in the hollow table leg.

After these things Jesus went over the sea
of Galilee, which is the sea of Tiberias. And
a great multitude followed him, because
they saw his miracles which he did on them
that were diseased.

Here was a part of the Holy Bible, written in English. No wonder Richard Sabyn was secretive. If the bishops had discovered he possessed a portion of Holy Writ in English, or was translating the Bible into English, he would have lost his place at Queen's College and perhaps much more. All scholars know Latin, so there was no reason to have a portion of the Bible in English other than to be translating it.

"You hold in your hand a dangerous document," Master John said, for he had read the words over my shoulder.

"Then I will give it up to you," I said, and handed it to him.

"This is from the Gospel of St. John," Wycliffe said as he began to read. "The sixth chapter, unless I mistake me. I wonder where the first five chapters may be. A man would not begin such a work in the middle of the text."

Three legs remained affixed to the table top, upon which it wobbled precariously. I lifted the table, turned it upside down, and inspected the bottoms of the legs. A hole had been bored in each.

Wycliffe immediately pushed a finger into the nearest leg and pulled from it another leaf of parchment. "Ha!" he exclaimed. "Here is chapter one: 'In the beginning was the Word, and the Word was with God, and the Word was God.' I am not surprised to learn what Richard was doing alone here in his chamber. I warned him more than once that he must not condemn the bishops for refusing to allow men to read the Scriptures in English. His point was well made, and I am in agreement. Nevertheless, to hold such a view and bandy it about is perilous."

"The lad spoke often of this?" I asked.

"Aye. He spoke with the enthusiasm of youth, with more wit than judgment."

"Mayhap one of his cohorts who disagreed with him learned how to make the explosive powder. But why slay him and risk a noose, or banishment to some Scots abbey? Another scholar would need only notify a bishop or archdeacon and Richard would have been dealt with."

"If," Master John said thoughtfully, "evidence of his guilt could be found. Were it not for the shattered table leg we would know nothing of Richard's activities. His thoughts, although he promoted them vigorously, could not be proven transformed to deeds."

"So we know of two reasons some other might want to slay Richard," I said. "His peevish nature, which made foes of all others, and his assertion that Holy Writ should be available to men in their common tongue. Can you think of any other disputes which might provoke a man to slay Richard?"

"Nay, and these two are likely enough," Wycliffe replied.

"Which do you believe most likely to be the cause of Richard's death?"

"Oxford is a contentious place," Wycliffe mused. "No scholar likes to be bested in disputation. Gossip and backbiting are rife. But I've not heard of a scholar outwitted in debate who slew his antagonist. Nevertheless, 'tis my view that this is the case."

"Who among the scholars at Queen's did Richard vex the most?"

"Hah! One day 'twould be one, the next day another. But none escaped his disparagement. Some were better able to rebut his attacks than others, but his wit was a dagger thrust into all."

"Even you?"

"I am able," Wycliffe smiled, "to answer most who take issue with my views. This is why in some circles I am nearly as unpopular as Richard. 'Tis an odd thing. Men have little respect for those they can easily overcome, but loathe men who regularly defeat them."

I did not say so, but Wycliffe's appraisal of his status in Oxford is correct. He is respected, even admired, but not much liked.

"Martyn and Simon occupied chambers closest to Richard. Did they therefore attract his abuse more than others?"

"Are they the most likely to have slain Richard? Is this what you ask?"

"Aye."

"Richard insulted all men equally. And would his neighbors set off an explosive powder so close to their own abodes that its discharge might do harm to them?"

"They might," I said, "if they did not understand the force they were unleashing. This murder has been plotted for some time, I think. To distill enough saltpeter from urine would take many weeks, months even. And whoso did this murder was patient. They waited till a storm would cover their felony."

"I wonder," Wycliffe mused, "how the powder was placed under Richard's bed. Surely if 'twas in place very many days he would have discovered the stuff and wondered what it was and how it came to be beneath his bed."

"Mayhap. But how many youthful scholars sweep the dust from under their beds? A lass might do so, but lads are generally content to ignore filth not readily seen."

"Aye," Master John agreed. "But the stuff would not have discharged until a flame was put to it."

"Indeed. So Bacon wrote. And Albert Magnus also, as I remember."

"Some man plotted this death for many months," Wycliffe said. "Mayhap for a year even?"

"I believe that is possible."

"The provost must be told of what Richard was doing," Wycliffe said, "although I doubt he will bandy it about. 'Twould do him no good if bishops and archdeacons learned that one of his scholars was translating the Gospel of St. John to English."

I went to the blackened boards which formed the floor under Richard's bed and sank to hands and knees for a closer inspection. The planks were of oak, about as thick through as my thumb, as wide as my hand from wrist to fingertips, and most were longer than I am tall. They were fixed with nails to beams about a yard apart.

This inspection revealed what a more cursory examination had not. The nails fastening one of the planks to a beam showed signs of being pried free, then replaced. The wood about the nail heads had been crushed by some instrument used to lift the nail from the board. The nail had been replaced, so that unless a man peered intently at the nails he would not likely see anything amiss. I had not, the first time I observed the place where the blast had happened.

I saw another anomalous thing. Close by the end of the loosened plank was a tiny hole, smaller than my smallest finger. Was it but a cavity, perhaps gouged out by the blast, or did it penetrate through to the ground floor?

"What chamber is below this?" I asked Master John.

"A lecture hall. What have you found?"

"A plank has been pulled up. See where the nails have been drawn and replaced. And a small hole has been bored through this plank." I pointed to the tiny opening.

"Why would a man make such a hole?" Wycliffe asked.

"A hempen cord, infused with saltpeter, will burn slowly, like a candle wick," I explained.

Arthur, who had been standing silently during this exchange, now spoke. "Me father said at Crecy them what shot off the stone balls had cords what smoked an' spluttered but did not flame much."

"I would like to see the ceiling of the chamber below," I said.

"Come," Wycliffe said, and led us to the stairs, thence to the ground floor.

When Queen's College was built, not many years past, its builders – to save pounds and shillings, no doubt – did not plaster the ground floor ceilings but allowed the beams and planks of the upper story to remain open to the rooms of the ground floor. No doubt those who planned the structure assumed that the ceilings would be completed at some later time, when funds became available. In such circumstances funds rarely are. The lecture hall was much larger than the scholars' chambers above. It was nearly square, and six or seven paces long and wide. Three windows of glass opened to Queen's Lane and a view of the tower of St. Peter-in-the-East. I noted that the windows were unmarred. No broken panes gave evidence of the damage above.

Because the size and shape of this hall did not correspond to the chambers above, it was difficult to locate the place where, immediately overhead, the blast which slew Richard Sabyn had occurred. Difficult, but not impossible.

I found the hole which some man had bored through the plank, and moved a bench under it so as to more closely examine the aperture. A gleam of light came through the opening from the destroyed window above. Enough for me to see that the edges of the hole were blackened. Charred. A hempen match had been fed through the hole, no doubt.

"What do you see?" Wycliffe asked.

I told him.

"So the explosion which took Richard's life was set off here? If so, much planning has gone into this murder."

"Oxford is filled with intelligent men," I said, "who, if they set their minds to it, can devise many ways to do harm to others."

"Indeed. Although most so inclined limit themselves to cutting words rather than the thrust of a dagger."

Chapter 3

Arthur had remained silent throughout this discourse. Men of his station are likely to do so when in the company of gentlemen and scholars, but Arthur did not always conduct himself as the commons are expected to.

From the corner of my eye I saw him lean against a wall and with his hand rub his forehead. I had never known Arthur to be ill, and neither had I seen him seek a wall with which to keep himself upright.

The man is surely past forty years of age, although some years ago, when we discussed his age, he was unsure of the year of his birth, or even the month. March, he thought, of perhaps the year of our Lord thirteen and thirty-two. This uncertainty did not trouble the man.

From the other end of the building came the sound of a trumpet. "Supper," Wycliffe said. Evidently the scholars of Queen's College were called to meals with the blast of a sackbut. "'Tis Friday," Master John continued, "so the meal will be a simple pottage, with perhaps barley loaves. You are welcome to partake, or, if you desire fish, there will surely be an inn nearby serving whelks or stockfish, or some such repast."

"We will join you," I said. "We enjoyed a pottage of whelks for our dinner. At least, I did. Arthur had little appetite, though by now it has likely returned."

'Twas as Master John had suggested. The Queen's College cook ladled bowls of pease pottage from a great pot, and each scholar received also a barley loaf. The ale was fresh.

The scholars consumed little more than half of the pottage, for the kettle it was cooked in was quite large. Wycliffe told me later that the college charter required that pease pottage be made available each day to the poor who gathered before the college on Queen's Lane.

I was surprised to see Arthur linger over his supper. Usually he emptied his bowl and was seeking another before my own meal was half consumed. The man was out of sorts, there could be no doubt. Neither whelks nor peas tempted him.

The longest day of the year was approaching, so the scholars of Queen's were not ready to seek their beds when supper was past. Some went to play nine men's morris, whilst others set off for an inn where they might imbibe more ale. Mayhap a few found themselves on Grope Street.

"There are empty chambers for you and your man," Wycliffe said when the meal was done. Perhaps he had noticed Arthur's waxen complexion. "I will seek the porter's assistant and have blankets sent. Will you seek your beds now?"

"Mayhap Arthur will do so," I replied. "There are some matters I would discuss with you concerning what must be done tomorrow to seek a felon."

The porter's assistant led Arthur to an empty chamber on the upper floor whilst I and Master John repaired to his chamber. This lodging was twice the size of the students' cells of the upper story, where Arthur would soon be snoring his way back to robust health. So I hoped.

Wycliffe's chamber was fitted with a glass window, and the slanting sun produced a golden glow upon a plastered wall at the base of which was a bench. Master John motioned to the bench and sat at one end while I occupied the other. My stomach was full, the sun was warm, and lethargy threatened to overwhelm me. Wycliffe spoke, and brought my wandering thoughts back to the issue at hand.

"What is in your mind?" he began. "How will you seek whoso has slain Richard?"

"'Tis my view that the felon is of Queen's," I said. "What others of Oxford would have had association enough with Richard to develop such a hatred for him that they would slay him?"

"Mayhap he borrowed money from some other scholar, would not repay, and earned the man's wrath."

"Possibly. But if so Richard's death would guarantee that he would never be repaid. And how would such a man gain access to Queen's in the night so as to set alight the match cord which produced the blast mistaken for lightning?"

"Ah... aye. Your point is taken." Master John stroked his beard, then continued. "The porter bars the door at night."

"Would the man take a bribe to admit another after curfew? How well do you know him?"

"Not well. The provost hired him and his assistant. I know little of the man. I have no authority at Queen's College. I rent a chamber here, that is all."

"Prepare a list of all the scholars of Queen's College, with your estimate of their capacity for murder and also their opinions, so much as you know them, of Richard Sabyn."

"What of Richard's forbidden work translating the Gospel of St. John to English?"

"If you did not know he was about such a task, would any others?" I asked.

"'Tis not likely. He was not one to confide in even friends, and he had few of them."

"And a man will not unburden himself to enemies."

"Or even friends if he is doing something which, were it known, would bring trouble down upon his head."

"Might he have let something slip," I asked, "when he'd had too much ale?"

Master John shrugged. "I've never known Richard to consume too much ale. And when a man is prone to do so 'tis likely 'twill be with friends attending some inn or ale house."

"And," I continued the thought, "Richard had no friends with whom he might frequent an ale house."

"Just so."

"There is another matter," I said, "which if addressed may lead to the felon. Sulfur and charcoal may be easily found. But not so saltpeter. If a man were to distill a supply from urine he would need to save a year's worth, I think. There are places where a man might purchase urine; tanneries, dyers, laundries. But why purchase what may be had for free? It would be expensive for a poor scholar, to say nothing of raising eyebrows."

"Might he freely collect the urine of other men?" Wycliffe asked.

"That does seem more likely," I agreed. "But how would he do so without stoking curiosity and causing gossip? I suppose men would not have to know the reason for a man to do such a thing. Merely that he did so would create much talk."

"Unless he could do this without other men being the wiser. I have heard that the king's armorers in the Tower produce the explosive granules by collecting straw from the king's marshalsea and other stables in London, then soaking the straw and boiling the residue to extract the salt."

"Mayhap I will visit some inns to learn if any man has done this in the town. It seems unlikely that a scholar would do so. A man would need a cart and runcie to collect enough straw."

"Aye," Wycliffe agreed. "'Tis unlikely."

The sun which had warmed us was now low and behind Oxford Castle, which, perched on a mound, cast its shadow early and long over Oxford. If the sun had done aught to illuminate our thoughts, those also fell into shadow. We lapsed into silence.

Wycliffe stared out of the darkening window, then finally spoke. "'Tis my practice when night comes to thank the Lord Christ that I have survived another day, and ask that He will permit a few more before He calls me to His bosom. Will you join me? This bench is a suitable altar, I think. As good as any blessed by some reprobate priest."

I knelt beside the scholar as he expressed his gratitude for favors received. He concluded with a request that the Lord Christ extend His powerful hand over Bampton and save Kate and my progeny from harm whilst I was not present to protect them.

Scholars at Queen's College break their fast with a loaf from the kitchen. There was a ewer of ale and cups in the refectory with which to quench one's thirst.

I did not see Arthur up and about so sought him in the chamber he had been assigned. I found him half asleep and shivering in his blanket. He heard the door swing open and roused himself enough to shift his face to the door.

"Give me a minute an' I'll be up an' about," he said, and lifted himself to an elbow. That was as far as he got before his strength seemed to betray him. He swayed upon the elbow, then sank back to the bed. "You'll 'ave to seek a murderer w'out me this mornin'," he whimpered. "Me 'ead feels like Hamo Tanner took to me skull with a fence post."

Hamo Tanner is a wrestler and leader of a troop of jongleurs and acrobats. He is constructed along the same lines as Arthur, and if he smote a man's skull with a club, he who received the blow would have an aching pate for a fortnight. If he survived.

I approached Arthur and reached a hand to his forehead. It was hot to the touch.

"Be all right soon," he wheezed. "Feel better after dinner."

"Aye," I agreed, but did not believe it so. Word had come to Bampton a fortnight after Easter that plague had returned to Witney. And if there, no doubt it was in Oxford as well, or soon would be. Of course, folk are often made ill with fevers and headaches by diseases other than plague, and from which they may recover. I said a prayer that this might be so for Arthur.

Holy Church teaches that God hears only spoken prayers. But if He knows my thoughts, why would He not accept a prayer which does not pass my lips? I did not wish Arthur to hear me beseech the Lord Christ that his illness be something other than plague.

St. Paul wrote that men must pray without ceasing. I do not remember ever seeing men upon the streets of Oxford or Paris or Bampton, or any other place, who spoke prayers as they walked. Either all men disobey the apostle, or Holy Church is wrong and the Lord Christ regards a man's silent petitions.

I went to the kitchen, asked for a cup of ale, and from my instruments bag removed a vial of dried sap of lettuce. This I mixed with the ale. The sap of lettuce is a soporific. I took the mixture to Arthur and he drank it readily.

I wished then to consult Master Wycliffe, but found him busy at his work, preparing to conduct a disputation. Youthful scholars filled the benches of the lecture hall below Richard Sabyn's shattered chamber, and Wycliffe sat in a chair facing his charges. Although he had no position at Queen's College, his reputation was such that scholars would pay to hear his wisdom. And Master John was not opposed to sharing his thoughts and collecting a few pence to augment his livings. This exercise would last an hour or two, I thought, so whilst Arthur suffered his aching head and Wycliffe suffered empty heads, I would prowl the nearby streets to learn if any man, scholar or not, had visited inns and stables to collect straw.

None had. Nor did I expect it so.

A latrine occupied a corner of the ground floor of Queen's College. Could urine be distilled to saltpeter if it was befouled with excrement? I thought this unlikely, and Bacon was silent on the topic. If one or more of Queen's scholars had collected urine for the purpose of doing murder it seemed to me the bucket or barrel used would be found near the college. Any urine deposited in a chamber pot during the night would be removed by a chamber maid. So the villain would have had to relieve himself in a place not serviced by a maid. Would such a vessel still be close by, now that it was no longer needed?

Behind the college was a row of mulberry bushes which had somehow managed to thrive in Oxford's thin soil. A place distinctly unfriendly to vegetation. Could a scholar hide a bucket within this copse and visit it in the night? Possibly. The entrance door to Queen's was barred from within, but more than likely the porter and his assistant, once the college was closed for the night, would seek their beds, assured that no man could enter without their allowance. But if a scholar was cautious he might quietly lift the bar, open the door, relieve himself, return, and drop the bar while the porter snored through the night.

Did the entrance door to Queen's College squeal on its hinges? I went to the door and, with the porter watching, drew it open. The hinges had been greased with lard and the door swung silently open and closed. I put a thumb on the latch when I closed the door and discovered that it could be secured whilst making no sound in the process.

From the door, I circled the building to the sparse bushes which separated Queen's College from the city ditch, a wasteland where thieves prowled and folk who died when plague first struck were buried. The vegetation was not verdant enough to hide a man, even in full leaf as it now was. But it would not need to be if a man sought the place in the night, when it was lit by only the moon and stars. And a bucket could be hidden amongst the stems and there attract no attention, even in the day.

How much urine would a man need to collect in order to distill the liquid down to enough saltpeter to create an explosion? I did not know, and I did not know any man who did. As for sulfur and charcoal, also required, they were easily obtained. Shiploads of brimstone are brought to England from Sicily, and the mines of Cornwall provide more. And charcoal can be had by the sackful in Oxford and most other towns. But not all charcoal is alike. Must the explosive powder be made only from the charcoal of certain woods? If so, what are these? Here was another thing I did not know. And again, I knew of no man who could tell me.

I walked the line of shrubbery behind Queen's but found no receptacle, nor was there any sign that in the past such a thing might have been hidden amongst the stems. I dimly heard the trumpet calling scholars and fellows to their dinner. My stomach took the opportunity to remind me that it was empty.

What of Arthur? I could not imagine the man being so ill that he would neglect his dinner, so I hurried to his chamber to learn if he was yet abed, or had roused himself.

I found him as I had left him. He had drawn the blanket to his chin and observed me entering with glazed eyes. He did not try to lift himself to an elbow as he had a few hours earlier. "Heard the trumpet call the scholars to their dinner," he whispered. "Ain't up to a meal meself. You'll have to seek the felon without me. Mayhap I'll be fit tomorrow."

Of this I had doubt, but I would not say so to Arthur. "I will bring you a loaf," I said. "Meanwhile, rest, as you are doing. This afternoon I will visit a herbalist and seek a supply of saffron and hemp seeds. These may reduce your fever and sore head."

'Twas again a fast day, so dinner was more pease pottage. I did not think the pale green repast would, in his condition, tempt Arthur, but I did take from the refectory a barley loaf and a cup of ale.

He found strength to raise himself to an elbow and empty the cup of ale. He managed to consume half the barley loaf, then sank back to his pillow.

A small table stood near the bed, where a scholar might bend over his books and set a candle or cresset. I placed the uneaten portion of the loaf upon the stand and told Arthur that he should eat it when he felt able, so as to regain his strength. He nodded, blinked, then closed his eyes.

I left him and made my way through Oxford's crowded streets to the castle. I did not know how much saltpeter was needed to make a blast powerful enough to slay a man, nor was I sure of the proper portions of sulfur and charcoal. But while eating my dinner I had thought of a place where men might know these things.

I sought Sheriff Roger de Elmerugg. He and Lord Gilbert had been companions on several of King Edward's campaigns and he knew as much about warfare as any man found in Oxford. The sheriff had been of great help a few months earlier, when I sought a silver cresset from an uncooperative burgher, so knew me as a man who served his friend Lord Gilbert Talbot.

The serjeant at the castle gatehouse told me that Sir Roger was at his dinner in the hall, and so he was. I entered the hall just as he was pushing back from the high table. He had not dined upon a pease pottage. Even his serjeants and constables had consumed fish, and there was enough remaining that the poor, who thronged the castle drawbridge each day at this hour, would receive a small portion.

Sir Roger glanced my way, recognized me, and waited at the opening to the screens passage when he saw me approach. I bowed when I came near, and he spoke. "I give you good day. How may I serve Lord Gilbert's bailiff?"

I looked about me and saw that several knights, serjeants, and constables lingered as if they also had business with the sheriff. Or awaited his instructions for their afternoon assignments.

"I wish to speak to you privily," I said. I could not say at that moment why I preferred that no other men should know of my interest in the explosive powder used at Crecy, but on the spur of the moment thought it best that as few others as possible were aware of the reason for my visit to Oxford Castle. Knowledge is power, and knowledge known to all is power diluted.

"Come," Sir Roger said, and led the way through a warren of passages to his chamber. A constable sat in the antechamber and sprang to his feet when the sheriff banged through the door. Sir Roger dismissed the constable and shoved open the door to his inner chamber. He motioned me to enter, then pushed the door closed behind me.

"What is so secret, eh?" Sir Roger said, and seated himself behind his table. As he did so he motioned me to a bench.

"Do you remember, a few days past, a scholar of Queen's College asked you to send a constable to investigate another scholar's death?"

The sheriff stroked his beard. "Aye. Day after the storm. Lad struck by lightning, wasn't it?"

"So men thought. You decided the death was not worth the time of one of your men and dismissed Master Wycliffe when he approached you about the matter."

"Wycliffe. Oh, aye. Suspicious fellow. Not content with the simple explanation of a lightning strike. Why do you bring this to me again?"

"There is strong evidence that the scholar died at some other man's hand. Not from lightning."

"Oh? What evidence?"

I explained the condition of the chamber when Richard Sabyn was found, the state of his corpse, the blackened planks under his bed, the hole bored through a plank to the lecture room below, and the unusual fact that, were it lightning which took the scholar's life, the bolt did not strike either the peak of the roof or the church tower across the lane, but rather blasted a hole in a lower portion of the college roof.

"Hmmm. Curious. So you wish me to send a man to confirm your suspicions and report back?"

"Nay. Master Wycliffe has engaged me to look into the matter. I'll not trouble you about it unless I find the lad's killer. Even then 'twould be a matter for the bishop. There was a blast, and it took the scholar's life, but 'twas not caused by lightning."

"What, then?" Sir Roger's brow furrowed as a new-plowed field.

"At Crecy, some thirty years past, an explosive powder was used to hurl stone balls at the French. The blast which propelled the missiles was deafening, I am told."

"Aye. Wasn't there myself. Too young. Began service

as page to Sir William Hopton soon after. Sir William told me of it later."

"He was at Crecy?"

"Aye. When a match was put to the explosive powder a great roar and cloud of smoke sent the stone ball at the French. Did little harm, Sir William said. 'Twas our arrows, not stone balls, that told against King Philip."

"Is it true that the king's armorers now produce the explosive powder in London, at the Tower?"

"Aye, they do. I see where you are going. You believe some man blasted that lad into the next world? No lightning involved?"

"Aye. I do."

"Hah. Where in Oxford would a man find the stuff?"

"He might make his own," I replied.

"Oh, aye... suppose so. The makings are easy enough to come by," Sir Roger agreed.

"Just so. Saltpeter, sulfur, and charcoal. Have you had words with any of the king's men at the Tower who make the stuff as to the proportions of each ingredient?"

"Aye. So happens I have. And I have seen it with my own eyes. Of every one hundred parts of the whole, seventy-five parts are saltpeter, fifteen parts are charcoal, and ten parts are sulfur. 'Tis the salt which is most trouble to obtain."

"Of what wood is the charcoal made?" I asked.

Sir Roger pulled at his beard. "Don't remember. Quite sure 'twas not pine. I remember the armorers saying the sap in pine will make for poor charcoal. Alder. Aye, that was it. 'Twas alder used to make the charcoal for explosive powder. Or willow, was alder not to be had."

I thanked Sheriff Roger for his time and knowledge, departed the castle, and sought a herbalist's shop. Saffron powder and hemp seeds, crushed and dispersed in a cup of ale, might help Arthur – the first to reduce his fever, the second to dull the pain of his aching head.

I purchased a vial each of powder and seeds, then hastened to Queen's, where I sought the cook. From him I acquired a cup of ale, dropped in the herbs, then took the potion to Arthur's chamber.

I was much distressed at what I found there. Arthur had spewed up the ale and loaf he had consumed for his dinner. The mess lay upon the floorboards. The man slept, snoring fitfully, and was in no fit condition to drink more ale. So long as he slept, his fever and headache would not trouble him. I set the cup upon the table beside the uneaten portion of the loaf and slowly, silently, departed the chamber.

When I had visited the college kitchen seeking ale, I noticed a scullery maid at work, scrubbing the bronze pot in which the cook had prepared the day's pottage. I sought the lass, explained that in a chamber upon the upper floor there was a man quite ill, and that he had vomited his dinner. I offered two pence if she would clean the foul discharge, which duty she was pleased to accept.

"Be as silent as you can," I urged. "The man sleeps and I would not wake him can it be avoided."

The maid promised to do so, collected a scoop and bucket, and hurried away to see to the task. I set off for Wycliffe's chamber, to tell him of what I had learned at the castle.

"What will you do with this new knowledge?" Master John said when I told him of my visit to Sir Roger.

"I will seek charcoal burners and men who sell sulfur, to learn if they have sold to a scholar in the past weeks."

"The past weeks? What if the felon purchased the goods many months past and hid them away?"

"Mayhap he would have done so. But if he had, what seller would remember a customer so long in the past? And where in Queen's College would the miscreant store sulfur and charcoal where it would not be discovered?"

"Do you still believe a Queen's scholar slew Richard?" Wycliffe asked.

"Why ask you that? Had he made foes of scholars at other colleges and halls?"

"Who can know?" Master John shrugged. "'Tis possible. A man is not likely to go about telling others of new enemies he has made in the last fortnight."

"Unless Richard spoke indiscreetly of translating the Scriptures to English. If some churchman heard of it he might decide to do the bishop's work for him."

"But you think not," Wycliffe said.

"How would such a man know which chamber was Richard's? How would he gain entry to Queen's College in the night, in a storm, to set a match alight? And how would he find opportunity to bore a hole beneath Richard's bed from the lecture hall below? Nay, the felon is most likely of Queen's. How many scholars study at Queen's?"

"Not so many as in the past. The pestilence has struck down many at all of Oxford's colleges and halls. Queen's College charter calls for a dozen or so of fellows and chaplains, and seventy-two poor lads. So far as I know there have never been that many. Funds are lacking. There are now eight fellows and five chaplains, and nine boys."

"Among them is a murderer," I said.

"Or mayhap more than one," Wycliffe replied. "It could be that Richard's death was the product of a conspiracy."

"The easier to discover, then. The more felons involved in an evil deed, the more likely one will do or say something which will lead to uncovering the wickedness."

"I have heard that your man is quite ill."

"Aye. I gave him a loaf and ale for his dinner, but he ate only a portion of the loaf, and when I looked in on him a short while ago he had spewed up even that small meal."

"What ails him, you think?"

"I hardly dare mention it."

"The great pestilence?"

"Aye. So I fear. Shortly before we came to Oxford I learned that plague has reappeared in Witney."

"The town is near to Bampton, is it not?"

"Aye. Eight miles or so."

"But Bampton is so far free of the disease?"

"So far – but for Arthur... if such is indeed the cause of his complaint. And he fell ill before we came to Oxford, I believe. Have you heard of plague returning to the colleges?"

"Nay." Wycliffe shook his head. "But if it does, all in the town will know of it, and the halls and colleges will empty."

"As they did when I studied at Balliol," I replied. "Men say the pestilence is a punishment from God, and surely men provide cause enough for His wrath, but when folk are taken ill many others will flee their presence, which if a man's sin be the cause of the disease should do no good."

"True," Master John agreed. "When plague first appeared at Oxford I was a young master, and I saw that a few scoundrel priests who fled from their parishes survived, whilst virtuous clerics, who attended their suffering congregants, died. Is it sure that the pestilence has infected Arthur?"

"Nay. 'Tis too soon to know. But if buboes appear it will be clear."

"What is then to be done for him?"

"I am a surgeon, not a physician."

"Bah!" Wycliffe exclaimed. "If physicians could cure

a man of plague none who could offer a few pence to a leech would ever die. When plague first came, physicians would go about with masks over their mouths and noses, filled with sweet-smelling herbs. They resembled ravens with oversized beaks."

"I remember well," I said. "'Twas of no benefit, so far as I could see. The priest who attended my father when he was struck down had a bag of herbs tied about his neck with a hempen cord. I remember the sack swinging over my father's body as the priest administered Extreme Unction an hour before my father breathed his last."

"The priest also perished?"

"Four days later."

"May the Lord Christ requite his unselfishness."

"Amen," I said.

"It may be that plague has returned," Wycliffe said. "If so, the felon who slew Richard may flee and never be heard of in Oxford again."

"Then we must discover the man soon. If a scholar departs Queen's with no good excuse, he will lay suspicion upon his shoulders, and he would know this. But to flee the town if plague appears will seem a wise thing, and the felon will be but one of many who will do the same. So I will seek those who sell charcoal. Oxford's smiths and farriers will know the charcoal burners who supply the town."

Chapter 4

In the next two hours I visited four smiths and two farriers. I learned that three families supplied nearly all of the charcoal brought to Oxford. One was from Cowley, another from Littlemore, and the third from Eynsham. I asked each smith and farrier if a scholar had asked to purchase charcoal from them. From most of these I received incredulous looks. Why would a scholar need charcoal? Mayhap whoso had sought to purchase charcoal had appeared incognito, leaving his scholar's robe behind. Nay, the smiths all said. No youths had asked to buy charcoal, wearing red robes or black, or no gowns at all.

If only fifteen parts of a hundred are required to make the explosive granules, how much of the powder would be needed to blast a man from his bed to the next world? Surely not much. Charcoal is sold in sacks which tax a large man to lift. Any man wishing to acquire only a few pounds would likely be remembered as unusual. I resolved to seek the charcoal burners of Cowley, Littlemore, and Eynsham.

The trumpet sounded, announcing supper, as I entered Queen's College. I expected another pease pottage and was not disappointed. For this meal the cook had provided an onion or two, which flavored the plain fare. When I had eaten my fill I took a bowl and spoon to Arthur, hoping I could induce him to take a portion.

He did make an effort and swallowed perhaps three spoonfuls of the pottage before he retched and the little he had consumed came up. He had managed to raise himself on an elbow so that he did not foul his blanket. But with a groan he then collapsed back to his pillow.

As he had raised himself free of the blanket I saw what I had feared. Arthur's neck was swollen and the lumps were dark against his otherwise pale visage.

"Sorry to be a bother," he whispered. "Wish I might die in Bampton, rather than 'ere. Where will you bury me? Plenty o' churchyards in Oxford."

Arthur had survived three recurrences of the great pestilence. He knew the signs of its appearance, he knew its progression, and he knew the consequence.

"Wish I might see Cicely again, and me lad."

"I will take you home," I said, without thinking. Had I considered the matter I hope I would have said the same.

"You got a felon to catch," he murmured.

"The man will still be here when I return… probably."

"Mayhap. If folk of Oxford learn I've brought plague amongst 'em they may abandon the place."

"Some," I agreed. "But set your mind at ease. One man is not likely to introduce the pestilence to an entire town. There are most certainly others who are suffering as you are, but no one yet knows of it. Their families will not want it known, for fear of isolation."

"Can't climb to the back of an 'orse," Arthur said. "Not goin' to get 'ome before the pestilence takes me."

"I'll hire a carter. We will depart at dawn."

"Sunday? You'll be absent for mass."

"The Lord Christ will forgive me, for doing His work. Rest now. I will send the maid to clean the floor, and seek a carter for the morrow."

I gave the lass another two pence, then set off for the stables where our palfreys were housed. I had seen a cart stored against the back wall of the mews. The owner drove a hard bargain. A shilling to hire the cart, a runcie, and a lad to drive the beast to Bampton and return cart and runcie to Oxford.

"There is no doubt Arthur is ill of plague?" Wycliffe said when I told him that I was, for a few days, abandoning the search for a felon in Queen's College.

"None. Buboes are beginning to appear."

"He will die, then, within the week."

"Aye. Mayhap he will live until I can return him to Bampton. He wishes to be buried in St. Beornwald's churchyard. If the journey does not kill him."

"You believe it might?"

"The jolting of the cart would try even a healthy man."

"Take his pallet to cushion the bumps. No man will want to use it now. When you get him home, burn it. No reason to return it."

At dawn on Sunday I sought a maslin loaf from a baker on Holywell Street, refreshed myself with a cup of ale, bid Master John good day, and hurried to the stable. I hoped that an early start would allow for a completed journey before nightfall. 'Twas not to be.

The stable proprietor had cart, runcie, Lord Gilbert's palfreys, and the driver ready as promised. I led cart and carter to Queen's College and went to Arthur's chamber.

I had not seen Arthur for twelve hours. I was dismayed to discover how his affliction had worsened. He was in no fit state to rise from his bed, walk the corridor to the stairs, then descend to the cart. Likely he could not have done so a day earlier either, but 'twas sure he could not now. The buboes upon his neck were larger and darker. No doubt similar lumps had appeared in his armpits and groin, where the disease most often made its presence known.

I rapped upon chamber doors until I found three scholars willing to assist me in moving Arthur's bed to the cart. Two lads refused. Arthur's illness was now known in Queen's College hall.

'Tis not an easy matter to maneuver a bed down a flight of stairs, especially if the bed is occupied by a man who weighs fifteen stone or so and it is desirable that the occupant not be pitched out upon the steps. Arthur was alert whilst he was carried from the building. His eyes observed, but he said nothing.

I told my helpers to set the bed behind the cart, then, with one at each corner, along with myself, we hoisted Arthur and the pallet to the cart. The lad who served as driver gazed down upon this operation wide-eyed. I feared he might abandon his obligation, for Arthur's swollen neck was now visible above his cotehardie, but he did not.

Master Wycliffe appeared in the doorway to Queen's as I mounted my palfrey. The other of Lord Gilbert's beasts I had tied to the cart. Wycliffe called out a wish for safe travel and urged a speedy return.

The cart jolted over Oxford's rutted streets, thumped across Bookbinders Bridge, and creaked and rattled as we left Oxford behind. Several times Arthur was wracked with coughing, and I noticed blood upon his lips. Soon, over the squeal of the cart's ungreased wheels, I heard a muted groan. And then another. I slowed my palfrey and waved to the carter to take the lead whilst I followed.

Arthur was in mortal discomfort. Each time a cartwheel struck a rock or dropped into a rut Arthur gasped with pain. The straw-filled tick did little to soften these thumps. There was nothing to do but slow our pace so that Arthur would not suffer so. I told the carter to rein in the runcie and we proceeded so slowly a grandmother could have overtaken us. I know this because a crone did so when we approached Swinford. But Arthur rested more easily. Only rarely did the bounce of the cart elicit a groan from him.

Crossing the Thames at Swinford brought more stifled moans from Arthur as the cartwheels banged against the riverbed. The spring flow was high and I feared the cart might be swept away. Wood floats. But we reached the western bank successfully.

We would not see Bampton this day. 'Twas past the ninth hour when we approached the gatehouse of Eynsham Abbey, a mile past the ford. Would the porter admit a man dying of plague? If he would not we would not see Bampton till midnight.

I dismounted before the abbey gatehouse and asked to speak to Abbot Gerleys. The porter might turn us away, but I thought the abbot would not. Nevertheless I would not seek a place for the night under false pretenses. The pestilence rages through monastic houses once introduced. Why should this be so if the malady is the result of God's wrath against sinful men? Do monks not strive to serve the Lord Christ?

The porter did not ask why a man lay in the cart and I did not tell him. He sent his assistant to inform the abbot that Sir Hugh of Bampton was at the gatehouse and wished to speak to him. A short time later Abbot Gerleys and the assistant appeared. No doubt the abbot was curious as to why I sought him. Many times I have found shelter at Eynsham Abbey's guesthouse, and this is the guest master's business, not a concern of the abbot.

"Sir Hugh," the abbot greeted me, "I give you good day. Or nearly good evening. How may this house serve you?"

"I would speak to you privily," I replied.

Abbot Gerleys glanced to the cart, thence back to me, and his puzzled expression deepened. "Very well. Come."

I told the carter to remain as he was, and that I would return shortly. I would return either to continue our journey to Bampton, or to announce that we had found a place of rest for the night.

Abbot Gerleys led me to the church door, where no monks or lay brothers were at this hour as Nones had just been completed, then turned and asked again how Eynsham Abbey might serve me.

"Do you remember Arthur, a groom to Lord Gilbert? He assisted me some years past when I discovered who had slain a novice of this house."

"Aye. A brawny fellow."

"He has been brought low and now rests upon a pallet before your gatehouse. He accompanied me to Oxford two days past, but now at his request I am returning him to Bampton."

"Is the man near death?"

"He is. And you must know the cause before you offer hospitality for the night. 'Tis plague which has seized him."

"And he wishes to return home to die?"

"Aye. I hesitate to ask of you shelter for the night. If you deny us I will understand. The journey from Oxford this day has been difficult for Arthur, and if we continue he may die before we come to Bampton. Of course, even if you permit us to stay the night he may die tomorrow before the journey ends."

"You have no doubt of his illness?"

"None. The buboes grow large and dark."

"I will not turn away a man who needs our care, but I must protect this house. You and the carter may stay the night in the guesthouse. I will assign lay brothers to carry Arthur to the church and leave his pallet in the north transept, where he will disturb no one, and no man will trouble him. Others will take your beasts to the stables for the night. Mayhap keeping your man from places where others live and sleep and eat will prevent the pestilence from taking root here, and the Lord Christ will defend His Holy Church. I will not ask the infirmerer to admit him to the infirmary. A brother and an elderly lay brother occupy the place at present, and I would not send plague upon them to vex them further.

"Has Arthur been shriven?"

"Nay. I thought to get him home, where one of St. Beornwald's priests could perform the sacrament."

"Are you confident he will live to see Bampton?"

"Nay. This morning I thought so. Now I am unsure."

"My chaplain can perform Extreme Unction if you wish it."

"It may be wise."

"After vespers, then. I will see to it."

Abbot Gerleys spoke and his commands were carried out. Lay brothers took runcie, palfreys, and cart to the stables, and four others each seized corners of Arthur's pallet and carried him to the church. I noticed that when the abbot told the lay brothers of their task he said only that the man they were to transport was ill. He did not name the disease.

Once the days grow long monks will partake of a simple supper as well as their meal at mid-day. So it was that as the guest master showed me and the carter to the guesthouse I heard a thumping upon the tabula.

"I will return with loaves and ale," the monk said, then hurried off to his own supper.

He returned with maslin loaves and ale, and bowls of beans eyffred also. I had only just consumed the meal when I heard the bell call the monks to vespers. I left the carter to finish his supper and joined several villagers who attended the office. I leaned against a pillar and listened to the monks sing the office. I hoped Arthur also heard and took solace in the voices praising the Lord Christ.

Abbot Gerleys had seen me, so after leading his charges from the church immediately returned. "I told my chaplain to attend us when vespers was finished, but his clerk is not to precede him nor is any bell to be rung."

As if in response to the abbot's words I heard footsteps and saw the chaplain approach, his slender form cutting through the slanting sunbeams which illuminated the interior of the church.

"Where is the dying man?" the chaplain asked. "And why is my clerk not to know of this?"

"Follow me," Abbot Gerleys said. "As for clerks and bells, that you will understand soon enough."

I followed the abbot and his chaplain to a shadowed corner of the north transept. "Here is the dying man," Abbot Gerleys said softly.

"His name is Arthur," I added.

"Why is he hidden away here?" the chaplain asked. "And if he is not of this house why is he dying at the abbey rather than in his own bed?"

"He is a groom to Lord Gilbert, Third Baron Talbot, in Bampton," I said. "He was taken ill whilst in Oxford, and wishes to die and be interred in Bampton."

"Why do you wish him shriven here, now?"

"He yet lives, but may not tomorrow."

"Very well." The priest bent to kneel over Arthur's prostrate form. I saw Arthur's head turn as he followed the chaplain's movements. He surely had heard our conversation and understood why the priest now knelt at his side.

The chaplain asked the seven interrogations, to which Arthur managed to whisper replies. From a pyx the priest then drew forth a wafer and held it to Arthur. He opened his mouth and the chaplain placed the bread upon Arthur's tongue and spoke the paternoster. The sacrament was over in minutes. It seemed to me the priest had hurried the rite.

He stood, addressed Abbot Gerleys, and I knew why this haste. "This man is dying of plague, is he not? I saw dark carbuncles upon his neck."

"Aye," the abbot agreed. "Now I will thank you to say nothing. The man will be taken away at dawn. None of the brothers need know of this. I do not wish fear to find a home in this house."

The carter was asleep when I returned to the guesthouse. Young lads who possess a clear conscience find sleep comes readily. As for older men who feel the weight of murder and pestilence upon their shoulders, for such men Morpheus approaches hesitantly.

I lay upon the bed and considered Richard Sabyn's death. From this subject my mind wandered to Arthur's impending death and the end of our work together seeking scoundrels and felons. Kate then entered my thoughts – although she is never far from them – and Bessie and John. Was I introducing the pestilence to Bampton and my own family? Would the Lord Christ permit that my charity to Arthur be answered in such a way?

The Lord Christ told His followers that His yoke was easy and His burden was light. But there is a yoke, and there is a burden, for those who obey. I prayed that the burden I would carry for what little kindness I could offer Arthur would not be the death of Kate or Bessie or John. Such would not be a light burden, but a heavy one. This I know, for Sybil awaits me and her mother and her sister and brother in St. Beornwald's churchyard. Her death was a heavy burden, especially for Kate, for I was with Lord Gilbert at Limoges when a fever took Sybil's life.

I awoke in the night when the sexton rang the church bell to call the brothers to vigils. After the call to lauds I prodded the carter awake and told him to seek the abbey stables and ask the lay brothers assigned there to make ready our beasts and the cart. We faced a slow journey if Arthur was yet living and was not to be jolted overmuch, and I wished to set out as soon as daylight allowed.

I sought the abbey kitchen whilst the runcie was hitched to the cart, and was provided with ale and four fresh loaves for the journey. The carter and I drank our ale, he took his place upon the cart, and I led the palfreys to the church door.

Abbot Gerleys greeted me there. "Your man yet lives," he said, as if this was good news.

Which is worse, I wonder: knowing that one is about to die, or the dying itself? This is a question which all men will someday answer, but they will be unable to share the information with any other. So Arthur faced a few more hours of affliction before death set him free.

"I have assigned lay brothers to await your departure. They will carry Arthur and the pallet from the church when you are ready... as I see you now are."

"Indeed. Have them bring him forth."

The lay brothers, one to each corner, carried Arthur and the pallet from the church and placed their burden in the cart. I was pleased to see that they did this as gently as could be, sparing Arthur yet more torment.

The buboes upon Arthur's neck were immense, and I saw a watery red stain upon his cotehardie under his arm, where one of the growths had ruptured in the night. He said nothing, but looked from me to the lay brothers, then to the abbot, before closing his eyes.

Abbot Gerleys bade me good day and safe travel, and waved us on our way as we passed slowly under the gatehouse. As before I told the carter to keep his runcie to a gentle walk to spare Arthur the jolts from ruts and rocks. He was not much pleased with this slow progress, as it delayed his return to Oxford.

The day was cloudy, so Arthur was at least spared the sun in his eyes. Of course, his eyes were closed for most of the journey, but as we passed Cote he opened his eyes and spoke. I was riding close beside the cart, else I might not have heard him, so feeble was his voice.

"Will you speak to Lord Gilbert for me? Cicely has no money to pay a priest to pray me from purgatory. Mayhap Lord Gilbert would provide a shilling or two."

"You need not concern yourself with purgatory," I replied.

Arthur looked up at me. At that moment one of the cartwheels struck a rock and the lurch brought forth a gasp from the doomed man. He did not speak again for some time.

"Why not?" he finally said. "Will you pay the priests? I have been a sinful man. I am condemned to thousands of years in purgatory."

"You are no more sinful than any other man. I know you well. As men judge others you are a good man. We are all sinners for whom the Lord Christ died. Holy Writ says that in His death He purged from sin all who believe in Him. If He did so, and the Scriptures speak true, why must our sins be purged again? Was His death in our place not sufficient to atone for our wickedness?"

Speaking seemed to tax Arthur. He did not reply for several minutes, as if gathering the strength he would need to voice a few words.

"The bishops say not," he finally said. "They say we must suffer in purgatory for our sins. The only way to shorten the time a man must spend in that awful place is to pay priests to pray that we might sooner be released."

"Aye, so the bishops do say. But the Bible says nothing of purgatory, or the need for such a place. The bishops tell men there is a purgatory so as to enrich themselves. How many great men and nobles have gifted Holy Church with lands so they might be released soonest from a place which is not and never was? The Lord Christ said 'twas difficult for a rich man to enter heaven, but the bishops say otherwise. 'Tis the poor man, they tell us, who must endure the torments of purgatory whilst the wealthy may be soon released."

Arthur again closed his eyes and lay silent. We were near to St. Andrew's Chapel, only a few hundred paces from Bampton, when he spoke again.

"I trust you to speak truth to me, but what if them bishops be right?"

"I will pray for your soul," I replied. If this would comfort Arthur in his last moments, I would say it, even though I knew that no prayers for a man after he has died will avail. A man must cleanse his ways whilst he yet lives. No other can do so for him after his death.

The youthful carter had listened silently to this exchange. What he thought of my opinions I neither knew nor cared. I should have.

As we entered Bampton I considered what to do with Arthur. I would not take him to Galen House and introduce the pestilence to my family. But would Lord Gilbert permit him to enter the castle? Arthur had been a loyal groom for many years. Would that matter to Lord Gilbert, when a cough from the stricken man could send even a lord to his grave before the sun set the next day?

I decided to take Arthur to the castle. His wife and his younger son were there, and he had wished to see them before he died. Would fulfilling this desire mean that they would follow him to the churchyard?

All of life is a risk.

I was too late. As the carter turned his runcie from Mill Street to the castle forecourt I glanced to Arthur and saw his eyes, unblinking, staring at the grey clouds above. Sometime after passing St. Andrew's Chapel he had succumbed.

I instructed the carter to wait before the drawbridge for my return, then rode across the planks and dismounted. I told the porter's assistant to take my palfrey to the marshalsea, then set off for the hall, where I assumed that at this hour I would find John Chamberlain overseeing the setting up of tables and benches for dinner. I did, and he was.

"Sir Hugh," he exclaimed. "Lord Gilbert told me you were in Oxford, dealing with some malfeasance."

"The malfeasance remains to be dealt with. I have returned with Arthur, and must speak to Lord Gilbert immediately."

The chamberlain heard the urgency in my voice. "He is in the solar, with guests. Come."

Sir Ranulph de Braose and his lady, Matilda, were in conversation with my employer when John rapped upon the door to announce our presence. He then pushed it open in response to Lord Gilbert's reply to enter.

Lord Gilbert did not expect my return from Oxford so soon, I think, and when he saw me behind John gave evidence of surprise. "Ah, Sir Hugh," he said. "Tell us of Oxford and the scholar's death. Was it truly a lightning bolt which struck the lad down, or was Master Wycliffe's suspicion correct?" Then, to his guests, Lord Gilbert said, "Sir Hugh is my bailiff, and is adept at ferreting out the truth of felonious events."

I did not wish to speak of plague before Lord Gilbert's visitors, so stammered out something about beginning the investigation into the scholar's death, whilst trying to collect my thoughts. I needed to speak privily to my employer, but how does one tell noble guests tactfully to go away?

Lord Gilbert is no dolt. I glanced to his visitors and he discerned that I had words for his ears alone. "Perhaps," he said to Sir Ranulph, "you would like to retire to your chamber to make ready for dinner whilst I consult with my bailiff."

When a great baron makes a suggestion, even the most witless knight will understand the message. Sir

Ranulph and Lady Matilda withdrew, and with a nod from Lord Gilbert so did John Chamberlain.

"What have you to say which others are not to hear?" Lord Gilbert said when the door closed behind John. "Why are you secretive about a death in Oxford?"

"'Tis a death in Bampton you must learn of," I said. "Arthur lies dead in a cart before the drawbridge."

Lord Gilbert's eyebrows lifted. Both of them. "Some felon has struck him down? I would not have thought that possible."

"He is dead of plague. Shortly after we arrived in Oxford he showed symptoms, so I do not know if he contracted the pestilence there, or here, before we departed. He wished to return home to die, and to see Cicely and Richard again."

"He knew he was dying?"

"He did. We spent the night at Eynsham Abbey, and he was shriven there."

Lord Gilbert crossed himself.

"Will you permit the corpse to enter the castle?" I asked.

"There is no doubt he is dead of plague?"

"None. The buboes are large and dark, and one has burst. Are any of your grooms or valets or household knights ill?"

"Not that I have been told. You believe the contagion might have begun here, before he went with you to Oxford?"

"Mayhap. Word came from Witney a fortnight past that the pestilence has reappeared there."

"So I heard. But we of Bampton seem free of plague. So far... Can a man dead of the pestilence yet pass the disease to the living?"

"I don't know. I am a surgeon, not a physician."

"Bah. Most leeches likely don't know either. I heard tell that when plague first struck, the French king asked the scholars of the University of Paris for the cause, and their opinion was that a conjunction of planets in Aquarius in 1345 caused the pestilence. If so, why has it so often returned?"

"There are many opinions," I said, "but few answers. Experience tells that distancing oneself from those who are afflicted may prevent contracting the disease. Which is why I ask if you will admit Arthur."

"To what purpose? I'll not hold a wake for him. Who would attend the wake of a man dead of plague and possibly leave the event doomed?"

"Indeed."

"What is your opinion, Sir Hugh?"

"Arthur should be taken straight to St. Beornwald's churchyard and buried. Cicely and Richard must be told, of course, and may follow behind the cart to honor husband and father. I will notify Father Thomas. He can sprinkle holy water upon the gravesite and after Arthur is interred speak the funeral mass. All must be done properly, but soon."

"I will send for Cicely and Richard, tell them of Arthur, and walk with them to the churchyard. Arthur was a loyal servant, and I would see him brought with respect to his grave."

"The cart where he now rests is too large to pass under the lychgate," I said. "Men will be required to carry Arthur from the street to his grave."

"Oh, aye. And a shroud. I will send John to collect four grooms and find a shroud. Uctred will be willing, I think, and three others."

I returned to the carter, told him that we would soon take Arthur to the churchyard, and bade him turn the cart in the forecourt. Cicely appeared a few moments later, weeping, stunned at the news that her husband was no more. Richard walked dumbstruck beside her, the sudden loss of his father being too much for the lad to comprehend. Lord Gilbert, Uctred, and three other grooms soon walked under the portcullis, and with a nod Lord Gilbert indicated that we were to set off.

Our procession would pass Galen House, and Cicely wailing for her husband would attract Kate's attention. She would surely come to the door to learn who had died in Bampton. I decided to hurry on ahead of the cart and mourners, so told the carter to slow his runcie's pace. Kate would be shocked to see me at Galen House door.

She was, but after a brief explanation cast off her apron, left Bessie and John with Adela, and joined Cicely behind the cart when it passed our door.

From Galen House I ran ahead to Father Thomas's vicarage, told him he was needed at the churchyard, and why, then returned to the cortège in time to halt with the others at the lychgate.

Father Thomas brought with him his clerk and John Sexton. The clerk was sent to ring the passing bell, and the sexton and two of Lord Gilbert's grooms applied shovels to the gravesite upon which Father Thomas had sprinkled holy water.

'Twas the hour for the noon Angelus by the time the grave was filled. I paid the carter four more pence for his troubles and sent him on his way back to Oxford. Lord Gilbert, Cicely, Richard, and the castle residents returned to their delayed dinner – although I suspect appetites were much reduced.

At the churchyard I had thought to speak to Cicely of her loss and mine, but hesitated. I find that regularly in such circumstances I say the wrong words, and later, in the night, reflect upon the error. I have often thought 'tis better to say later what one should have said than to unsay later what one should not have said.

I walked with Kate to Galen House, where I might tell her more completely of events since I had departed three days past. Was it but three days since Arthur had been well yet was now in his grave, awaiting the Lord Christ's return?

"So now you will return to Oxford alone, to seek a felon who slew the young scholar?" Kate asked when I had told her more completely of the events of the past days.

"Mayhap I will take Uctred, if Lord Gilbert will permit and he is willing to go."

"You think he might object to leaving Bampton?"

"He might. His friend is dead after making the same journey."

"Is there no other who might accompany you? I do not like the thought of you upon the roads alone."

"No more than I. Perhaps Sir Jaket might accompany me."

"I would be much relieved if he did so. His squire would travel with you then also?"

"Surely."

"Three men upon the road would travel safely, I think. I wish it may be so."

After a dinner of hanoney, which Adela had prepared, I went to the castle to consult again with my employer. I nearly missed him. He and Sir Ranulph were mounted, preparing to ride behind the hounds, half a dozen of which were yapping and straining at the fewterer's leashes, eager to chase after a fox. Sir Jaket, his squire, and two other of Lord Gilbert's household knights and their squires were also mounted and ready for the hunt.

I had to shout to make myself heard over the excited hounds, but eventually Lord Gilbert – whose hearing at the best of times is not what it once was – understood my request. As Sir Jaket was present and listening I did not name him as a possible companion, but said only that if a man of the castle could be spared, his aid would be appreciated. I hoped that Sir Jaket would hear and volunteer. He had been a worthy assistant a few years past in the matter of a lady who had disappeared whilst traveling to Bampton with her husband. He knew the reason for my summons to Oxford. I hoped that, hearing my desire for assistance, he would offer to take Arthur's place. He did so, much to my Kate's satisfaction.

Chapter 5

At Kate's insistence I stayed another day and night. On Tuesday I instructed the marshalsea to have two palfreys ready next morn for me and the squire. Sir Jaket's previous squire was now knighted. His new squire, a lad of about sixteen years, was one Thomas Bennying. Sir Jaket would ride his ambler, a horse of which he was quite fond, and no wonder. I would like such a beast myself, but such animals cost six or seven pounds, far too much coin for a bailiff's purse, even one as well paid as I. And Kate would not likely approve the expense. Ah, well, life is a series of compromises. Although in some cases should probably not be.

Sir Jaket, Thomas, and I crossed Bookbinders Bridge at the fourth hour after a quick ride from Bampton. Sir Jaket, upon his ambler, set a fast pace. I led them to the Green Dragon – are not all dragons green? – and we shared a porre of peas for our dinner. From the inn 'twas but a short walk to Queen's College and its red-gowned scholars.

The porter remembered me and we were admitted readily. The fellows, chaplains, and boys had finished their dinner by the time we arrived. From the aroma which wafted down the corridor from the refectory I suspected that pease pottage was again on the menu. This day likely flavored with a bit of pork. As the college charter required that the poor be fed pottage at the college entrance it was good economy to boil up a pot of the green comestible large enough to feed both scholars and the indigent.

Master Wycliffe was in his chamber, in a customary posture, bent over a book. When he was not reading a book he was likely to be found writing one. I had told him when leaving Oxford that I would return as soon as possible, so he was not surprised to see who darkened his door.

I greeted Master John and introduced Sir Jaket and Thomas. Before I could tell of the journey to Bampton and Arthur's death he spoke.

"I am pleased you are returned so soon. There is news. A scholar of Merton College is found with plague, and some are making plans to abandon Oxford. Simon Duby has already left us, I think."

"The lad whose chamber adjoined Richard Sabyn's?"

"The same. Said nothing about leaving when I saw him yesterday. Probably did not wish to be dissuaded of his choice. This morning he was gone. Did not come to dinner, and no one has seen him. A disputation is scheduled for the ninth hour. Mayhap he will appear then."

"But you think not?" I said.

"Nay. Simon is not a brave lad – timid when provoked to defend his opinions, if an opinion can be drawn from him, which is unlikely. I suspect that at first word of the pestilence he set off for home."

"Where is that?"

"Cumberland. Most of Queen's scholars are from that county. The college was founded for the purpose of educating lads from there."

"He will have a long walk," I said.

"Aye, and I doubt he will return. He did not seem to enjoy a contentious life, debate and such."

"He would not have liked Richard Sabyn, then?"

"Nay. Tried to avoid Richard if he could. Of course, most others avoided Richard also."

"Are there others considering flight?"

"There are, I'm sure. But no man knows if he might flee a place where plague is rare, as it is yet in Oxford, and find himself where the pestilence is well entrenched."

"What of you?" I asked.

"I shall remain. I have survived three episodes of plague. If the Lord Christ wishes for me to perish of the disease He has had ample opportunity to strike me down. As I am yet among the living it is my opinion He has other plans."

What the Lord Christ intends for me I know not. I pray He desires me to live long enough to bounce grandchildren upon my knee. Of course, if I choose to do something dangerous I may then interfere with His plans. Decisions have consequences.

"You will now resume the search for a felon?" Master John continued. I was unsure whether the phrase was a question or a command.

"I will. As it is my belief that Richard was slain by someone of this college I will seek the provost and ask him to require his charges to cooperate with the investigation."

"I wish you good luck with such a request," Wycliffe grimaced.

"Why so?"

"Henry Whitfield is, uh, not popular at Queen's." In response to my lifted brows Master John continued. "He is not from Cumberland, as the provost is supposed to be."

"He is unpopular for his origins?"

"That, amongst other reasons. Most of the fellows wish him replaced."

"With one of them?" I guessed.

"Just so. And when he learned of Richard's death he was quick to agree that the cause was lightning. 'Twould do the college no good were it thought that one of its scholars slew another."

"And the reputation of the provost would suffer harm as well," I said.

"Indeed."

"Nevertheless, I will need his authority, weak as it may be, to press this inquiry. Will your opinion persuade the provost to support my investigation?"

"Perhaps, though I have no position at Queen's. I am but a tenant."

"But you are known throughout the town, and your opinion is valued."

"Hah. Not always."

"Mayhap. But if Henry Whitfield was thought to be covering a murder in his college his reputation would suffer, and if his grip on his post is tenuous, such gossip might force him out. He would know that."

"Aye, so he would. And you desire me to speak to him and suggest this?"

"I do. This day, if you will. I will speak to him tomorrow, after he has had time to consider his decision."

Although 'twas not his prerogative Master Wycliffe assigned three empty chambers to me, Sir Jaket, and Thomas. Perhaps he told Henry Whitfield of the arrangement when he called upon him that afternoon. It is unlikely the provost would have objected too strenuously. Wycliffe paid handsomely for a large chamber – funds which the college fellows would not wish to lose – and having Master John under Queen's College roof lent distinction to the school.

I awoke next morn in my chamber as the skin of the window was growing yellow. But 'twas not the dawn which drove away sleep. The chamber door rattled upon its hinges as some man thumped upon it and called my name. 'Twas the porter's assistant.

"Master Henry and Master John wish you to attend them at the entrance. Quickly, sir, if you please."

"Why so?" I asked as I drew on chauces and pulled my cotehardie over my head.

"'Tis Simon Duby."

"The lad who fled when 'twas known plague had returned?"

"Aye. He's dead."

My thought upon hearing this was that the young scholar had perished of the pestilence, and Arthur and I had introduced the disease to the college. I was much grieved. Evidently the lad had not traveled far before he died, and his red gown would identify him as a scholar of Queen's College, to which place he might be returned.

That part of my conjecture was correct. Little else was.

I hurried down the stairs and saw Master John and the provost looking to their feet in the dim light. Several other men I did not recognize stood about, one of these garbed in the sheriff's livery – a constable or serjeant, no doubt. These also gazed at the ground. As did I, when I came close enough. A red-garbed form lay motionless upon a pallet. Simon Duby. But not dead of plague. I saw when I came near that his robe dripped water to the ground under him. He had been fished from the river, I thought. Drowned. That also was wrong. Well, not the fished from the river part. I crossed myself in the presence of untimely death.

'Tis indeed startling how many young scholars drown in the Thames and Cherwell. Too much ale or wine, a tipsy walk home along the riverbank, a drunken misstep in the dark, and plop, into the current they go. Few of these lads have learned to swim, and even if they had, entangled in a wet gown with a belly full of ale or wine they would find it difficult to keep their head above water.

I learned to swim at an early age. I lived as a lad in Little Singleton, alongside the River Wyre. My older brothers took delight in tossing me into the stream, and when I managed to paddle to the riverbank they'd pitch me in again, until they tired of the sport. These thoughts passed through my mind as I peered down at the pale, waxen face of Simon Duby.

"Simon did not flee the pestilence," Master John said softly, "as you can see. This officer said he was found in the Cherwell at first light."

"Who found him?" I asked.

"A man checking his fish traps," the constable said.

"Where?"

"Near to the East Bridge."

"So it may be that he tumbled into the river from the bridge," Whitfield said.

"Tumbled?" Wycliffe said skeptically. "Not unless he chose to walk the bridge atop the wall. Jumped, more likely, or was pushed."

All those present looked up from the sodden corpse to Master John. His suggestion was unwelcome.

"Bah," the provost scoffed. "Simon was well liked and a threat to no man."

"We do not know that he entered the river from the East Bridge," I said. "Fallen, jumped, or pushed. 'Tis all conjecture."

"If there is evidence the lad was pushed from the bridge or riverbank the sheriff will set me to inquire into the matter," the constable said. "Until then, I've other duties. You," he said to the provost, "may dispose of the corpse in whatever churchyard you choose. If evidence of a felony is discovered, send word to Sir Roger." With that he turned away and disappeared into the growing number of pedestrians clogging the High Street. Those who had assisted him in hauling Simon from the river also began to drift away.

"Wait," I said. "Is one of you the fisherman who found Simon?"

"I am," one of the men said, and tugged a forelock. The fellow was all hair and unkempt whiskers, garbed in muddied chauces and a short cotehardie which would permit him to wade into a shallow stream without soaking the hem of his garment. His feet were bare.

"When do you set your traps?"

"In the evening, just before dark."

"And you always return to them at dawn?"

"Aye. If I wait too long others get to 'em and steal what may be caught."

"So when you placed your traps last evening there was enough light to see had there been a corpse in the water?"

"Oh, aye."

"I wonder," I said, "where Simon was yesterday. He was not seen all day. Is this not so?"

Wycliffe and the provost both nodded.

"Yet the corpse did not appear 'til this morning. If Simon went into the river from the East Bridge, or anywhere near it, the current would have carried his body to the Thames and beyond in the course of a day."

"Mayhap the lad sat upon the riverbank all day, considering whether or not to take his own life," Wycliffe mused. "Or his body was caught for a time upon some snag."

"Was Simon one of those Richard Sabyn was most likely to abuse?" I asked.

"Aye," Master John said.

"Why would he take his life now, when the scholar who made his life miserable is no more?"

Neither Wycliffe nor the provost had an answer.

"We must not leave poor Simon here in the street any longer," Whitfield said. Many Queen's scholars, having heard of the death after rising from their beds, had gathered on Queen's Lane. The provost looked to them and said, "Some of you take Simon to the lecture hall. I will seek the rector of St. Peter-in-the-East and have the boy shriven. Then we will prepare him for burial."

This was done, the sacrament concluded, then the corpse stripped of gown, kirtle, and braes for washing before burial. Simon had spent some time in the river, so washing the corpse was a mere formality, but there are traditions which must be followed. Blood will stain fabric and the discoloration is nearly impossible to eradicate, no matter how diligent the laundress. I had no particular reason to observe preparations for Simon's interment, but I had nothing else in mind to do and the death troubled me.

The damp kirtle, braes, and robe were laid aside and whilst two of the college servants washed the corpse I lifted the garments for a closer look. I had no reason in mind, simply idle curiosity.

Then I saw the holes. One each, in kirtle and gown. They were hardly larger than would be made by a large needle. When the kirtle was held up against the robe, the punctures matched. It was then that I saw a slight discoloration about the hole in the kirtle, a darker patch about the size of the palm of my hand, and barely visible. No such stain was noticeable against the red of the robe.

I held the robe against my chest and Sir Jaket, who had been silently observing all the while, spoke. "You have found something amiss, have you not?"

"Indeed. Fetch Master Wycliffe and the provost. Here is something they must see."

The tiny hole in Simon's robe was slightly to the left of the center of his chest. An awl pushed through a man's breast in such a place would enter his heart, were it long enough. Even though the puncture would be small, blood from a beating heart would seep from such an orifice. How much? No matter the answer, if a man so pierced was immediately plunged unto the Cherwell, blood oozing on to his garments would soon be washed away. Except, perhaps, for some slight trace apparent on a white kirtle.

The servants completed their loathsome task and departed. I was temporarily alone with the corpse. I peered at Simon's chest and saw there what I had expected. A tiny red mark. The wound was barely larger than a hemp seed. A man who saw it but not the holes in gown and kirtle would think it nothing but a scratched blemish.

I was holding Simon's robe before me when Master Wycliffe and the provost hurried into the lecture hall, Sir Jaket and his squire close behind. Henry Whitfield is not young, and in the course of a long life has taken opportunity to enjoy his many meals. He was red-faced and breathing heavily when he entered the room.

"What is it we must see?" he demanded. "Simon drowned. We all saw his state. He was drawn from the river."

"Aye, so he was. But 'tis possible he was dead when he went into it, and whoso did away with him expected the Cherwell to carry Simon beyond Oxford and remove evidence of the felony as well. See here," I held the robe up to the provost. "Note the hole in the garment."

Whitfield scowled and studied the robe. "What? This perforation is likely a moth hole, nothing more."

"Do moths also consume linen kirtles?" I set the robe aside and produced the kirtle. "Or flesh? Look here." I took the provost's elbow and guided him to the corpse. "See below his breast where some slender weapon has penetrated."

Whitfield gazed silently at the wound. I believe he rejected the idea of murder because of the opprobrium such a death would bring to Queen's College – and his administration of the place. "Likely some twig caused this injury after he went into the river," he said.

"Possibly. There is one way to know. No twig so slender could be forced through flesh and past ribs and sinew into a man's heart. If Simon's heart were to be examined and a hole found in it we would then know he was slain, not drowned."

"You wish to desecrate a corpse? Holy Church forbids such a thing."

"The bishops forbid dissection for the purpose of instruction," I said. "There is no rule against seeking the cause of a man's death."

"Nay. I forbid it. Simon will be buried tomorrow in St. Peter's churchyard and he will be interred whole and unabused." And with those words he stalked from the room.

Master John had observed this conversation silently. Now he spoke. "Three small holes, through robe, kirtle, and flesh. Small, but are they large enough to cause death?"

"So I believe. I suppose," I said, "that such a little wound might not bring instant death, but it could so disable a man that he would be unable to resist when his attacker cast him into the river."

"So he would then indeed drown," Wycliffe said.

"Aye, but only because he had first been grievously wounded."

"And there is no way to know if this is so but to open the corpse and inspect Simon's heart?"

"Not so far as I know. But regardless of what the provost thinks or says, or will or will not allow, 'tis my opinion that there have now been two murders done in Queen's College."

"Will you seek two felons?"

"It is possible I will need to find but one."

"One man slew both Richard and Simon? How could that be? They were opposites. Their behavior could not have angered the same man."

"There are many reasons a man might slay another."

"How many of those would exist in an Oxford college?"

"Some would not, I think. Two scholars bound for the church would not quarrel over a maiden," I said.

"Don't be too sure of that," Master John replied.

Two scholars suddenly appeared at the lecture hall door. They did not appear pleased to be there. Sir Jaket and Thomas stood aside to allow them to enter.

"The provost sent us," one said. "We are to stand watch over Simon till noon."

No doubt two other lads would be appointed to watch over the corpse for the afternoon, and several more for the evening and night hours until Friday morning, when Simon would be carried to the churchyard. By that hour nearly all of the lads of Queen's College would have gazed down upon their deceased companion. Such assignments would allow me to interrogate those closest to Richard Sabyn and Simon Duby.

The two scholars who watched over Simon's corpse in the morning agreed with the two who performed the service in the afternoon. No one of Queen's was sorry to learn that Richard was dead; all were saddened to discover that Simon was. Who might have slain Richard? Nearly anyone. Who might have slain Simon? No one. Richard had many enemies; Simon none.

After supper – pease pottage yet again – I told Sir Jaket that we would walk the riverbank and seek the fisherman as he set out his traps for the night. We pushed through the mob of poor folk who, with their bowls, awaited distribution of pottage, and walked the river in the twilight. 'Twas a pleasant stroll, or would have been but for the cause.

I found the fisherman knee-deep in the Cherwell, placing a contraption made of thin wooden strips and netting of hempen cord under an overhanging tree branch. I watched as he fixed the trap to the bank with two stakes and more cords, then went to work locating a second trap. He saw us observing his work but did not stop to inquire of our curiosity. The man surely recognized me, for I had questioned him in the morning.

He finally finished his work and scrambled from the water. He wiped his feet on the grass, drew on a pair of well-worn shoes, then deigned to notice me.

"I am Sir Hugh de Singleton. Mayhap you will remember that I spoke to you this morning regarding the scholar you found in the river."

The man nodded, but said nothing.

"Do folk often walk the riverbank here? I see what seems to be a path worn in the grass."

"Aye, folk do."

"Do you often see the same people, alone or with companions?"

"Don't come 'ere much in the day. An' scholars like to lay abed in the mornin', so most often them as comes by do so late, like now."

"And some who do so are regular?"

"A few."

"Do some lads come past with lasses?"

The fisherman smiled through his thick beard. "They do. Not all of 'em garbed as scholars."

"But some?"

"Aye. Some."

"Are some of the scholars who frequent this path of Queen's College, garbed in red gowns, as was the lad drawn from the river this morning?"

"Some be."

"Did you see any such last night when you placed your traps?"

"Not 'ere, along the path."

"Does that mean you saw some Queen's scholars elsewhere?"

"Aye, crossin' East Bridge."

"How many?"

"Two."

"Which way were they traveling, east or west?"

"East. Odd, though."

"What was odd?"

"They stopped in the middle of the bridge an' seemed to argue."

"Seemed to?"

"One lad poked 'is finger to the chest of 'tother."

"Ah," I said. "Not a thing one is likely to do in amicable conversation. If you saw these scholars again would you recognize them?"

"Nay. East Bridge be too far away an' me eyes not so good as when I was a lad."

"But you could see well enough that you are sure one of these scholars jabbed a finger into the chest of the other?"

"Oh, aye. No doubt about that. Them young scholars is always arguin' 'bout somethin'."

"Indeed. Did these disputatious scholars look into the river whilst they argued?"

"Aye, now you mention it."

The occasional twig floated past with the current as I spoke to the fisherman. "How long, would you say, would it take for an object to pass from the bridge to this place?"

"Not long. No more'n half an hour. Mayhap less."

"Show me where the scholar's corpse was when you found it."

"Right there; 'is arm was tangled in me net."

If that was the case Simon could have gone into the Cherwell hours earlier and been arrested for hours at the trap. As I had suspected. He was likely put into the river well before the fisherman found him – perhaps not long after the man had set his traps the night before. And long enough for the current to wash blood from garments and skin, except for the faint discoloration on Simon's kirtle.

I thanked the fisherman for his time and gave him a farthing. I told him that, did he remember anything else of last night and early this morning which might pertain to a corpse in the Cherwell, he should seek me at Queen's College. I hoped the coin might jog his memory.

"Would a man slay another," Sir Jaket said, "then toss the corpse from a bridge? The splash could be heard, I think."

"Aye," I agreed. "And the sound would travel in the night – although it could be that no one was about to hear it. Look where this path approaches the bridge. There is no space to walk under, so any who walked here must climb the verge to the road, then descend on the other side. 'Twould be easy enough to plunge an awl into Simon, then drag him down the slope and place him in the river."

"Aye. And this could be done silently," Sir Jaket agreed. "If the lad did not cry out when he was pierced."

"The fisherman saw two Queen's scholars arguing upon the bridge. Mayhap two did the murder, one put a hand over Simon's mouth and the other drove the bodkin to his heart. Or perhaps one of the two the fisherman saw was Simon, quarreling with the scholar who slew him."

"Does this murder have to do with the death of that other scholar – the one who was supposed to have perished of a lightning strike?"

"What do you think?" I said.

"'Twould be most strange for two lads of the same college to be slain within a few days of each other and the deaths be unrelated."

"Indeed. But are the felons responsible the same?"

"Seems to me once a man has killed he will be less troubled about doing so again."

"Especially," I said, "if the second murder is needed to conceal the first. If found out, he can hang but once."

"Would Simon have known who slew Richard?"

"He might have. Or the felon who slew Richard thought he did."

I slept fitfully that night, and left my bed at dawn bleary-eyed. In the night I had decided to seek the provost's permission to examine Simon's chamber. This was granted, as Whitfield was becoming more concerned by the hour, I believe, that two deaths at Queen's reflected badly upon his tenure. And he was already viewed as an interloper, not being from Cumberland.

Sir Jaket and Thomas accompanied me to Simon's chamber. The provost had assured me that the small cell was as Simon had left it. Nothing had been disturbed. All of the scholars' cells were equipped with a table, a bench, and a bed. A small chest rested in a corner of Simon's chamber, and sometime between Richard Sabyn's death and Simon's disappearance the chamber had been swept clean of the dust and plaster which littered the place a few days past.

"What do you seek?" Sir Jaket asked.

"I don't know," I shrugged. "When I find it, then I will know."

The table and bench were copies of those in other scholars' chambers. The desk top was bare but for a cresset which had lighted the scholar's nocturnal study. If Simon had been studying a book before his death, some other had cleared it away despite the provost's assertion.

I prodded the mattress and felt nothing but the straw with which it was filled. I lifted the bed frame to learn if the lad had stored some possessions under it. I saw only traces of plaster dust which had not been completely swept away

The chest was of oak, small, iron-bound, and well crafted. It was furnished with a hasp, but there was no lock. I lifted the chest to the table and raised the lid. Spare kirtle and braes were folded atop other objects lower in the box. There was a leather pouch containing a handful of coins, mostly farthings and pennies, but also a groat. Many Queen's scholars own black gowns as well as red, as they are required to don red only whilst in the college. But some fellows and boys are too poor to own two gowns. Simon was one of these. The chest contained no black gown.

Three books rested upon the bottom of the chest: *Categories* by Aristotle; *Sentences* by Lombard; and *Topics*, Book Four, by Boethius. I found four quills, two of them sharpened and stained with use, and a pot of ink with a wooden stopper also. Just above the books I found eight sheets of parchment and a copy of the Gospel of St. Matthew. This was likely rented, as few scholars can afford their own Bible. Mayhap Simon had ink and parchment ready so he could make his own copy of the gospel. This is also commonly done.

Who, I wondered, would now claim Simon Duby's few possessions? Queen's College could make use of the books, although they were set books and many surely already possessed copies. The parchment, ink, and pens would also find use. Who would claim the coins? And the clothing? I decided to inform Master Wycliffe of what I had found. He could tell the provost.

I closed the chest and replaced it upon the floor. As I bent to lower the chest I noticed that one of the table legs was split at the bottom. Could the blast in the adjacent chamber have done the damage, I wondered? The leg was yet serviceable and in no danger of collapse, but having had recent experience of table legs which were more than they seemed I decided the cracked leg should be inspected.

I upended the table and was startled at what I saw there. Holes, like those in the table legs in Richard Sabyn's chamber, had been bored into the bottom of each leg. The hole in the cracked leg was off center, thus the weakness of the wood which caused the split. I felt certain of what I would find if I examined the holes.

Two of the bores were empty, but from two I extracted leaves of tightly rolled parchment. I turned the table back to its proper position, then unrolled one of the parchments. Sir Jaket and Thomas looked on, open-mouthed.

The first scroll I flattened upon the table contained, in tiny script, chapters three and four of the Gospel of St. Matthew, written in English. I was sure that when I unrolled the other parchment I would find chapters one and two. And I did.

"What have you found?" Sir Jaket said. The man can read and write, but he stood behind me, some distance from the scrolls, and the writing was small. "What did Simon hide?"

"'Tis the Gospel of St. Matthew," I told him, "or part of it, written in English. Simon was slain before he could complete the translation. If that is what he was about and 'twas the reason for stuffing his work in a hollow table leg."

"Such a thing is forbidden," Sir Jaket exclaimed. "Why would he do such a thing? Certainly he knew better."

Simon had known that what he did was prohibited. Whether or not he knew better depended upon what he thought was better. Sir Jaket had no Latin, so trusted his priest to tell him what the Lord Christ required of him. Some priests can be relied upon to do so truthfully. Not all.

"Thomas," I said, "take word to Master John that he is wanted here."

The lad bowed and scurried off.

Wycliffe appeared a few minutes later, curiosity creasing his brow. "What have you found?" he asked.

"The provost granted me permission to search Simon's chamber. Look here." I upended the table again and pointed to the holes bored in each leg.

"Hmmm. The same as Richard's table. This is odd. Did you also find parchment rolled into the holes?"

I pointed to the scrolls, which I had laid upon Simon's bed. "The first four chapters of the Gospel of St. Matthew."

"In English?" Wycliffe asked.

"Aye."

"This is indeed strange. Two scholars who disliked each other at work at the same business."

"There are four gospels," I reminded him.

"What?" Wycliffe exclaimed. "You believe there may be two other scholars translating the Gospels of St. Mark and St. Luke to English?"

"I would wager a shilling on it," I said.

"I would not take the bet," Master John replied.

"That chest," I said, changing the subject, "contains all of Simon Duby's possessions. Amongst these are three books and a purse with perhaps two shillings of coins."

"Likely his next of kin are in Cumberland," Wycliffe said. "What books are there?"

I told him.

"There is always a market for set books. They can be sold and the funds added to what he had in the purse. Whitfield can deposit the total with Osney Abbey, then write a letter to Simon's parents, if they can be found, which, with his seal, will allow them to receive the funds from an Augustinian House near to them. Carlisle is near, and Carmel also. They might honor the exchange as well."

"The Gospels of St. Mark and St. Luke trouble me," I

said. "If the provost learns that Richard and Simon were doing forbidden work at Queen's, and there may be others at the business, he will upend every table in the college seeking holes bored in the legs. If two hid their work in such a way, two others may also have done so."

"And woe betide the scholars he discovers," Wycliffe said.

"Indeed. We must find them first," I said.

"And do what?"

"Warn them to desist. Or, if they will not, tell them to conceal their work in some other way."

"That will do them little good," Wycliffe said, "if the provost learns what has been found in the chambers of Richard and Simon. Even if the other scholars remove their work and hide the translations elsewhere, the holes bored in the table legs – if that is how they also are concealing what they are doing – will tell Whitfield of their actions."

"Then he must not learn of the translations," I said. "Do you agree?"

"Aye. I have long believed that men should be able to read God's word in their common tongue."

"And you have spoken of this belief. I remember when I sat under your teaching at Balliol you suggested such an opinion."

"I am more careful now than when I was a young master," Wycliffe grimaced. "Yet if the scholars at Queen's believe they have discerned my opinion and have decided to act upon it, I am responsible for what may befall them."

"Then we must discover the other translators and tell them to look to their safety."

"How will we find them?" Wycliffe said. "We must not ask each of them. To do so would alert those not involved, and likely at least one would go to Whitfield and the cat will be out of the bag."

"Is there a time when all scholars will be absent from their chambers?"

"Aye. At disputations."

"Is such a debate scheduled today?"

"This morning, at the fourth hour. 'Twill last till noon, and dinner."

"Must you take part?"

"Nay. I sometimes participate, and offer my views if asked, but my absence would not be noted as unusual. I believe I see your scheme. We must enter each chamber and upend the tables to learn if two more have holes bored in the legs."

"Just so," I replied.

We four waited in Wycliffe's chamber until the upper corridor was silent and empty, and we could hear voices from the lecture hall. I assigned Master John and Sir Jaket to investigate the chambers on one side of the passage whilst I and Thomas entered those on the other. 'Twas Wycliffe and Sir Jaket who found both hidden gospels, secreted in drilled table legs as with the Gospels of St. John and St. Matthew. Neither of the discovered translations was complete.

Chapter 6

Master John took the rolled parchments to his chamber and buried them deep in his chest, where he had previously hidden Richard and Simon's work. He then told me that he would speak to Gospatric Map and Robert Talley, in whose chambers we had found the gospels, that afternoon and tell them of their danger and what had been done with their work.

I told Wycliffe I wished to be present when the scholars were told of our discovery. Two of four translators had been slain. Were Gospatric and Robert also in danger? Did they know of, or could they guess, who the felons were who had murdered their collaborators? And surely Richard and Simon, dissimilar as they were, had worked in concert with each other and with Gospatric and Robert. Each was translating a separate gospel, and all hid their work in the same way.

At dinner I saw Master John approach Robert and Gospatric, and when the meal was done they followed him. As did I. And also Sir Jaket and Thomas.

Although Wycliffe's chamber was large, six men found the place crowded. Two of those present were perplexed about the cause of the assembly. Wycliffe motioned to Thomas to close the chamber door, then pointed to a bench and invited Gospatric and Robert to sit.

"The work of our Lord Christ on earth is told," he began, "in four gospels. Sir Hugh has discovered that two Queen's scholars, engaged in translating these books to English, have been slain. We know not why, but may guess. This morning we learned that you are also engaged in this laudable but dangerous work. Nay," Wycliffe said as Robert made to speak a denial, "the Gospels of St. Mark and St. Luke were found rolled into bored-out table legs in your chambers. Just as Richard and Simon hid their English translations of the Gospels of St. Matthew and St. John."

"Who," I asked, "of Queen's scholars know of your work? Other than Richard and Simon, who are now in St. Peter's churchyard?"

Robert and Gospatric glanced to each other. It occurred to me that, 'til then, they had not looked to each other or even acknowledged the presence of the other.

"None others," Robert finally said. "The fewer who know a secret, the less likely 'twill be bandied about."

"Are you certain no others know?" I said. "Did you ever suspect that any other Queen's scholars might have learned of your work? Would Richard or Simon have been careless and let slip an incautious word?"

Gospatric shrugged. "Who can know?" he said. "Not within my hearing." Robert nodded agreement but said nothing.

"Two of four who were translating the gospels to English are dead," I reminded them. "You should be careful. Whether or not their work was the cause of Richard's and Simon's murders I do not know. If any other scholar lets slip a word which might indicate a suspicion of what you have been about, come to me and tell of it."

"Is there any more to be learned from Gospatric and Robert?" Master John asked.

"Probably... if a question occurs to me, I know where to find them. You may go," I said, "but take care to whom you speak."

All during this interview Robert and Gospatric had said nothing to each other, nor did they, but for that one moment, even admit the presence of the other. I thought this strange.

I had yet to discover who had concocted the explosive powder which sent Richard Sabyn to meet the Lord Christ, so plotted the afternoon's business with Sir Jaket, with Wycliffe looking on.

"Only a pound or less of charcoal would be needed," I said, "to create the blast which killed Richard. Charcoal burners would remember if a youth purchased such a small amount, whether he wore a scholar's robe of black or red, or was plainly garbed. Most charcoal is sold in hempen sacks so large even a strong man will find them troublesome to carry. Sir Jaket, you and Thomas travel to Cowley and Littlemore to seek the charcoal burners there. The villages are not far. I will go to Eynsham and seek the charcoal burner who resides in that village."

I wondered whether I should tell the sheriff of Simon's death and the holes in kirtle, gown, and flesh which pointed to murder.

Aye, I should. I decided to do so before I rode to Eynsham.

"So at first 'twas thought the lad had drowned," Sir Roger said when I had gained audience with him. "But now you believe murder has been done?"

"Aye. There is evidence to suggest it." I told the sheriff of the holes in Simon's robe, kirtle, and flesh.

"But he may have drowned and these punctures be mere happenstance?"

"Mayhap."

"Hmmm. If you find more evidence to prove murder, seek me and I will assign a constable to assist you. Although, as the death involves Queen's College 'tis the bishop's bailiwick, not mine. Until then, as the evidence

93

for felony is conjecture, I'll leave you to sort out the matter. You have, in the past, proved yourself capable of doing so. Keep me informed." With that Sir Roger stood and I was dismissed.

From the castle I sought the mews where our beasts were stabled and set off for Eynsham. Finding the charcoal burner was no trouble. The first man I encountered when I entered the village directed me to the fellow. "Nay," he said, when asked if any man had approached him to purchase a small amount of charcoal. He sold only by the sackful, to smiths and farriers of Eynsham, Abingdon, and Oxford.

Because of time lost speaking to the sheriff I was late returning to Queen's. Although 'twas yet light, supper was past and I had to content myself with a stale maslin loaf from the kitchen. The ale was also gone stale. The afternoon had been most unsatisfactory.

Whilst I was consuming the stale loaf the cook opened a sack and strew corns of sulfur about his kitchen floor. I had heard that mice and rats and other vermin dislike the smell and will vacate a place where the stuff is. I now knew where a scholar of Queen's might collect sulfur to make the explosive powder.

Sir Jaket and Thomas had received the same answers as I did when they called upon the charcoal burners of Cowley and Littlemore. No buyer had purchased less than a sackful for years.

"I suppose," Thomas said, "a man might purchase a sack of charcoal, remove what he required, then toss the residue in the river."

"He might. But this would be a waste of money, and most scholars have few coins to spare. Without a cart the charcoal could not be transported back to Oxford. Renting a cart and runcie would also be an expense."

"'Twas but a suggestion," the squire shrugged.

"There are many smiths and farriers in Oxford," I

said. "Perhaps the felon went in the night to one of these and stole a pouch of charcoal. A pound or so of the stuff would not be missed, and I suspect most smiths store their supply in a shed, just to keep it from the weather."

"What of the brimstone needed to make the explosive powder?" Sir Jaket asked. "Where in Oxford might that be had?"

I told him of the cook's use of the yellow stuff to rid his kitchen of pests. "Not much is needed," I added. "Only one part in ten."

"And the saltpeter? What of that? You said that three parts in four of the explosive must be saltpeter."

"The salt is simple to obtain, but it cannot be done quickly. Unless one can collect the urine of many men."

"Urine?" Sir Jaket said skeptically.

"Aye. Urine is collected and boiled until the water has evaporated and all that remains is the salt. The whole process is more complicated than that, but there you have the rudiments. If but one man is involved 'twould take many months, a year mayhap, to collect enough."

"Where in Queen's College could that be done?" Thomas asked.

"Nowhere, I think. Oh, the urine might be collected here, but the processing would need to be done elsewhere."

"Unless the explosive powder could be obtained elsewhere and brought to Oxford ready for use."

"'Tis possible, I suppose. But the only place in the realm where the stuff is made is in London, at the Tower, where the king's armorers produce it. I've not heard of it being made elsewhere."

"So all which is necessary to blast a man to the churchyard may be had here, in Oxford," Sir Jaket said.

"Aye. And no doubt there are leather workers near who have awls and bodkins with which a man might be pierced. If a man wishes to slay another, there are many innocuous tools which can be converted to the purpose. Even a man's urine.

"According to Master Wycliffe," I continued, "there were two reasons why a man might slay Richard Sabyn. The scholar insulted all others, and he was at work translating a gospel to English. All men knew of his objectionable character, but did anyone know what he was doing, alone in his chamber? And if they did know, would they care enough to slay him? And as for Simon Duby, he would not have been slain for his offensive behavior."

"Then someone knew of Simon translating a gospel to English?" Sir Jaket said.

"Mayhap. But if so, why not simply tell the provost of it? He would have been expelled from Queen's, but even an archdeacon's court would not do more than that, I think."

"Hmmm." The knight scratched his head. "Is there another reason a man might have for slaying Simon of which we know not?"

"I believe so. But I cannot think what it might be. Perhaps he was slain not for what he had done, but for what he knew, as we have already considered."

"You think he might have known who killed Richard?"

"It's possible that he might, and may even have had a hand in the deed."

"A conspiracy?"

"Perhaps."

"Of scholars Richard had abused?"

"Just so."

"That might include all who study at Queen's College, according to Master Wycliffe."

"And some who conspired with Richard to translate the Lord Christ's deeds and words to English," I added. "Conspirators both for and against Richard Sabyn."

"If so, the matter will be complicated to sort out,"

Sir Jaket said. "No wonder the sheriff is willing to allow you to work without imposing his jurisdiction. If you succeed in discovering a murderer or two he can insert himself into the arrest. If a felon or felons are not found he suffers no loss of prestige, as he can claim the failure not his, but yours. He has likely asked," Sir Jaket concluded, "that you keep him informed, has he not?"

"He has."

"So if he believes you close on the trail of the killers he can send serjeants to step in ahead of you and take credit for solving these crimes."

"You believe Sir Roger would be so duplicitous?" I asked.

"Of course. He did not rise to be Sheriff of Oxford because he was an innocent."

I slept well that night. Likely because of exhaustion from the day's investigations. Certainly not owing to a mind at ease. Master John would want to know what Sir Jaket and I learned the previous afternoon, as well as what we did not learn.

I sought him next morning after splashing water upon my face to wash sleep from my eyes. He had procured a loaf from the kitchen, and a ewer of ale. He invited me to break my fast with him and I told of the past afternoon as I did so.

"The sulfur, then," he said, "could be collected from the kitchen floor, and charcoal purloined from some smith's supply. Because so little would be required, what was missing would never be noticed."

"So I believe."

"Then 'tis the source of the saltpeter which must be found."

"Aye," I agreed. "More of the stuff is needed than any other ingredient to make the explosive powder, and it is more difficult to acquire."

"Sheriff Roger told you that alder and willow make the best charcoal for explosive powder. What did the Eynsham charcoal burner have to say?"

"He said only that pine and suchlike wood makes poor charcoal. Trying to do so makes a puddle of pitch. Any tree which loses its leaves in autumn," he said, "will make good charcoal. Alder and willow," he claimed, "are difficult to obtain, and in his view elm, oak, and beech serve just as well."

"If the felon who slew Richard knew this he would not trouble himself to know whence came the charcoal he stole."

I heard the sound of a hammer. Master John saw me turn my head to the door, whence came the pounding noise.

"Whitfield has employed men to repair Richard Sabyn's chamber," he said. "A rafter must be reinforced, new slates fixed to the battens, and the wattle and plaster of the walls replaced. The ceiling, also."

"The provost is not likely pleased for the expense," I said.

"He is displeased at any expense," Wycliffe smiled.

Sir Jaket appeared as I consumed the last of the half-loaf Wycliffe had broken off for me. He could not disguise his hunger. I told him that loaves might be available in the kitchen, and if so he should get two – one for Thomas.

"'Tis good that Master Henry has decided to set the repairs in order. Yesterday, whilst you were out," Wycliffe said, "I saw some of Father Hubert's doves exploring the hole in the roof. The priest would be upset if his birds abandoned their dovecote for the college attic."

"Who is Father Hubert?"

"Rector at St. Peter-in-the-East. Enjoys a squab for his dinner now and then, does Father Hubert."

"Does he have a dovecote near the church?"

"Aye, between church and rectory, just outside the churchyard wall. Proud of it. Few gentlemen have one better."

"How many doves does he keep?"

"Who knows? I've never asked. Fifty, at least, from what I've seen flocking at dusk. Mayhap a hundred."

"Saltpeter," I said, thinking aloud, "can be got from the urine of men and beasts. I wonder if it can be distilled from the droppings of birds."

"You have me there," Wycliffe said. "I'm thought a wise man, but no man can know all."

"The sophists thought so."

"So they did. They were wrong. But Sir Roger would know, I think."

"He might. I will pay him another visit."

"Who?" Sir Jaket said. The knight entered Master John's chamber with two loaves and Thomas close behind.

"The sheriff."

"I'll accompany you. Sir Roger and my father fought side by side at Poitiers. I've not seen him since I was a lad."

"You are welcome. And Thomas, also."

Could saltpeter be collected from dove droppings? Sir Roger did not know. He'd not heard of such a thing, but the king's armorers at the Tower used all sorts of ordure to collect the salt, he said, and whether the excretion came from man, beast, or fowl he thought it could be used.

We departed the castle in time to return as the trumpet sounded for dinner. Somehow Master Whitfield had found a few shillings for stockfish, so we and the scholars were spared another meal of pease pottage. But there was surely a kettle of it in the kitchen. Whitfield would not feed the poor at the college gate with stockfish.

Master John sat beside me as I consumed fish and bread. He knew where I had gone from his chamber, and why, and asked what I had learned.

"Very little. Sir Roger knows of no reason saltpeter could not be extracted from dove droppings, but does not know that it can be, either. The armorers at the Tower have enough urine from men and beasts that they do not, I suspect, need to experiment with other sources.

"Do you know the rector of St. Peter's well?" I continued. "Would he be offended if I asked of his doves?"

"Aye. Know him well. A portly, jolly fellow is Father Hubert. He'd be proud to display his birds. Although pride is, of course, a sin."

"Is that why the Lord Christ said 'twas difficult for a rich man to gain heaven? The poor have few goods of which to be proud, whereas the wealthy have much."

"A man – or a woman –" Wycliffe said, "may be proud of many things. Richard Sabyn was poor, but I've rarely seen a scholar so proud."

"And Simon Duby was humble?"

"He was. But may a man be proud of his humility? When a man recognizes his humility he no longer is."

"You are wading in waters too deep for me," I said.

"To return to your question. I know Father Hubert well, and the bell rang for the noon Angelus half an hour past. He will be free. Come, we will seek him."

A misty rain began to fall as Wycliffe, Sir Jaket, Thomas, and I crossed Queen's Lane and entered the church. A clerk was busy in the vestry, told us the priest was in his rectory, and pointed to a door which opened from vestry to the churchyard.

I saw the dovecote as we passed from church to rectory. It was separated from the churchyard by a low wall, so as not to profane the place where so many of the parish awaited the Lord Christ's return. Wycliffe rapped upon the rectory door and a servant opened to us. When Master John asked to speak to the priest, the servant told us to wait in the hall, tugged a forelock, and hurried off.

The rector was as Master John had described him. His belly pushed his robe before him, and his belt and rosary were long enough to encircle my waist twice. His jowls were heavy, and his eyes peered at the world from lids crinkled from mirth. So I thought.

"Father Hubert," Wycliffe began, "here are Sir Hugh de Singleton, Sir Jaket Bec, and Thomas Bennying. Sir Hugh is bailiff to Lord Gilbert Talbot, at Bampton, and also a surgeon."

The priest bowed slightly in greeting. "How may I serve Lord Gilbert's bailiff?"

"You have a large dovecote. How many birds make their home there?" I asked.

The priest turned to Master John, curiosity creasing his brow.

"You remember the great storm a week past? When a portion of the roof was torn from Queen's College?" Wycliffe said.

"Aye. I see that repairs have begun this morning."

"There is evidence that 'twas not a bolt of lightning which caused the damage."

"Oh? What then?" Father Hubert said.

"Have you heard of the explosive powder which can propel a stone ball with great force?"

"Aye."

"The blast which killed a Queen's scholar was likely caused by a pouch of the stuff, not lightning. Sir Hugh has investigated many felonies and discovered the perpetrators. I have asked him to seek the malefactor who did this evil."

The priest's eyes widened under his heavy lids. "Murder was done? How could this be?"

"The explosive powder," I said, "is made of three elements: charcoal, brimstone, and saltpeter. We know whence the charcoal and sulfur came, or believe we do. 'Tis the origin of the saltpeter which vexes us. And more of the salt is required than of the other two elements."

"What has this to do with my doves?"

"Saltpeter may be extracted from the urine of men and beasts. Mayhap from other excrement? Such as the droppings of fowl," I surmised. "Who clears the offal from your dovecote, and how often does he do so?"

"My servant, Hucca. I require that he collect the dung every fortnight."

"Is the fellow near? I would like to speak to him."

"'Twas Hucca who opened to you. I will seek him."

The priest bustled off and from the next room I heard him call for the servant. The man replied, and soon both re-entered the hall.

"This man," Father Hubert said, gesturing to me, "is bailiff to Lord Gilbert Talbot, in Bampton. He has questions for you."

"You care for Father Hubert's doves, I understand. How many has he?"

"Not sure. Ain't easy to count 'em."

"A hundred? More? Less?"

"Likely more'n a hundred. Hundred an' fifty, mayhap."

"And you are charged with clearing the droppings every fortnight?"

Hucca wrinkled his nose at being reminded of the repulsive duty. "Aye. Every fortnight."

"Most who care for dovecotes put down straw. Do you also?"

"Aye. Helps to keep droppin's from gettin' hard, like. Easier to clean the place."

"Where do you place the straw after you rake it from the dovecote?"

"Just behind the wall."

"Show me."

Hucca looked to Father Hubert, shrugged, and said, "Follow me."

The wall behind the dovecote was crudely made, the stones simply laid haphazardly, and was barely waist-high. High enough to keep out stray pigs, and to signal to unwanted visitors that here was a place they should not enter. The ground behind the churchyard sloped toward the stone wall so that rain would gather and flow through the base of the wall.

The servant stopped at the wall and pointed to a pile of moldering straw nearly as high as the wall. The heap was about four paces in diameter, and located between the wall and a little-used path which meandered toward St. John's Hospital. A shallow ditch bordered this path, and mud in the ditch indicated that when rain fell, water would flow toward the path, the hospital, and beyond to the Cherwell.

Before entering the ditch rainwater would soak the pile of straw, and water would leech residue from dove droppings into the trench. If a man collected this befouled drainage, could he boil it down 'til naught but saltpeter remained?

"Do folk often use this path to travel from Queen's Lane to the hospital?" I asked Hucca.

"Nay. High Street goes same way. Mostly see men walk this way after rain, when the street is mud."

The path was so little used that sparse grass grew along its course. The thin sod would protect a man's shoes from the muddy street. If he knew the path existed.

"After rain does this ditch flow with water?"

"Aye. Near dry now, 'cause we've had little rain since the storm what blew a hole in Queen's roof. Rainin' now some, so likely there'll be water in the ditch tomorrow."

"When the ditch flowed with water in the past did

you ever see a man with a bucket scooping water from it?"

"Aye, so I did. Thought it strange."

"When was this?"

"Oh, long ago. Last autumn. After Martinmas it was, I think. But not much after."

"Did the fellow see you?"

"Aye, think so. 'Twas near dark, an' rain come down all day, so there was water in the ditch. I come with a pitchfork o' straw I'd just taken from the dovecote an' was about to throw it over the wall when I seen the fellow. Had two buckets. 'E looked up, saw me, an' 'urried away, like 'e'd been caught stealin' somethin' of worth."

"Which way did he go?"

Hucca pointed east, toward the hospital. "Dark enough I couldn't see if 'e went to the hospital. Didn't much care."

"What did the man look like? Can you describe him?"

"Nay. Near to dark, wasn't it?"

"Did he wear a scholar's gown?"

"Oh, aye."

"Tall or short? Fat or thin?"

"Thin, 'e was, an' taller than most."

"You saw this man but once?"

"Aye. Never seen 'im again."

Eight months had passed since Hucca saw a man drawing befouled water which had drained from the pile of straw and droppings. What if he had become more cautious after being seen once, and so visited the place only after dark? In winter months rain falls often. Nearly every day if it doesn't snow. How many buckets of ditchwater could the fellow collect? Enough to distill a pound or so of saltpeter? Even Sir Roger would not be able to answer that question.

The mist continued to fall, and became a light rain

as I questioned the servant. If it continued through the night might the ditch fill with water drained from the heap of straw and droppings? Mayhap. Could this be of importance to my investigation? Best wait and see, rather than speak my thoughts and see them come to nothing.

When we had first come near the dovecote, birds had taken flight, startled that so many men had gathered about their home. Now, as we departed the churchyard, they returned. Perhaps they liked rain no more than I. The precipitation had begun as mist, became rain, and by the time we entered Queen's was become a downpour. The hole in the college roof could not be patched too soon. A few slates had been replaced this day, but most of the work was yet to be done. The hole had been covered with a waxed hempen canvas in recent days, to keep out the rain, and this was now in place again.

Rain did not much deter the poor, who huddled under the eaves awaiting the distribution of pease pottage. Where, I wondered, did these folk spend their days and nights? Most would have a roof over their heads, I thought, however mean it might be. But mayhap some slept wherever they might. Even against a churchyard wall? It might be worth asking. But not then. I was sodden, and wished to be out of the rain.

I would need buckets, as many as could be found, and a brass pot, or iron. After mass next day I set about collecting these. Henry Whitfield looked askance at me when I asked how many buckets the college possessed. He knew not, so sent me to the caretaker.

"Three," the fellow replied, and as none were currently in use I took all three. Queen's cook showed me a bronze pot which could hold perhaps four gallons, and reluctantly gave me permission to use it for a few days. From Father Hubert I collected another bucket, then returned to the college refectory in time for dinner.

The cook had prepared aloes of lamb with maslin loaves this day, and whilst we ate I explained to Master John, Sir Jaket, and Thomas my intention. I would collect ditchwater which had drained through the pile of straw and dove droppings behind the dovecote. This I would place in the cook's bronze pot, then build a fire under it. So long as water remained in the ditch I would refill the pot, boil off the liquid, and keep careful record of how many buckets of water I had boiled away.

"Ah," Wycliffe exclaimed. "I see your scheme. You wish to discover if saltpeter could come from the droppings of Father Hubert's doves, and if so, how many buckets a man would need to fill to make enough to send a man to the next world."

"Just so. Thomas, will you assist me in filling the buckets after dinner? And the fire under the bronze pot must burn continually. If it is allowed to go out each night 'twill take twice as long to boil away the water."

"I often rise in the night," Wycliffe said. "I'll help keep the blaze going. Where will you build this fire?"

"In the toft behind the college. There is a space between the building and a row of mulberry bushes. I will need permission of the provost."

"Which he will grant," Master John said. "The fellows of Queen's are displeased that two scholars have died and he is unable to discover why."

"I have told him why they perished," I said.

"He is unwilling to accept murder as the cause. To do so would reflect badly upon his governance. Either way, murder or not," Wycliffe said, "he would seem incompetent. If you can prove murder and ferret out the felon he will be pleased, I think. Especially if he can take some credit for the apprehension."

"Even if the wickedness is found within Queen's College?"

"Aye, even so."

"How many buckets of that ditchwater will you need to boil to have enough saltpeter?" Sir Jaket asked.

"Don't know. I'm not even sure a film of saltpeter will result, no matter how much water I distill."

"If you are successful and produce saltpeter, what then?"

"We may know whence all three ingredients came which blasted the life from Richard Sabyn."

"What of Simon Duby?" Wycliffe said.

"One murder at a time."

When the meal was done Thomas came with me to collect the buckets and fill them with water from the ditch. Although the rain had ceased, the water in this channel was yet ankle-deep and the four buckets were soon filled. We carried them behind Queen's and from there I entered the kitchen and brought out the bronze pot. It balanced upon three legs, each longer than a man's middle finger, so a sizeable fire could be lit under it.

The cook was not pleased that I also carried off an armload of his firewood, and even less so when I told him that in an hour or so I would return for more. A small iron scoop rested near the kitchen fireplace. I filled it with embers, took these to the toft, and set ablaze the wood under the pot. Half an hour or so later bubbles began to form in the pot. A faint white skin appeared on the surface of the water, and a foul odor offended my nostrils. Of course, foul odors are common in Oxford, but this was different.

Half the water in the pot had boiled away by nightfall. I took two buckets to the watery ditch, filled them, and returned whilst there was yet enough light to see my way carrying two heavy buckets without stumbling.

Sir Jaket had taken a turn tending the fire. After I emptied the buckets into the pot and refilled it to the brim I dismissed him and took the next watch. Master John had promised to relieve me at midnight, but I told him that he need not do so 'til nearer dawn. Thomas would replace him at sunrise.

How many days and how many buckets of ditchwater would be required before I would know if a heap of straw and dove droppings could produce saltpeter? And if I learned that it could, would the knowledge lead to a felon? Sometimes there is no way to learn the destination of a path but to travel it.

Chapter 7

$\mathcal{F}$or three days I hauled water from the ditch to the boiling kettle. By Monday evening the water level in the ditch had fallen so that I was unable to fill both buckets. I used one to top off the other. Tuesday morning dawned grey and rainy, so the stream was replenished. But the rain nearly extinguished my fire. Wednesday, after supper, I procured a large wooden spoon from the kitchen and scooped the accumulated skin from the pot and set it aside. By Thursday morning the pot had boiled dry, the fire beneath it reduced to a few glowing ashes.

When the pot had cooled sufficiently I removed it from the pile of ashes and with the spoon scraped the pale residue from the sides and bottom of the pot. This powder I added to what I had skimmed from the pot on Wednesday, then poured the flour-like accumulation into a vial and secured it with a wooden stopper. The vial was somewhat over half full and slightly larger than my thumb.

Master John, Sir Jaket, and Thomas had watched this process. "What now?" Wycliffe said.

I must find a goldsmith and have this powder weighed. When I learn how much I have I will know how much sulfur and charcoal to blend with it. And if it detonates, the size of the explosion will give me an idea of how much of the mix was used to slay Richard Sabyn."

"Hah," Sir Jaket said. "Will you set a match to it?"

"Aye. If the powder explodes I will know where the fatal explosive mix may have been made, and how."

"I will stand well back when you put a flame to it," Wycliffe grinned. "Just in case you have been successful."

"You hope for failure?"

"Nay. I am eager to hear the blast."

At that moment Henry Whitfield appeared. The man's face was pale and drawn with worry. He appeared not to have slept for some nights. He spoke, and we soon learned the reason for his appearance.

"Ah... I was told I would find you here." He glanced to the pot, the ashes, and the vial I held in my hand. "Henry atte Brooke is taken ill. The pestilence has come to Queen's, I fear. I learned just yesterday that two scholars of Balliol are taken, and a canon of St. Frideswide's Priory." The provost wrung his hands as he spoke, as well he might. Plague will jump from man to man as a flame from one scrap of tinder to another. "I have commanded that no others enter Henry's chamber. I told him that meals and ale will be shoved through the opening when his door is pushed ajar."

"Who will carry off his slops?" Wycliffe asked.

"That he must deal with for himself."

"If 'tis the pestilence he will be unable to rise from his bed. You would have him die in his own filth?"

"Better that than another perish caring for him."

"What better cause for a man to die? I would willingly meet the Lord Christ if that was the reason for the encounter. And the dead must be shriven. I will do so now, if he is as near death as you believe."

Whitfield looked at Master John, shook his head, then said, "Very well. You may enter his chamber if you wish, and die with him."

"If plague has come to Balliol and St. Frideswide's

and Queen's," Sir Jaket said, "it will affect others soon, if not already."

"Aye," Master John agreed. "Then the scholars who can will flee to their homes, and if one is the felon who slew Richard Sabyn he will escape the penalty due him." He looked to me. "Haste is important."

"Haste may lead to error," I said. "I would rather fail to apprehend the felon than accuse an innocent man. But for now, I intend to take this," I held up the vial, "to a goldsmith and have it weighed."

Sir Jaket and Thomas accompanied me to Fish Street, while Wycliffe went to Henry atte Brooke's chamber to learn how ill the lad was, and offer Extreme Unction if he was as near death as the provost believed.

I knew of a goldsmith who did business near the South Gate. The burgher brought out his scales. I emptied the vial to one pan, and he placed his weights upon the other. "An ounce," he said. "Mayhap a few grains more."

I thanked the man, gave him a penny for his trouble, and with Sir Jaket and Thomas hurried back to Queen's College. On the way I turned from the High Street to an alley which ran behind a blacksmith's forge. I thought I might find some discarded charcoal fragments there. I did.

At Queen's I went to the kitchen and asked the cook for a small portion of the brimstone he used to expel vermin. He produced a fragment the size of my thumbnail and asked if that was sufficient. I assured him it was.

I needed also a mortar and pestle, which any cook was likely to have. These I took to my chamber, telling Sir Jaket that what I was about to do might be dangerous and he must not accompany me. He should seek Master Wycliffe, I said, and meet me in the toft behind Queen's in half an hour.

I poured the powder, which I hoped was saltpeter, into the pestle, then added a minuscule portion of sulfur and a slightly larger amount of charcoal. These I carefully ground into the saltpeter. I did not believe a wooden mortar and pestle would produce a spark when forced together, but intended to take no chances.

When the three elements were crushed fine, I poured the mixture into a leaf of parchment, then with a length of silk from my instruments bag I tied the parchment into a pouch.

Wycliffe, Sir Jaket, Thomas, and the provost awaited me in the toft. I would need fire, or a spark, to apply to the parchment pouch. There would be fire in the kitchen, for 'twas near time for dinner and the cook would be roasting or boiling something.

I asked Thomas to go to the kitchen and return with a scoop of embers. The lad was enthusiastic about this experiment and hastened to the kitchen door. I held the perilous pouch in my left hand, and noticed that the three remaining onlookers seemed to be sidling away from me. I might have created something as fatal as the pestilence.

The squire soon returned holding the scoop filled with embers which glowed hot from the speed of his approach. He held the scoop before me and I took it and blew upon the already reddened coals. I then dumped the contents of the scoop on to the cold ashes where for three days I had boiled ditchwater. I was about to tell the others to step back, but there was no need. They were already some distance away.

Fire had to be applied to the parchment pouch, but I did not intend to be near when this happened. In my instruments pouch I had a coil of cheap hempen twine. I cut a dozen or so feet of the twine and tied one end to the pouch. Then I placed the pouch one pace from the embers, took the other end of the twine and hurried to the opposite side of the ash pile. 'Twas a simple matter then to pull the pouch into the embers. When the parchment touched the ashes I dropped the twine and ran. I would have felt foolish if nothing had happened.

I had not gone three strides when the explosive powder ignited and discharged a cloud of ash and embers into the air with a resounding blast. The kitchen door flew open and the cook and his assistants plunged through the opening to learn the cause of this report. They saw five grinning men standing at the far fringes of the toft, with a dissipating cloud of ash and smoke at their center. Well, four of us were grinning. Henry Whitfield looked on with sober countenance.

Queen's scholars began appearing, brought by the blast to see what had caused such thunder when no storm darkened the sky. And men appeared behind the hedge separating Queen's from the town ditch and wall, peering quizzically through the mulberry branches.

The breeze soon dispersed the ash cloud and I went close to better view the result of the explosion. Embers and ash were gone, and where they once were was a small cavity in the ground, perhaps two inches deep and as large around as my two hands together. If an ounce of saltpeter added to a puny supply of charcoal and brimstone could do such damage, how much more would be required to slay a man? Would a pound of the stuff be enough? I thought it likely, and did some mental calculations whilst Sir Jaket, Thomas, and Master John found their tongues and began to exclaim over the successful experiment.

I had heated four buckets of ditchwater the first day, then two or three on each of the next three days. About twelve or thirteen buckets of befouled water had gone into the bronze pot, each bucket containing perhaps a gallon and a half of liquid. Eighteen gallons had produced an ounce of saltpeter. If the felon had exploded a pound of explosive powder under Richard Sabyn's bed, using the same ratio I had discovered he would need to boil three hundred gallons of the ditchwater, or thereabouts. And would one pound of the explosive be enough? How would the killer know, if he had no experience of saltpeter?

Mayhap he did have such experience. Where would he come by it? Perhaps, to be sure of his intent, he set off more than a pound of the powder. Then what? Did he collect four hundred gallons of the foul water? Alone? Would a single perpetrator be able to do so? Probably, but 'twould be easier with another to help. Or a third.

Where could a man boil so much water 'til the liquid was gone and only the salt remained? Certainly it could not be done in the toft behind Queen's College. But the work must have been done nearby. Who would carry heavy buckets for a great distance? Unless the water drained through the straw cast off from Father Hubert's dovecote was not where the saltpeter used to slay Richard had come from.

What had the past few days taught me? I knew how to make the explosive powder Roger Bacon had described nearly a century past. Did that bring me closer to discovering a felon? Who could know until – unless – the man was discovered? Had I wasted these few days, the only benefit being a curiosity now relieved? Meanwhile Kate, Bessie, and John were without me and the pestilence had returned. When I next entered Galen House would I find my family hale, or awaiting me in St. Beornwald's churchyard?

I wanted to be free of this business and off to Bampton, but I had promised Master Wycliffe that I would find whoso had slain Richard Sabyn. And there was Simon Duby's death also, which the sheriff and provost wished to ignore. If I did not keep my word to Wycliffe, who would take my place and seek justice for the dead?

"Why so solemn?" Sir Jaket said. "You have succeeded."

"At what?"

"Making an explosion."

"Is that what I should have been doing? Master Wycliffe summoned me to find a felon, not play about with sulfur and charcoal and bird droppings."

"But," Wycliffe said, "we now know that Richard could have been slain by a scholar of Queen's using ingredients found nearby."

"Aye, could have been. But was he? Have I wasted four days?"

The question hung in the air, unanswered, for at that moment the trumpet called Queen's College to dinner. The novelty of an explosion could not dull young men's appetites. Nor could the knowledge that one of their number was not present, but lay dying in his chamber. I wondered if Wycliffe would really follow through with his vow to care for the suffering scholar.

He did. "Physicians have discovered no cure for the pestilence," Master John said when the meal – an egg leech – was done. "But are there herbs and such which will ease a man's torment as the buboes grow and rupture?"

"There are. The dried sap of lettuce will induce sleep, and crushed hemp seeds can reduce pain. And henbane. But that must be delivered in small doses or it may cause death."

"Which Henry might welcome."

"Aye, but not by my hand."

"These herbs are mixed in a cup of ale?"

"Aye. The problem is that if a man is too ill he may not be able to rise from his pillow to drink."

"Have you a supply of these physics?"

"I do. And surely more are available from herbalists. These are common remedies and are easily come by."

Wycliffe approached the cook for a cup of ale, then accompanied me to my chamber, where I poured a sizeable dose of the lettuce sap and crushed hemp seeds into the cup. I had no henbane, as I rarely use it. Sir Jaket and Thomas had followed us to my chamber, but when they understood that we were now to treat the ailing scholar they held back. I could not blame them. All men desire admittance to heaven and the presence of the Lord Christ, but few wish for the event to happen soon.

Master John pushed open the door to the doomed lad's room and did not hesitate to enter. I admit that I halted in the doorway. I had cared for Arthur in his illness, and survived. So far. How often could I consort with plague and escape its ravages? Here was a discovery I preferred not to make.

The lad had drawn his blanket to his chin. The day was mild, yet he shivered. Wycliffe touched the scholar's forehead, then looked to me and grimaced. The fever was surely acute. Master John told the youth that he had a cup of ale for him, in which there were herbs which would ease his discomfort. The scholar succeeded in raising himself on an elbow high enough to drink. The provost had ordered a ceramic slops jar be brought to the room. Wycliffe asked the lad if he needed help to use it. He nodded, and Master John drew back the blanket and assisted the youth in relieving himself.

After my experience with Arthur I was concerned that the lad would spew up the ale with its herbs, but Wycliffe managed to get the boy back to his bed without him retching. Whilst the scholar was free of his blanket I saw his neck. The buboes were large and dark and would soon rupture. But he did not cough. Had he done so Master John would have been in great peril. So would I. When plague attacks a man's lungs he can take others with him to the gates of pearl in but a few hours.

Wycliffe told the youth that he would return with a bowl of pottage for his supper. The lad did not reply, but managed to find strength to draw his blanket to his chin. Master John turned, approached the door, and I backed to the corridor to allow him to pass.

"Will he be able to consume some pottage, you think, if I bring him a bowl?" Wycliffe asked.

"I doubt it. Should he do so he will likely vomit what he consumes, as did Arthur."

We returned to Master John's chamber, where Sir Jaket and Thomas awaited us. We passed the entrance hall to do so, and saw the porter admitting a white-robed figure. An archdeacon, come to visit the provost, no doubt.

The cleric was immaculately garbed in fine white wool. From his belt dangled a silken purse and a rosary of what appeared to be amber, each bead glowing in the slanting afternoon sun. Behind him walked three attendants: a clerk and two servants.

Wycliffe said nothing about this visitor 'til we were in his chamber with the door closed behind us. "Archdeacons," he then said, "do not visit an Oxford college to exchange pleasantries with the provost."

Archdeacons are nearly as unpopular as bailiffs, and for similar reasons. Bailiffs see to it that residents of a lord's manor obey his commands and pay their rents and fines. Archdeacons are employed to seek out troublemakers for the bishop in whose diocese they serve. In the case of Oxford, the Bishop of Lincoln. The diocese is so large that the bishop has eight archdeacons assigned to monitor discipline. As archdeacons are employed to root out theological error, they, to keep their position, must find it. No error, no need for archdeacons.

So the appearance of such a cleric, like that of a bailiff, brings no joy to his host. "What," I wondered aloud, "has Henry Whitfield done to cause an archdeacon's presence?"

I knew how the explosive powder which ended Richard Sabyn's life could have been made, but that did not mean I knew how it was made. There is a gulf between the possible and the probable. If I could find the place where two or three hundred gallons of foul water were boiled down to salt I might find the probable. To produce the saltpeter needed to slay Richard would require not only a cauldron, but a large supply of wood. Or charcoal. As none of the three charcoal burners had reported selling to a scholar, I thought it more likely that the boiling was accomplished with wood. Bought or stolen? Or collected? And if the fuel was stolen, then charcoal might have provided some of the heat. Were any Oxford smiths missing the occasional sack?

Was the ditchwater boiled continuously, 'til enough saltpeter was produced? Or did the felon boil but a few gallons at a time? And if he was a scholar of Queen's College, how would he explain his absence from lectures and disputations, which would be necessary to keep his pot simmering?

Hucca had said the man he saw collecting ditchwater in the autumn wore a scholar's gown. Black or red? Was it too dark to see the color? Or was the felon from some other college? Was there a conspiracy against Richard Sabyn, made up of the many he had apparently belittled and insulted? Or did some scholar of Queen's hire a man to collect the ditchwater and keep it aboil? There is little difference to be seen between a scholar's gown and a long cotehardie. Especially on a dark evening.

A dozen or more poor gathered each day at Queen's with bowls and spoons to receive a portion of the pease pottage the college charter required be dispensed. A poor man might think it good fortune to be hired to watch a boiling pot.

No matter what the cook prepared for dinner, supper would be pease pottage. The poor who gathered at the entrance to Queen's knew this and the queue generally began to form by the ninth hour. Most of the regulars understood that there would only be enough in the kettle for twenty or so, so when the line reached that number latecomers wandered off seeking other sustenance, recognizing that this day they must find another way to fill their bellies. Few seem emaciated, so there must be places in Oxford where a man can cadge a meal.

A thumping upon Master John's door brought my thoughts back to the present. Wycliffe and Sir Jaket had been discussing plague and its avoidance whilst I was wool-gathering.

Master John called for the visitor to enter, and the provost's clerk entered the chamber.

"Master Whitfield," he said, "wishes to speak to Sir Hugh."

Wycliffe looked to me with a furrowed brow. The last we knew, the archdeacon was in conversation with the provost. Now was I asked to join them? What wisdom could I impart to such eminent men? Perhaps they wished to know of developments involving discovery of the churl who had slain two scholars.

I followed the clerk to the provost's chamber. This room combined lodging and office and was nearly twice the size of Wycliffe's chamber, which was itself more than twice the size of a scholar's simple abode. Whitfield and his visitor sat upon ornately carved chairs which bordered a fireplace now cold as 'twas June. I noticed that the clerk disappeared after announcing me at the door, and none of the archdeacon's retainers were present.

Neither man stood when I entered. I am but a knight with no land or ancestral title. Of course, most archdeacons are the same. Had they lands and titles they would be bishops rather than a bishop's lackey.

The provost pointed to a bench drawn up between the two and invited me to sit – though I am being too kind with "invited". 'Twas a command layered in honeyed tones.

"Here is Roger Fryde," Whitfield said, introducing the archdeacon. Presumably the man already knew who I was. Why? I was about to learn the answer to that question.

"It has come to the attention of Bishop Bokyngham that you hold heretical views," Fryde said. The man wasted no time in making his point.

"Indeed? Of what does the bishop accuse me?"

"You have denied purgatory."

"I have never said anything of purgatory not found in Scripture," I replied.

The archdeacon seemed taken aback. He could not reply, as Holy Writ says nothing about purgatory. A man who denies purgatory cannot be accused of denying sacred texts. He pulled at his chin and quickly found his footing.

"You deny the teaching of Holy Mother Church?"

"Who says so?"

"You were heard telling a dying man he need not fear purgatory." The only man who had heard me soothing Arthur's fear was the youthful carter. I had not counseled any other dying man.

"The dying man was a friend. A good man, who had served the interests of the Lord Christ. How is it you believe you know what I said to him?"

"You were taking him home to die. Is this not so?"

"It is. Plague has returned." I thought I saw the archdeacon shudder, but he quickly collected himself.

"The lad who drove the cart reported your conversation."

"To whom?"

"Makes no difference. The carter admitted to being influenced by your malign words."

"He sought you to complain that I led him astray?"

"Nay. He confessed his error to his parish priest."

"What error?"

"That for a time he was ready to believe your falsehood, but now wished to repent that he was so easily deceived."

"And this priest told you of the confession?"

"He did."

"What has become of the sanctity of confession? The priest has sinned. As now have you. This evil will require eons in purgatory to erase. So the bishops do say."

The archdeacon's face turned red. I have learned in the course of service to Lord Gilbert that when attacked, a counter-attack may be more effective than defense. I have also learned that mentioning my employer's name – he being one of the great barons of the realm – has generally salutary effects.

"Lord Gilbert would be displeased that a bishop would act upon a breach of the seal of confession."

"Lord Gilbert Talbot?" the archdeacon asked.

"The same. I serve as his bailiff in Bampton."

Bishop Bokyngham and Lord Gilbert had surely met in the House of Lords, and would again were parliament to be called. And it will be, for the king, it is said, has brought the realm near to bankruptcy paying for hostilities in France and buying baubles for Alice Perrers (two of the most expensive things with which men may entertain themselves being war and women). King Edward needs new taxes. I wonder what he will concede to the Commons in exchange.

"Why... surely Lord Gilbert would be displeased," the archdeacon said, "to learn that a trusted retainer has contradicted Holy Church."

"You should ask him," I replied. I could advance such a thought because I knew my employer. After Lady Petronilla died in a return of the pestilence some years past he had grumbled that he must pay to release her from purgatory, and alluded to the fact that purchasing the prayers of the priests of St. Beornwald's Church was a profitable sideline for the clerics. Especially as no one could know whether or not such hired prayers were effective. Well, the bishops said they were, and surely they would know. But no man deceased has ever returned to comment upon the matter.

My complaint about the violated confession, and my mention of Lord Gilbert, had served to reduce the archdeacon's indignation. Mayhap he genuinely believed in purgatory, and worried that he was now charted for an extra thousand or so years there for being party to the breach of the confessional. That might or might not be so, but Lord Gilbert Talbot's displeasure could be measured, he knew, even if time in purgatory could not.

"Well," the archdeacon harrumphed, "I see that your views were perhaps misconstrued. Nevertheless," he continued, in order to salvage something of the exchange, "I shall be keeping a close eye on you in the future. You must not think that you can defy Holy Church without penalty."

I did not think it wise at that moment to mention praemunire, which for more than twenty years has allowed King Edward to defy the pope with impunity. Of course, I am no king. But neither is the archdeacon a pope.

The provost had listened to this conversation in silence. Now he spoke. "Sir Hugh seeks the cause of two deaths at Queen's. Master Wycliffe has engaged him." This last sentence Whitfield spoke as if a spoonful of rotting cabbage had been thrust into his mouth. He wanted the archdeacon to know that my presence at Queen's College was not his doing.

"Nay," I replied. "I do not seek the cause of two deaths. That is known. The lads were murdered. I seek the felon or felons who slew them."

Whitfield's lips drew tight. He did not like being contradicted. Few men do. But as I had already scorned the archdeacon's accusation I thought I might as well perturb the provost as well and make their opinion of me unanimous.

There are times when my sarcasm runs out of control. As I left the provost's chamber I considered that this was such an occasion. Master John would wish to know the subject of my interview with the archdeacon. His views are much like my own. Or, I should write that my views are much like his. I determined to ask him how he would have responded to the archdeacon.

"Hah," he said when I related the conversation. "Hoisted on his own petard. Wonderful! Violating the sanctity of the confessional and suggesting he will rue the action in purgatory. Should a similar occasion confront me I will have to remember your response."

The interview with the archdeacon had interrupted my plan to question the poor who were gathered awaiting the pottage distribution. I explained my purpose to Master John and he offered to accompany me, but I demurred. Too many cooks spoil the broth, and too many questioners close mouths.

Those who awaited pottage knew their fellows. They were regulars at the door to Queen's, and respected each other's place in the queue. A man who attempted to crowd ahead would be dealt with by his resentful companions.

A man may be poor for many reasons. I discovered most of them by the time I had questioned those in the queue. Three of the beggars were simple. So much so that I was surprised they could find their way to Queen's for a free meal, or remember where they had last seen their bowl.

Half a dozen of the supplicants had suffered injuries or illness which made them unemployable. One was a tiler who had fallen from a roof. His arm had been broken near the elbow, and badly set, or more likely not set at all. Had he visited me when the injury was new I could have mended the fracture. But he had not, nor had he known of my existence. A broken bone which has healed wrongly cannot be made right. The man's right arm extended away from his body from elbow to hand, making it nearly impossible for him to use the appendage for any useful purpose.

Two others, quite elderly, gazed at the world through eyes white with cataracts. To see anything at all they fixed their eyes to one side so as to gain a narrow glimpse of their surroundings. Although these cataracts were severe. I could couch them if the sufferers were willing, but without lenses the world would then be a blur to them, and how would they be better served than with no treatment? Such lenses are costly, the best made in Milan, and beyond what a poor man can afford.

The pestilence has much reduced the number of laborers, so that those who survived are able to demand greater wages. Parliament saw fit to thwart that by enacting the Statute of Laborers, restricting wages to what was customary before 1348, when plague first assailed England. The statute has been a failure, as with most such ordinances. The wealthy will pay what they must to attract workers, and a laborer will charge what he may for his toil.

So men able and willing to work have little need of alms. All of the men – and two women – to whom I spoke had genuine needs. The most troubling were two venerable codgers, bent with age and crowned with thin white hair and unruly whiskers. They tottered along, each with a cane, and struggled to stand and keep their place in the queue. To leave it and sit might mean no meal. Their curse was that they had survived the pestilence and its frequent return when none of their family had, so neither had a child to care for them in their decrepitude. These ancient ones could barely support themselves. They would not be able to carry wood or water to a boiling pot. But most of the others awaiting pottage would have been capable of doing so.

I asked each man to whom I spoke if he sought employment. Nearly all agreed that, was the work something they were capable of, they would be pleased to accept. Of course, they would say that until the offer was actually made. Then an arm or knee or shoulder would be afflicting them, or their back would be wrenched.

Then I asked if, in months past, whilst they stood before Queen's awaiting a supper, some scholar had offered work. At this question most became reticent, fearing, I believe, that if they said "aye" and had accepted, the provost might question their need now for charity.

I heard the trumpet call scholars to their supper. Those in the queue heard also, and shifted from one foot to another in anticipation of their meal, which would come to them after those attached to the college were fed.

I left the mendicants and sought Sir Jaket, Thomas, and Master Wycliffe, to join them for supper. In the past hour or so I had learned much about human frailty and discovered a few men who, despite their infirmities, might watch over a steaming kettle and perhaps even haul the water and wood the process consumed.

I had also learned that half or more of those who consumed pottage at Queen's College resided in St. John's Hospital. The hospital is beyond Long Wall Street, near to New Bridge, out of the center of Oxford. Not far from the hospital, beyond the river, are meadows and forest where a man might hide a bubbling pot and buckets used to replenish the liquid in the kettle. Well, a pot might be hid in the forest, if not the meadows.

When supper was done Master John took a bowl of pottage and a spoon from the kitchen to feed Henry atte Brooke. I followed.

There was no point in rapping upon Henry's chamber door. When we had last seen him he was too feeble to rise from his bed to open to a visitor. Wycliffe pushed the door open and approached the lad's bed.

I thought at first that my potion had succeeded in bringing rest to the sufferer. Perhaps it did, in his last moments. But his stillness now was not due to the herbs. The lad was dead.

"Too late," Wycliffe said. "I should not have suffered the lad to die alone."

"He did not," I replied.

Wycliffe peered at me from under raised eyebrows. "Who was here?"

"The Lord Christ was present, as with all who die in faith and are baptized."

"Oh... aye. You are a better theologian than I. The Lord Christ is also present with we who live, even if there are those who would prefer His absence. No man wishes to think his wickedness is seen by another, especially a heavenly observer, but it is so."

"Indeed," I agreed. "I wish the Lord Christ would provide me with a hint as to the felon who has done two murders, for He has seen the evil and mourns for it."

"Mayhap He has made a suggestion."

"And I am too witless to comprehend?"

"That was not my meaning," Wycliffe protested.

"Yet it may be so."

"Whitfield must be told of this death," Master John

said. "Father Hubert must send his sexton to ring the passing bell, and then prepare a grave for Henry. Perhaps the provost will have a shroud in which to bury the lad. If not, he should seek a few of them. I fear he will need more than one in the next months."

Sir Jaket crossed the lane to the church to tell the priest of Henry's death, while Wycliffe hastened to tell the provost. Whitfield collected four scholars to carry Henry's pallet to St. Peter's churchyard. I suspect the provost of some coercion, as most folk desire to be as far as possible from the corpse of one who has perished of plague.

The passing bell rang as we departed Queen's, and the poor who remained, waiting for their pottage, crossed themselves at the sight of the shrouded corpse.

Whether or not those who have perished of plague may yet infect the living, it is the practice to hasten the funeral mass and inter the deceased as rapidly as possible. The four scholars who bore Henry atte Brooke had barely set down his corpse under the lychgate before Father Hubert spoke the paternoster and directed the lads to carry the dead scholar to a far corner of the churchyard. Three men were at work opening a grave. The priest intoned a brief homily, and Henry was lowered into the hole.

So long as only a few met their death of plague, those who perished would await the Lord Christ's return alone. If the pestilence should begin to slay many, as when it first appeared, great pits would be needed to bury the dead. I pray the realm will not again come to such a pass.

Were new graves needed in other towns and villages? Likely. Men and women die every day, for many reasons. Were new graves disturbing the sod of St. Beornwald's churchyard in Bampton? Because of the pestilence? Who would rest in them? I shuddered to think of Kate and Bessie and John, and my ignorance of their state. What good would it do me to know if they were well or ill? I had no power to cure disease or prevent its appearance.

The longest day of the year approached, so after Henry was buried, there was yet an hour or two of daylight remaining. I asked Sir Jaket and Thomas to accompany me, and we set off down the path between St. Peter-in-the-East and St. John's Hospital.

I sought the hospital's warden, Robert de Tyve. The fellow was sour-looking and seemed to resent the inhabitants of his institution, as if the place would be improved if no men cluttered the building with their presence.

I introduced myself and asked if, in the past months, he had noticed the smell of burning or seen wisps of smoke drifting from the forest to the north and east.

"We bake our own bread," he replied. "And when we have a supply of flesh 'tis roasted, so there is always a scent of smoke from the kitchen. But from the forest? Nay. Why do you ask?"

The man did not need to know all of what had recently transpired at Queen's College and St. Peter-in-the-East. So in a few brief sentences I explained that I sought some man who might, in the past months, have been boiling tainted water to produce a potion.

"A potion, you say? What good could come from such a brew? And what was it which tainted the water?"

The warden's curiosity was aroused, so I decided to tell him more. "The water was polluted with urine and dung, and was boiled to produce saltpeter."

"Saltpeter? What use could a man find for that? Odd, but now that you mention it a great pot went missing some months past."

I was not required to answer the warden regarding

the use for saltpeter, but immediately asked him of the missing pot.

"Bronze," he said. "And capable of containing pottage enough to feed all who reside at St. John's Hospital... sixteen gallons or more. Cook would know. 'Twas worth eight shillings."

"Have you searched for the missing vessel?"

"Of course. 'Twas not to be found. I even sent men to spy out other kitchens. Colleges and halls and inns must prepare pottage to feed dozens at each meal, so would find such a cauldron useful. And the kettle was recognizable. It stood upon its own trivet. Nothing unusual about that, but it had 'St. J' engraved upon the lip."

"Such letters could be ground away," I said.

"Indeed. But the scraping would leave a telltale abrasion."

"And no such mark was seen in any pots found at other kitchens?"

"Nay, sir... none. The kettle is gone and we make do until we can afford a replacement."

A pot such as the warden had described could boil away vast amounts of water. Was this how some villain produced enough saltpeter to make an explosion? If so, where was the work done? A kettle the size of the one missing would require great strength to carry off, especially because its shape would provide no convenient handles. Most of the residents of the hospital of St. John were too frail to carry away even a pot of middling size. But two likely could. And carrying ditchwater and fuel to feed the boiling would be more productive done by two men rather than one. Or mayhap three.

A search of the forest east of the hospital, across the Cherwell, might prove profitable. Bronze pots and buckets of water and enough wood to boil away two or three hundred gallons of water would be heavy. If the business was done as I suspected, the place of boiling would not be far. But night was nigh. A search must await the dawn.

Chapter 8

$\mathcal{I}$ awoke with the dawn as the Angelus bell sounded from the tower of St. Peter-in-the-East. I was eager to seek the kitchen for a loaf and a cup of ale, then prowl the wood and hedgerows to the east of St. John's Hospital.

The bell fell silent, but a few moments later rang again. I knew why, and crossed myself. The sexton was announcing a death in the parish, for this peal was a passing bell. Was another Queen's scholar taken, or was this the death of a townsman? I thought Master Wycliffe might know and hastened to his chamber. Sir Jaket and Thomas fell in behind me as I approached Wycliffe's chamber door.

"One of the carpenters," Master John said when I asked the reason for the passing bell.

"One of those repairing the roof?" I asked.

"Aye. Took to his bed with a cough yesterday, I was told, and was found dead this morning, his pillow drenched in bloody sputum. When the pestilence settles in a man's lungs he will not survive long."

I told Wycliffe what I had learned the evening before, and said 'twas my intention to prowl the wood and lanes and hedgerows to the east of the hospital of St. John this day.

"I'll go also," Master John said. "Let's fetch loaves from the kitchen and be away."

131

Wycliffe was as excited as a child with a new toy. He was convinced, he told me and Sir Jaket as we munched our loaves, that we were close on the trail of whoso murdered Richard Sabyn. We were not so near as Master John thought.

A plan was needed. If we four simply wandered the wood to the north and east of the hospital without some design to our steps we would likely pass by some places which should be inspected and mayhap search another area twice. I told Sir Jaket and Thomas to explore east of the river, along the north side of the road across East Bridge. Master Wycliffe and I would seek to the east of Sir Jaket for any sign of ashes now cold. We would meet at Queen's for dinner and describe what we had seen. Or not seen.

We saw forests and hedgerows and meadows where sheep grazed. We saw fields planted to barley and oats and wheat. Also peas and beans. We saw no evidence that any quantity of wood had been burned in some hidden location.

The pottage this day was flavored only with leeks and onions, as 'twas a fast day. Dinner was a somber meal. Three men having some association with Queen's College – though for two of them it was tenuous, to be sure – had perished of plague in but a few days. No man could be reproved for considering his own mortality. As scholars bent over their meal I saw that hung about several necks were lengths of twine. This string likely supported bags of sweet-smelling herbs hidden under the scholars' gowns, to perfume the air and ward off pestilence.

When plague first appeared I was a child, and saw our village priest bending over my father on his deathbed, a small bag of herbs dangling from his neck. The precaution did the cleric no good. He died but a few days after my father. A physician who refuses to treat the ill will earn no fees, but 'tis dangerous to be near those who are afflicted. The contagion may slay the physician along with his patient, so most physicians prepare favorite concoctions of herbs to suspend under their noses. These are to ward off the pestilence. I am not convinced that such preparations are efficacious, but they will do no harm. A bag of herbs and spices can be had without payment of a physician's fee, so men are eager to prepare their own physic and clearly a number of Queen's scholars had done so.

Surgeons do not share the risks physicians encounter when they attend their patients. When I stitch up a lacerated arm I am in no danger of the same affliction, and when I place a plaster upon a broken leg, my own legs are in no peril of fracture due to the proximity of my injured patient.

My thoughts roamed as I consumed my dinner. Nothing of value entered my mind but that in the afternoon we four should explore south of the hospital of St. John, since the wood north and east offered no evidence that anyone had boiled away large pots of water.

But when I announced this plan Wycliffe demurred. He had scheduled a tutorial with half a dozen Queen's scholars, and neither plague nor felony would interfere with his instruction. I would send Sir Jaket and Thomas off as a team, but I would seek cold ashes alone.

To the south of the hospital of St. John was a meadow. One of the colleges likely owned the field, and wool sheared from the sheep which grazed there would help finance the scholars. Some of the sheep had already been sheared, and seemed gaunt beside their yet fleecy companions.

I sent Sir Jaket and Thomas to explore the wood bordering the south side of the meadow whilst I went east along the road until I came to a wall which hemmed in the sheep. "We will meet at supper," I told Sir Jaket as we separated.

A forest in June is a pleasant place. Jackdaws and robins chirped and scolded. New leaves cast a green hue to the shaded ground. A light breeze wafted pleasant odors, the air delightfully free of the stink of Oxford.

I wandered the wood in a jagged pattern, deviating from my chosen path only when some fallen branch obstructed my way. And this was rare. Whoso owned this wood had allowed tenants to glean broken boughs for winter fuel, so that limbs now upon the ground had dropped since autumn.

I so enjoyed this forest stroll that I nearly ignored the scent of damp ashes. Nearly. The smell eventually overcame my wool-gathering and I stopped in my tracks. For how many steps had the odor come to my nostrils before I recognized what it was? Not many, I decided, and if I pushed my nose into the wind I might find the origin of the smell.

How far had my crooked wandering taken me from the gate of St. John's Hospital? I had paid little heed, being attuned to the enjoyment of nature and the search for some place where a cauldron of water might have been boiled. I was likely five hundred paces past the East Bridge, and the hospital entrance was another two hundred paces beyond that. If Sir Jaket had found the evidence I sought he was too far away for me to hear his shout, and if I called for him he would not respond.

In centuries past, the lands about Oxford were the possession of Norman nobles, but now most land belongs to monastic houses and colleges. Gentlemen know that they will not take their estate to the next world, so in return for perpetual prayers for their souls they have deeded properties to those who promise to speak to the Lord Christ on their behalf. Their sons and heirs lose much, but the abbeys and halls and colleges prosper. Whose forest was this, I wondered, and what had been burned nearby? Was this the site I sought, where foul ditchwater had become saltpeter?

I followed my nose through the wood for thirty or forty paces and came upon a low swineherd's hut. The shelter was dilapidated, probably used only for a few weeks in autumn when pigs were allowed to pannage for acorns and beech nuts, fattening themselves for slaughter come Martinmas. Would they behave so if they knew the result of their appetite? Probably. Men, who are thoughtful creatures, behave in like manner even though they know the result of their excesses.

This shelter was fallen in at one end, with a flimsy door of boughs tied together with vines, and with vines serving as hinges. The roof, such as it was, consisted of layers of bark fallen or peeled from nearby trees. The hut was much like others used for the same purpose. I assumed the scent of wet ashes came from beyond the hut, but when I walked past it the stink vanished.

Had some swineherd warmed himself within the hut? Apparently so, for when I turned back to view the shelter from the rear I saw that what I had assumed to be decay was actually the result of burning. A warming blaze had got out of control and set part of the shelter afire before it was extinguished.

Curiosity killed the cat, 'tis said. It can do harm to men, as well. I decided to investigate the hut, so drew open the makeshift door and entered. This I did on hands and knees, for even the undamaged part of the shelter was too low to allow me to stand upright. The swineherd who first built this hut must have been a small man.

As I had supposed I found inside the hut a bed of sodden ashes as thick as the width of my hand, where water leaking through the bark roof had penetrated. And there was indication that a fire had kindled part of the rear wall and roof. 'Twas gloomy within the place, but some light entered through the burned wall and leaky roof. Enough that I could see three impressions in the bed of ashes. Much like would be made by a large pot cast with its own trivit so to rise above the burning fuel.

Was this the place where a few hundred gallons of ditchwater had become saltpeter? It seemed possible. The hut was far from the eyes of men, and if some man wandering the wood did happen to see smoke wafting from the openings and crevices of the shelter's walls and roof he would think as I had, that a swineherd was warming himself.

I peered closely at the ashes and the three impressions equidistant from each other in a circular pattern. If there had been a bronze pot here, it was now gone, but not so long past that the marks made in the ash pile had been obliterated. The close inspection convinced me that a kettle had at one time seen service here. Why? To cook a swineherd's pottage? Not likely. I was convinced that I had discovered the place where some man had distilled saltpeter.

A twig snapped nearby. I thought perhaps Sir Jaket, having found nothing in the place I had sent him, had come searching for me. Or mayhap he had discovered something of interest and sought me to tell me of it. But why had he not called out my name as he looked for me?

Still upon hands and knees I turned to the open entrance and saw before the door the legs and feet of some man. I scrambled out of the opening to greet the fellow, and as I made to stand I suddenly saw all the stars and planets of the heavens flash before me. I remember falling face down in the leaves, attempting to rise, and then all becoming black. I had been struck twice across the back of my head. What happened next I must relate from hearsay, for I was laid insensible.

Sir Jaket and Thomas returned to Queen's College for their supper, expecting to find me there. They had discovered nothing of interest in their inspection of the territory I had assigned them.

When I did not appear for supper, nor for an hour after, they went to Master Wycliffe to voice concern that some evil might have befallen me, or that I had made some discovery which prevented my timely return to Queen's. In either happenstance the three thought it possible that I required assistance. There were yet a few hours of daylight remaining, as the solstice was near, so they set off in the direction I had taken, past the hospital of St. John and the East Bridge.

They prowled the forest and shouted my name, they said, 'til darkness settled over the wood. They did not find me, nor happen upon the swineherd's hut, and I did not reply to their calls as I was face down in last year's fallen leaves, insensible.

Returning to Queen's College they agreed to assemble at dawn and resume the search for me, sure now that some untoward event had befallen me. A man will not choose to spend the night in a wood when he has a bed and blanket awaiting in his chamber.

I awoke from my slumber some time in the dead of night. Why did I write that? I am sure that dead was what I was intended to be.

As conscious thought returned I realized that I was supine upon the forest floor with a mouthful of moldering leaves. I made to stand, but the world began to spin and I collapsed to hands and knees. A second time I tried to stand, but could not do so, and fell to the base of a tree. With the tree as a prop I was finally able to gain my feet, but to take a step away from the trunk would mean again tumbling to my knees.

As my wits returned I considered what had happened to me. Some man had followed me as I searched the forest, or happened upon me by chance. The fellow was not pleased that I had discovered the swineherd's hut and its bed of wet ashes, so picked up a fallen limb and when I emerged from the hut upon hands and knees he brought the limb down upon my head. Twice. As the thought came to me I reached to the back of my pate and felt there a great lump under my cap, and crusted blood matting my hair. As with most men who think themselves fashionable I had wrapped a long liripipe about my head. Mayhap this had softened the blow and saved me from greater harm.

What if my assailant lingered, to make sure of my death? I must depart the wood before he returned. I was in no condition to defend myself against another attack. A man who wished me ill would find me easy prey.

But to leave the tree meant collapse. The dark world yet spun, and any movement of my head caused a resumption of the flashes of light which the blow had produced. If I was to leave the wood, I decided, 'twould be upon hands and knees.

I slid down the tree and began to crawl toward what I hoped was St. John's Hospital, which would be the nearest place I could find succor.

Every few minutes I came upon fallen boughs which impeded my progress, and I was constantly finding twigs which tore at my hands and ripped holes in the knees of my chauces. Stars and planets continued to flash before my eyes whenever I turned my head to find some easier path through the dark wood. At some time in the night I tired, and slept. Briefly. The stars and planets vanished. Briefly.

'Twas near to dawn when I awoke. I was comforted to see that I had been crawling to the west, toward the East Bridge and St. John's Hospital rather than away from them. The grey eastern sky told me this.

I was near a slender beech tree, so crawled to it and

rose to my feet. I hoped that, with the passage of a few hours, I might have regained my wits enough to walk. Not so. I took a step from the tree and tumbled to my knees. It is important that a man choose his friends wisely, but the knot at the back of my head reminded me that I must also choose my enemies more carefully.

I crawled another hundred or so paces under a lightening sky and then heard a distant shout. At first I could not discern what was said, but as the man who called out came nearer I realized 'twas my name being bawled through the wood. I attempted to cry out a reply and discovered that a whack upon the head can influence many things. I raised my voice, but felt bile rise in my throat and the whirling stars and planets reappeared. I did, however, manage to croak a response.

"Here!" I heard a voice yell. "Over here! I heard something."

A moment later I heard men crashing and stumbling through the wood. Was my assailant returning, with companions, to complete his work? I thought the voice sounded like Sir Jaket's, so raised myself to my knees and called out as loudly as I could. Immediately I recognized Sir Jaket's voice. "This way!" he shouted, and a moment later I saw him plunging toward me between the trees. Master John and Thomas were close on his heels.

Wycliffe said, "We must take Sir Hugh to his chamber and seek a physician. Thomas, hurry to the hospital and get a pallet. Surely they will have one. And hire some of the more robust inhabitants to bear the pallet."

Thomas hurried away, whilst Master John and Sir Jaket sat upon the decaying remains of a stump. They were silent, understanding, I believe, that I had little desire for discourse.

As my wits returned, my thoughts considered the moments just before the blows fell upon my head. Whoso smote me wore brown woolen chauces. Nothing unusual about that. I could not remember seeing his cotehardie, which spoke of a younger man. Most lads wear short cotehardies so as to show a manly turn of leg to passing maidens. The shoes were of leather and quality. A skilled cobbler had made them. One had been torn and repaired, the rent stitched as well as I could place a suture in lacerated flesh. Of one thing I was certain: the man did not wear a scholar's gown. Did the man who smote me wish me dead? Surely. He struck a second time when it would have been clear to him that I was badly injured but yet lived.

Master John and Sir Jaket remained mercifully silent. They recognized that it required effort for me to speak, and knew that, when I could, I would tell all of what had transpired. Thomas arrived with a pallet and two men of St. John's Hospital, and as they lifted me to the pallet the squire spoke one question after another, not allowing me time to answer even had I a mind to do so. Sir Jaket finally silenced the lad, for which I was most grateful. Master John understood my silence and added: "Sir Hugh will tell us all when he is able. Which he is not now. Come, we will return him to his chamber. And be careful, he needs no jostling about."

My bearers were indeed solicitous. There was discomfort when the lump at the back of my skull made contact with the pallet, but if I turned my head the pain passed. So much so that I fell to sleep for part of the journey to Queen's.

It was inconvenient to maneuver the pallet up the stairs at Queen's College, so with Sir Jaket under one arm and Thomas under the other I was lifted to the first floor, my feet barely touching the stairs. The treads were blurred before my eyes, passing in and out of focus. Master Wycliffe followed, and when I was settled upon my bed he announced that he would seek a loaf and a cup of ale at the kitchen. I thought this a fine idea. Until

I swallowed a mouthful of maslin loaf and drank half a cup of ale, and promptly spewed up the small repast. I saw Wycliffe and Sir Jaket exchange worried glances. I was rather apprehensive myself.

The only useful clue to locating the man who had laid me low was the repaired shoe. I could not seek the fellow, weak as I was, but Sir Jaket and Thomas could. I motioned for them to come near.

"I found the place where water was boiled to make saltpeter. I am sure of it. 'Tis a broken-down swineherd's hut. The roof was so low I inspected the place on hands and knees. I heard someone approach, thought 'twas you, and as I crawled from the hut I was struck twice upon my head. But I remember that the man who delivered the blow wore a shoe which had been torn and mended. Seek the cobblers of Oxford and ask if any have recently stitched a ripped shoe."

The exertion required to deliver this message taxed me. I sank back to my bed as Sir Jaket replied that he would begin the search immediately. Meanwhile Master John left to seek a servant with a mop to clean the mess I had vomited to the planks. I was alone with my thoughts, and they were not pleasant.

My Kate had come near to being a widow, my children fatherless. What price must honest men pay to root out wickedness? Was the cost too high? My resolve had been tested in the past, but never so severely as this day. I had seen men who suffered blows to the head and were ever after afflicted with headaches and staggered as they walked in the manner of drunken men. How could I perform my duty to Lord Gilbert should this be my fate?

A servant entered my chamber with mop and bucket and interrupted my thoughts. Master John stood in the doorway until the floor was cleaned, then entered, sat upon the bench, and spoke.

"Your injury is my doing. I wish to discharge you of your agreement to seek Richard Sabyn's slayer. One death is enough."

"What of Simon Duby?" I said.

"Ah. I confess I'd forgotten about the lad, what with other matters."

"Simon was a retiring sort, I remember. Forgettable."

"Aye, to my shame," Wycliffe grimaced. "No man, nor woman either, should be forgotten."

"Although many are."

"Indeed. But the Lord Christ remembers all," Master John said. "And will reward men according to their deeds."

"Then mayhap in heaven the blow to my skull will be requited."

"Mayhap, although you will not wish to be sent there soon to discover if it is so. Whoso smote you will not be pleased to learn you are alive, I think, and may try again to do you harm. Which is why I absolve you of your pledge to seek a murderer – or two."

The trumpet calling scholars to their dinner echoed through the college. Wycliffe stood. "There will be pease pottage again for dinner. I will return with a bowl and some ale. You must try to eat. No man will recover from a blow such as you endured if he does not eat. Starvation is not a cure for any ill."

I found it easy to fall to sleep. Even thoughts of revenge against my assailant could not keep me awake. So when Sir Jaket and Thomas and Master John finished their dinner and entered my chamber they found me asleep. The squeal of ungreased hinges woke me, and the scent of pease pottage caused my empty stomach to complain. I thought this a good sign.

Slowly, so as not to bring the whirling stars and planets back before my eyes, I sat up and placed my feet upon the floor. My vision blurred for a moment, but soon cleared. Wycliffe produced a bowl and spoon, and Sir Jaket set a loaf and a cup of ale upon the table. I took the bowl, lifted a small spoonful of the pottage to my lips, and ate. Never had pease pottage tasted so fine. I waited to learn if my gut would reject this offering. There was some gurgling from under my navel, but the spoonful stayed where it had been sent. So I ate another, and took a bite of the maslin loaf.

I was able to consume half of the bowl of pottage before a brief wave of nausea told me I'd had enough. A few sips of ale completed the meal, and I told Master John that his prescription had been correct. I did feel stronger for having eaten, even if only a small portion.

While I'd been eating, Sir Jaket spoke of visiting several cobblers. "'Tis astounding," he said, "how many men require their shoes mended. Every cobbler we visited this morning has recently sewed together a torn shoe. There are a few other shoemakers we will seek this afternoon, but I suspect we will find the same."

This news disappointed me. I had thought the repaired shoe of my attacker would lead to the man, and he would be the felon who slew Richard Sabyn. And perhaps also murdered Simon Duby. This prospect now seemed remote, but I told Sir Jaket to call on the other cobblers anyway. No stone should be left unturned.

"You seem sure that swineherd's hut the place where the saltpeter was distilled," Wycliffe said when Sir Jaket and Thomas had departed. "Why so? What evidence did you find?"

I told him of the three indentations in the wet ashes where a footed pot likely rested above the fire. "And if the ashes in the shelter were innocuous, why would some man strike me down for entering the place?"

"Hmmm. Indeed. No man would do such a thing except that he felt an itch upon his neck where a noose would fit. Perhaps you should lay down. You are swaying like a sapling in the wind."

Wycliffe's form had become unfocused. I reclined and immediately saw the ceiling become clear.

"Shall I seek a physician?" Wycliffe asked.

"Nay. He would sniff my urine and prescribe foods warm and dry, then measure out a packet of herbs and for this charge six pence. Herbs will not mend a broken skull, and I have a selection of herbs which will reduce pain. I need none to aid sleep."

"A broken skull? You think 'tis fractured?"

"Mayhap. My liripipe cushioned the blow, and the lump is too large and galling to poke about for a fracture. And even if 'tis so, there is nothing to be done but allow the break to knit."

"How long will that take?"

"Six weeks. Or mayhap eight. Thereabouts."

"And your pate will be delicate 'til then?"

"Indeed. 'Tis never a good thing to receive a blow to the head, but till Lammastide I must avoid men who wish me ill."

"And also those who fear you," Master John said. "I have no doubt that you are close to discovering the felon we seek. But you must rest. For a few days at least. What would you have me do in the meantime?"

"Alone? Nothing. Your head may not be so hard as mine, and a cowl not so effective a cushion as a liripipe. Tomorrow you and Sir Jaket and Thomas might seek colleges and halls and abbeys and such like places to learn if any have recently purchased a large, footed bronze kettle. The thing would be too large for a family's use. Some institution will have it. The three of you together should be safe from harm."

"You think the felon will have sold the pot after his use for it was done?"

"Why not? He had already slain a man, perhaps two.

144

What greater punishment could he receive for selling stolen goods? And the pot can be identified. The warden of St. John's Hospital told me that 'St. J' is engraved upon the lip."

"Which will, by now," Master John said, "likely be filed away. Even so, such grinding would identify the thing. You must rest," he continued. "I see your eyes wandering, as if they cannot remain fixed upon me. I will return after supper with more pottage and a loaf. And ale."

"I have a pouch of crushed hemp seeds," I said. "When you bring ale I will pour some seeds in the cup."

"Of what use are these hemp seeds?"

"They may reduce a man's pain. Not much, mind you, but when a man is suffering, any alleviation is welcome."

"Then I will get you a cup of ale immediately. Why did you not ask for one, or put the seeds into the cup you drank with your dinner?"

"The seeds are not that effective," I said.

"But any relief is better than none, so you said. I will return anon."

The truth was that I had brought with me to Oxford only a few of my instruments and half a dozen small pouches of medicinal herbs. If I used my hemp seeds for myself I would have none for some patient who might need the relief. There are herbalists in Oxford, but one can never be sure of their supply. And if plague had indeed returned, the afflicted would seek any palliative which might ease their passage to the gates of pearl. Oxford's herbalists might even now have sold their supply of hemp seeds.

Wycliffe returned whilst I was convincing myself to take some of the crushed hemp seeds in the cup of ale he had procured. I used but a small fraction of my supply. When I had swallowed the potion I reclined, fell immediately to sleep, and when I awoke found that Sir

Jaket, Thomas, and Master John had assembled in my chamber. Wycliffe held a bowl in his hands, and my eyes gradually focused upon the table, where a cup and a loaf rested. I sat upon the bed and carefully consumed the entire bowl of pottage and ate all of the maslin loaf. Wycliffe seemed pleased.

When I had finished my meal we spoke of what might be done by way of finding the pot stolen from St. John's Hospital. Sir Jaket wished to split our force, with him, Thomas, and Master John each visiting different establishments seeking the kettle.

"Not only colleges and halls and abbeys must be examined," Master John said, "but inns also."

I agreed, so we decided that, upon Monday, the three of them would seek a large bronze pot. But I was adamant that they not split up. Alone they might be overcome, even Sir Jaket, skilled in combat as he is, might be overwhelmed if two or three rogues set upon him. The search would take three times longer, but together they would be more than three times safer. And safety was to be considered. My lumpen head was proof of that.

With the plan in place my companions departed so that I might rest. 'Twas yet light, and the skin of my window bright, but shortly I was asleep. When I awoke, the skin was but a pale square in the wall of my dark chamber. I thought for a moment I had slept through the night and 'twas dawn I saw. Not so. I lay awake for some time and saw the window grow dark.

Sometime after darkness came to my room I again slept. I had spent so much time in the arms of Morpheus that now, when I fell to sleep, I was easily awakened. This was fortunate.

I awoke during the night with a need to use the chamber pot. I had resumed my bed for but a few minutes, dozing but not asleep, when I heard a sound which brought me alert.

146

Chapter 9

Scholars cannot be troubled with the mundane matters of life, intent as they are on debating the ethereal. So no man of Queen's College had troubled himself to grease a hinge since the structure was raised. What I heard was the faint squeal of a hinge as the door to my chamber was slowly pushed open.

All was blackness. I peered in the direction of the door but saw nothing. Then I heard the faint squeak again. No question but the sound came from the door. A man attempting to enter another man's chamber in the dead of night could be about no lawful purpose. If I shouted I could surely frighten the man from my room, but he would then escape. I thought it probable that the prowler was the felon I sought. And he now sought me. Likely the man who dented my skull, or an accomplice, was now but a few paces from me, intent upon completing his wicked deed.

I pretended a snore and thought I heard the intruder stiffen. Well, I heard something and 'twas not a squeaky hinge. If I was to capture the man I must not allow him to believe himself discovered. He would flee, and I was in no condition to chase him. I was in no condition to do much of anything, but if the man came near enough I might roll from my bed, wrap arms about his ankles, and shout until those who slumbered in nearby chambers – Sir Jaket and Thomas were in adjoining rooms – could hurry to my assistance. Many plans are excellent in the design and fail only in the execution.

Was that a floorboard which creaked? A loose nail? If there had been even a sliver of moon I might have seen a shadow gliding across my chamber, but all was dark.

There! I heard the floorboard again. And was that the shallow breath of a man so intent upon silence he tried to still his lungs?

When Wycliffe had brought my supper he moved the bench close to my bed, the better to converse with me and hear my weak replies. The man skulking toward my bed – how could he know where my bed was in such darkness? – pushed a foot forward and even though the contact was slight 'twas enough to scrape the bench across the floor for an inch or two. I lay silent, pretending deep sleep, awaiting the single opportunity I would have to seize and hold the interloper.

I felt a slight tug upon my blanket. The intruder was, I thought, reaching tentatively to locate my bed. I felt the blanket move again, at my toes. The rogue had discovered where I lay, but I had also discovered him. I steeled myself, swept back my blanket, and lunged into the darkness whilst shouting for help at the top of my lungs.

My aim was good. I felt my arms go about the man's knees, but then he stumbled back and drew me with him. I fell headlong upon the bench, which caught me in the ribs. My shouts failed as breath was driven from my lungs.

I lost my grip on the intruder and a moment later heard my chamber door slam. My breath returned, and I raised the hue and cry again. My shouts were quickly answered. I heard doors opening and running feet thumping in the corridor. A light flickered. One of those who answered my call had thought to light a candle.

'Twas Sir Jaket who carried the candle. He flung open the door and saw me upon the floor. Now in addition to a sore head I had tender ribs. I put hands upon the overturned bench, raised myself to my knees, then reached for my bed and managed to climb upon it. Sir Jaket's candle flickered before my eyes. First there was one candle, then two, then but one again.

All this while men and youths were squeezing into my chamber, each shouting questions about the cause of the uproar. Another candle appeared, and then I saw Master Wycliffe elbow his way through the throng. As scholars recognized him they moved aside.

Wycliffe turned to face the crowd and demanded silence. Such is his authority that the mob instantly obeyed. "What has happened here?" he asked.

I explained what had transpired and immediately Sir Jaket spoke to Thomas and they ran from my chamber to seek the intruder.

Master John stooped to pick up the overturned bench and I heard him exclaim, "What is here?" He lifted an object before me and even in the dim light from two candles I could see 'twas an awl. The prong was nearly as long as my hand, from wrist to fingertips, and the stub end was fixed to a palm-sized block of oak rounded upon the corners.

Here was evidence that the felon who murdered Richard Sabyn also slew Simon Duby. The awl which Master Wycliffe held was probably the instrument which had pierced Simon's heart. If not, 'twas much the same. Did some man intend to pierce me with it because I was investigating Simon's murder? Nay, for I was not. I sought the maker of saltpeter, and for that curiosity some man intended to slay me with the weapon used against Simon. How could the two deaths be unrelated?

I voiced these thoughts to Master John as I sat upon my bed. My vision was occasionally blurred. Sometimes I saw two candles, sometimes I saw four. And Wycliffe had a disconcerting habit of producing a twin. But although I spoke my suspicions to Wycliffe, all within the chamber and at the door heard.

Sir Jaket and Thomas returned, breathless, as I concluded, and announced that no interloper had been found, nor had the porter or his assistant seen or heard any man foreign to Queen's College. Either the intruder knew of some secret way to depart the college, or he was one of those who stood, gazing open-mouthed at me and Master John, pretending ignorance.

The provost puffed his way through the press of scholars behind Sir Jaket. As his chamber was upon the ground floor, and at the opposite end of the structure, he had not heard the ruckus when I first shouted for aid, then fell over the bench. He required of me that I relate again what had happened. I did, but when I completed the tale for the second time I asked that all depart. My head ached, as did my ribs. My vision was blurred, and I felt myself swaying as I sat upon the bed.

Wycliffe saw me lurching one way then another, and spoke. "Sir Hugh has been ill-used and must rest. All must depart. We will hear more of this and decide what must be done when day comes."

"Someone must remain to be sure an attacker does not seek Sir Hugh again," Sir Jaket said. "I will remain."

Master John agreed that this was a good idea. I thought so also. I had no desire to fling myself upon a hard-edged bench again.

I lay my head carefully upon my pillow, assuming that the night's events would drive sleep from me. Not so. My next conscious thought came as the skin of my window illuminated Sir Jaket sitting upon the bench, back against the wall. He would rise stiff and aching, I knew. But if no man had returned intent on doing me ill, it may have been his presence which deterred the rogue.

It was my intention to rise this day from my bed and attend mass at the Church of St. Peter-in-the-East. I had survived two assaults and I wished to thank the Lord Christ for His intervention. A cynic might say that I was alive due to the incompetence of the man who wished to slay me. But was it coincidence that I awoke in the night and needed to use the chamber pot? And was therefore my half-wakeful dozing at the moment some felon chose to enter my chamber with evil intent but coincidence? Bailiffs do not believe in coincidence.

So I rose from my bed slowly, to be sure, and drew on chauces and cotehardie. This awakened Sir Jaket, who could not have been in deep sleep, given his posture.

The awl which was meant to pierce my anatomy – why else would a man carry it to my chamber on a moonless night? – rested upon the table. My eyes and those of Sir Jaket were drawn to it. When Master John found it in the night 'twas too dark for an inspection, but now that sunlight was causing my window to glow, the thing might be closely examined.

The oaken grip into which the long skewer was fixed seemed nearly new. The wood was rough, not polished with use, and pale in color. Except for the area where the iron rod entered the handle. There I saw a dark circular stain, reddish brown in color. Blood?

Sir Jaket saw me peering at the awl and asked of what I saw. I handed it to him without a word, to see if he would come to the same conclusion I had. He turned the weapon in his hands, wrapped one hand about the wood, and pretended to thrust the bodkin into some imaginary target. When he tired of this he went to studying the wooden block again. The stain arrested his attention.

"Is this blood?" he asked. Although he had trained for battle, peace with France had kept him from combat. I had seen more blood, both fresh and dried, than he.

"Aye," I replied. "The blood of Simon Duby, or I miss my guess."

"What was the purpose for this tool?"

"Mayhap a carpenter would find it useful, or a cobbler or a glover. Someone who needs to make small holes in objects... leather and thin pieces of wood, I think."

I stood to make ready for Sunday mass, and the chamber suddenly came loose from its foundation. I swayed, Sir Jaket saw, and grasped me by the shoulders before I toppled to the planks. I had known I was about to fall and had aimed for the bed. Fortunately the knight caught me before I could discover whether or not I had achieved my goal.

"Master Wycliffe spoke true," Sir Jaket said. "Starvation will not improve your health. 'Twill be no insult to the Lord Christ if you consume a loaf and a cup of ale." He referred to the custom of neither eating nor drinking before Sunday mass. "You need to bolster your strength, and that will not happen on an empty stomach. Wait here. I will seek a loaf and ale at the kitchen."

What else could I do but wait? Whilst I sat upon my bed, the chamber remained fixed in place. I was not eager to stand and learn if I could make it wobble about again. The lump at the back of my skull was large and tender. Nothing about the sore had changed, but my headache was nearly gone. Either time or hemp seeds, perhaps both, had reduced the pain. Would it return if I stood and attempted to walk to St. Peter-in-the-East? I was not eager to find out, but I would worship this day if I could.

Sir Jaket returned with half a maslin loaf and a cup of watered ale. Wycliffe followed him into my chamber. I was embarrassed to eat before men who would not, but I did feel stronger after the brief meal. Strong enough that I was able to stand without the chamber spinning. Well, not much.

Sir Jaket would not hear of me attempting the stairs

alone. He grasped an elbow and when Thomas saw he seized the other. Together they steered me to the ground floor, out of the door and across Queen's Lane to the church.

Some churches provide benches for their older or feeble parishioners. St. Beornwald's in Bampton has a few. But at St. Peter-in-the-East the congregation is expected to stand. So I did. I noticed that Master John, Sir Jaket, and Thomas kept close watch on me, ready to spring to my aid if I seemed about to sink to the tiles.

Father Hubert's homily was brief. This was a mercy. I usually appreciate a priest who has some wise matter to relate and says it well, but this day I was pleased that the cleric seemed at a loss for words.

I was able to cross Queen's Lane without staggering, but Wycliffe and Sir Jaket kept close in case their stabilizing arms were needed. The longer I spent vertical, the stronger I felt.

We heard the trumpet sound for dinner as we entered Queen's. The cook had prepared fraunt hemelle. This is a popular dish among young men. I was sure that there would be none remaining for the poor, and that in the kitchen there would be a kettle of pease pottage simmering.

So long as I did not turn my head quickly the ache within my cranium was nearly gone. And leaving the refectory I was able to walk a straight path. I asked Sir Jaket and Thomas to meet with me in Master Wycliffe's chamber to plot what next might be done to discover a murderer.

"I thought," I said to begin, "that the torn and mended shoe would lead us to the man who bludgeoned me with a limb. But not so. Mayhap the pot missing from St. John's Hospital, or the awl, might show the way to resolving murder."

"Tomorrow," Wycliffe said, "we three will seek the

bronze pot. Together, as you wished. You," he said to me, "will remain here and rest. You seem to think yourself whole, but a blow to the head such as you sustained will not be soon forgotten."

"Are you a physician," I said, "to instruct me as to my welfare?"

"Nay. But neither am I without experience. I have seen a man fall and bruise his head with less damage than you sustained, yet he perished from the hurt."

"Master Wycliffe speaks wisely," Sir Jaket said. "We three will be your feet and eyes and ears for a few days."

"I am concerned that whoso tried to attack you in the night," Wycliffe said, "might return if he learns you are alone in your chamber."

"In the day?" I said. "Nay. No man would be so rash as to do so in the day."

"Not even a man who fears viewing the world suspended from a noose? Though if he is a Queen's scholar that is unlikely. The bishop will send him to serve in some dismal place. Scotland, perhaps."

"Attacking me whilst others are going about their daily business in Queen's would be a sure way to be found out. Even a dolt would see that. And as the felon is likely a scholar he will be no dolt."

"What if he returns again in the night?" Thomas said.

"I will sleep with my table drawn up against the door," I said.

I did. When I awoke Monday the table was against the door as I had placed it Sunday evening. I moved it to its accustomed place and was pleased to discover as I did that my chamber did not whirl before my eyes, nor did my head throb with the exertion.

Sir Jaket heard the hinges squeal when I opened my chamber door, and opened his own door to see what I was about. I told him I was off to the kitchen for a loaf and ale to break my fast. He insisted upon accompanying me. He would have grasped my arm when we reached the stairs, but I shook him off, complaining that I was no longer an invalid and would not be treated so. Nevertheless he stayed close.

We met in Wycliffe's chamber at the third hour. I felt strong enough this day to accompany Sir Jaket, Thomas, and Master John as they sought a bronze pot, but they would not hear of it. So a few moments later, when they departed Queen's College, I climbed the stairs – cautiously – and spent the morning dozing within my chamber. Other than the tender lump at the back of my head I felt no further consequences from being struck down. But I will surely try to avoid a repeat of the experience.

Wycliffe, Sir Jaket, and Thomas visited four inns and Balliol College before noon. They found large kettles in all five places, but those at two of the inns were of earthenware. The pot at Balliol had been in use there for many years, and as with the pot missing from St. John's Hospital, the owner's name was engraved upon the rim. This, I supposed, might have been newly added, but Wycliffe said the pot bore no sign of any other mark being scoured away. And Master John knew the provost of Balliol to be an upright man. If the Balliol pot was new to the college he would not deny it.

Of the bronze pots at the other two inns, one was likely too small to be the pot missing from the hospital, and showed no sign of any name being burnished from the lip. At the other inn the proprietor balked at allowing his kitchen to be inspected until Sir Jaket suggested that the sheriff might send a constable to ensure that the ale served there was not watered. It was, of course, as at all inns. But this persuaded the owner to allow access to his kitchen. The fellow possessed two bronze pots. Neither had any engraved letters on the rim, nor was there any indication that such inscriptions had been filed away. The morning had been a failure.

I said as much and Wycliffe corrected me. "Not so. We have learned where the missing pot is not. We now have five fewer places where it might be." He is an optimistic man.

Dinner that day was a pottage of ravioles, and again I thought it unlikely there would be any of the tasty morsels remaining for the poor. They must be content with pease pottage flavored with an onion.

Pottage. How many pots did the kitchen at Queen's College possess? I had used one, fairly small, in my experiment, but there must be others. The pot I employed was not large enough to boil ravioles for all of the scholars of Queen's.

When the meal was done I poked my nose through the kitchen door. I justified the incursion by seeking the cook and complimenting him upon his competence. The large kettle in which our dinner was cooked sat beside the hearth, the water within it yet hot and steaming. It had been swung over the fire by means of an iron bar fixed upon a hinge. An iron bail held the pot over the flames. There were no legs cast into the base. This was not the pot I sought. I did not believe it would be, but I was resolved to leave no pot unturned.

Wycliffe and Sir Jaket peered at me with curiosity writ in their eyes when I returned to the refectory.

"There are two bronze pots in Queen's kitchen," I explained. Then hastened to add, "Neither is the one we seek."

"We will visit Oriel and Merton and Canterbury Colleges this afternoon," Wycliffe said. "And St. Frideswide's Priory, have we the time. And on the way we may inspect a few inns along Fish Street."

"I will accompany you," I said.

"Nay," Sir Jaket said. "You are not yet strong enough."

"Not strong enough for a brawl, nay. But strong enough to seek a bronze pot. If we find it and the possessor will not tell how he came by it I will yield to you to persuade cooperation."

We found bronze pots in nearly every college and inn we visited that afternoon. And the priory. One inn possessed only an earthenware pot, and the cauldron at St. Friedeswide's was like the larger of the pots at Queen's; equipped with a bail by which it might be swung over a blaze, with no feet cast into the base. All the other kettles we inspected that afternoon had no identifying marks cut into the rim, nor was there any sign that such an identification had been polished away.

'Twas nearly time for supper when we gave up the search and set off toward Queen's College. I was weary, but made an effort to appear strong so as not to give Sir Jaket the satisfaction of rightly discerning my state.

Our path to Queen's took us between Canterbury College and St. Frideswide's Priory, to Merton Street. As we passed Grope Lane I glanced to my left and saw what I first assumed to be a heap of rags against the wall of one of the disreputable establishments found upon that street. But then the pile of rags moved. Another glance told me that what I saw was a human form wrapped within a tattered cotehardie. 'Twas a woman, and as I watched, she struggled to sit against the wall and clutched a mantle close to her.

Master John had been talking of the search to Sir Jaket and did not see me hesitate and peer down Grope Lane. Not immediately. But after a few steps he noticed I had fallen behind. Mayhap he thought I was fatigued. If so, he was not far wrong.

He, and then Sir Jaket and Thomas, followed my gaze. Shadow hid the woman, and her mantle and cotehardie were dark.

"What is there?" Wycliffe asked. The scholar's vision

is not good. Perhaps he has spent too much time closely examining his books. He took half a dozen steps into Grope Lane, then announced, "'Tis a lass."

The woman heard Wycliffe speak and turned her head to see who had appeared. Here was no lass. Her hair was streaked with gray. Her face was red and mottled, her lips blue, and what I could see of her neck was swollen and dark.

"'Tis the pestilence," I said. "Best not approach too closely."

"What is a dying woman doing alone on the street?" Master John said, then answered his own question. "Ah... 'tis Grope Lane. Well, we must not leave her to die alone. The Lord Christ told His disciples whatever they did for the least of folk they did for Him."

"What must we do?" Thomas asked.

The squire is fleet, as I was at a similar age before my Kate's cookery slowed my pace, so I told him, "Run to the hospital of St. John. Tell the warden to send men with a pallet. If he hesitates, say also we have spent the day seeking his bronze pot."

He had barely disappeared around the corner to the East Gate when the supine woman was wracked by a coughing fit. She slumped lower against the wall, and blood and mucus flew from her mouth.

"Approach no closer," I said. "The contagion has gone to her lungs. There is nothing to be done for her, and if your lungs become afflicted you will join her in the churchyard by tomorrow night."

Sir Jaket and Master John stopped where they were. They did not need to be told this, for all men know what will befall them if one so afflicted coughs in their presence. Occasionally, however, it is helpful to be reminded of matters we know.

Half an hour later Thomas returned with two residents of St. John's Hospital. One of these carried two poles with a hempen canvas wrapped about them. I did not wish to put these men at risk of their lives, so decided that when the stricken woman was placed upon the pallet I would cover her face with the mantle. She had not coughed since the fit shook her, but she might again at any moment.

I approached the woman and thought for a moment she had died, so motionless was she. But then I saw a slight rise and fall of her chest and realized she yet lived. Likely not for long. I directed the carriers to place the woman upon the pallet, covered her face with the mantle, and explained to the men why I did so. They nodded appreciatively. Together our party traveled to the East Gate, where I, Master John, Sir Jaket, and Thomas turned to Queen's and the men of St. John's Hospital carried their burden to the east. What comfort could the hospital provide for a sufferer in such a condition? Very little. But where else was she to be taken? I prayed the pestilence would not sweep through the hospital because of her presence, even if 'twas likely to be brief. The woman, I thought, would be dead by the same time the following day.

A queue of poor folk stood before Queen's College awaiting their allotment of pease pottage. The trumpet announcing supper had evidently sounded some time past, and by the time we entered the refectory the scholars had nearly finished their supper. We managed to collect bowls full of pottage before the leavings were taken to the waiting mendicants. When we four departed the refectory it was decided that next day we would again meet in Master Wycliffe's chamber and choose the colleges and inns we would visit.

I entered my tiny room. The awl which was intended to prick me to the next world lay yet upon the table in my chamber. Or so I thought. But as my eyes became accustomed to the fading light I saw that it was no longer there. Had it fallen to the floor? Nay. I bent to examine the planks under table, bench, and bed. The awl was not to be seen.

I castigated myself for not being more careful with the tool. If we had no success in seeking the bronze pot missing from St. John's Hospital I had hoped the awl might identify the man who employed it. How this might be I could not say. The torn and mended shoe had identified no malefactor, nor, so far, had a bronze pot been discovered which might lead to a felon.

I slept well that night, secure in the knowledge that no man would enter my chamber unless he could silently push open a door with squealing hinges blocked by a bench and table. I considered moving my bed before the door as well.

Chapter 10

"The awl is missing?" Sir Jaket said next morning when we assembled in Master John's chamber. I had but moments before told of its disappearance.

"Indeed. Someone crept into my chamber yesterday afternoon and made off with it."

"What could it tell of a felon?" Wycliffe mused. "I saw nothing about it which would lead to a murderer. Perhaps I overlooked something. No man, I think, would enter your chamber and risk discovery there except he thought the awl would give him away."

"Mayhap we should seek the provost's permission to examine all the chambers here at Queen's," I said. "'Tis unlikely some man not of the college entered to make off with it."

"I will seek the porter and learn if any man did," Wycliffe said. "Wait here."

Master John returned quickly. No man unknown to the porter had entered Queen's College yesterday afternoon.

"Your suggestion that we seek Whitfield's authority to examine the chambers is wise," Wycliffe said. "Come, we will approach him now about the matter."

The provost is not popular. He is not a Cumberland man, and the fellows from that county resent his authority. Most would be eager to replace him if it could be proved he was derelict in his duties. So when Wycliffe requested permission to examine the private chambers of all who resided at the college he immediately refused. No man, even the innocent, likes to have his belongings examined, and the scholars would lay the insult against Whitfield.

"Two of Queen's scholars have been slain," I said. "Most likely by one of their acquaintances. Some man would have murdered me in my bed. How will it look to men of Oxford if there is another death within the walls of Queen's College? Your governance will be mocked."

This was surely true and Whitfield knew it. He sat quietly, pulling upon his beard. "When would you do this search? And what do you seek?"

"Immediately," I replied. "We seek the awl that was intended to puncture me. 'Twas taken from my chamber yesterday. The porter claims no man not of Queen's entered the college yesterday afternoon, when it disappeared. So we believe some scholar of the college took it."

"Why would they do so?" Whitfield asked.

"Mayhap they used it to slay Simon Duby and intended the same fate for me. It may be that the villain fears there is something about the tool which may identify him. What that might be I cannot guess."

"Very well," Whitfield reluctantly agreed. "Shall I have the trumpet sounded so as to call the college together?"

"Nay," I said. "I wish no warning be given to any resident."

"Master Whitfield's suggestion might prove wise," Wycliffe said. "If all the scholars are assembled in the refectory their chambers can be examined without interference."

"Just so," I agreed. "We will do as you suggest. Have the trumpet sounded and when the college is gathered you may explain to all why they have been called together, and that they must remain in the refectory until the search is complete."

"There will be much anger," the provost said.

"It cannot be helped," Wycliffe replied.

Whitfield was correct. Queen's scholars were

incensed that their chambers were to be probed. I told Whitfield he should not say what we sought, and he did not. This caused even more discord as one scholar after another objected and suggested some malicious intent on my part. 'Twas their respect for Wycliffe which eventually brought the protests to a sullen end. He calmed the scholars and promised that care would be taken for their possessions. Clues, he said, were sought to help discover the felons who had slain Simon Duby. As Simon had been well liked it seemed to most of the scholars, after some thought, a reasonable thing to allow the search.

We decided to go separate ways to seek the missing awl. Four individual searches would be concluded in one-fourth the time otherwise required if we inspected each chamber together. The safety of an individual searcher did not seem to me to be an issue within the confines of the college. I hoped I was correct.

The search concluded within the hour. Sir Jaket found an awl and so did Master Wycliffe. Neither was the tool I sought. The bodkin of each was no longer than my smallest finger, whereas the awl intended to dispatch me was twice that length. And Wycliffe knew their purpose.

"These are used," he explained, "to prick out the measure between lines of a manuscript. The writer or copyist uses the point to make a tiny puncture on each side of the parchment, then with a straight edge connects the two. His script will then be fair and uniform on the leaf."

I knew of this use, and as it was sure that neither awl had been intended to be used against me or taken from my chamber I told Wycliffe and Sir Jaket to replace the tools in the chambers where they had been found. When this was done I returned to the refectory and released the impatient scholars. 'Twas by this time nearly the hour for dinner. We would wait to continue our search for a bronze pot or an awl till after the meal was past.

We visited Gloucester College, crossed the River Thames on Hythe Bridge and went as far as Rewley Abbey and Osney Abbey. On the return we questioned several innkeepers. Both abbeys and the college possessed bronze pots, and two of the inns. None were the pot we sought.

As always, the poor were queued before Queen's when we returned, footsore, to the college. There were yet some friaries – Dominican, Franciscan, and Carmelite – we might visit, and a few more inns. To what purpose? I despaired of finding the missing pot, of locating a man with a torn and mended shoe, or of recovering the missing awl.

I lay abed that evening – with bench and table against the door again, just in case – and despaired of discovering who had slain Richard Sabyn and Simon Duby. I awoke in the early morning, well before dawn, and considered my conundrum.

If the pot missing from St. John's Hospital had not been sold, where was it? Such a thing was too valuable to discard. Surely the man who stole and used it would seek to profit from his thievery. But would he perhaps be patient, knowing that selling the vessel immediately might lead to his apprehension? If so, where might the pot be hidden? 'Twas too large for one man to carry off unaided for any distance. Unless he was as burly as Arthur.

Arthur. I lost the thread as my thoughts went to my former companion. Where was he now? Was there a purgatory where he was atoning for past sins? Or was he in the blissful presence of the Lord Christ and the saints of ages past? I felt certain 'twas the latter, but even men most sure of their opinions are occasionally troubled by doubt. Mayhap doubt is the truest measure of faith. When doubt is overcome, faith is stronger. I must seek Master Wycliffe's opinion.

I fell back to sleep thinking of Kate and Bessie and John. The image was pleasing, until the specter of plague intruded. The Lord Christ told His followers they must not worry. Why would He so instruct them but that He knew they had in the past and would in the future? 'Tis not necessary to tell a man not to do a thing he is unlikely to do without the command. So I said a prayer that the Lord Christ would defend my family from the pestilence and finally fell back to sleep.

I met again at the third hour next day with Sir Jaket, Thomas, and Master John. Thus far none of my schemes had brought us closer to discovering a felon. I began to sense that my companions were losing faith that they ever would. Hardly surprising when I was losing faith in myself.

"Shall we visit the friaries today?" Sir Jaket said.

"To what purpose?" Wycliffe scoffed. Master John has often quarreled with the mendicant friars. He views them as lazy beggars. "They will pride themselves in having but earthen pots. Of course, if some man gave them a bronze pot they would accept it."

"But a man who stole a bronze pot would not likely give it away when his use for it was done," I said.

"Just so. There is a stolen pot somewhere near," Sir Jaket said. "But have we the wit to find it?"

"And if it is found, will it lead us to a felon?" I said.

"You may visit the friaries if you wish," Wycliffe said. "I will not. There is a disputation I am to attend this morning. My day will be more profitable here than examining the haunts of men who believe beggary the surest path to piety."

"I am beginning to think the pot is hidden, not sold," I said. "Whoever used it to distill saltpeter will sell it at some time, but I am becoming of the opinion that the man is wise enough to know that it would be a link to his wickedness if it could be identified whilst the evils are yet fresh in men's thoughts."

"Hmmm." Wycliffe pulled at his beard. "If I were the man, where would I conceal such a thing? 'Twould not be easy to do."

"Indeed. The warden of St. John's Hospital said 'twould hold sixteen gallons and weighed near forty pounds. No man would want to carry it far."

"I'd bury it," Thomas said.

"A worthwhile thought," I agreed. "Bronze is impervious to rot and rust, so a season in the earth would do little harm. If the man we seek decided to bury the pot, what better place than the wood, near to the hut where he brewed the saltpeter? He could sweep fallen leaves over the fresh-turned dirt, and would be relieved of having to carry a heavy pot any distance."

"But how would we find the thing if it rests underground?" Sir Jaket said. "We cannot plow up the forest seeking it. We'd need an army, with spades their weapons."

We fell silent, considering Thomas's suggestion and Sir Jaket's response.

"How would the felon find the pot after he buried it if he waited a year or two to recover it?" I asked. "He might, if he did not revisit the collapsed swineherd's hut, forget just where he had buried it. Would he not mark the place in some way?" I answered my own question. "Perhaps slash the bark on a tree, or dig his hole at the base of a rotting stump."

"Indeed," Wycliffe agreed. "But to find the thing, even if a suspicious indication were discovered, would require much digging."

"Mayhap not," I said. "If you were burying a pot would you dig a hole as deep as a grave? I would not. Why go to such an effort? Just deep enough to hide the thing, no more, then cover it with earth and last year's fallen, matted leaves."

"What is your point?" Sir Jaket said.

"We will go to the wood armed with a spade, a poker from the kitchen, and a mallet. If we discover near the swineherd's hut what appears to be a telltale sign, we can pound the poker into the ground a few feet. If a bronze pot is buried there the poker will find it."

"I will pound the poker into the soil," Sir Jaket said. "It might be wise not to exert yourself overmuch. I saw yesterday how, when we neared Queen's after searching all day, you stumbled once and your eyes seemed crossed."

I had thought none of my companions saw me stumble. As for my eyes, I cannot see them, so have no opinion as to their appearance. I no longer see two fingers when I lift one before my face, so there is an improvement.

"I wish I could explore the wood with you," Wycliffe said, "but 'tis near time for the disputation and I promised to attend."

"There are yet two hours 'til dinner," I said. "I will visit the kitchen and find a poker. You," I said to Sir Jaket, "seek the porter and learn if he knows where a spade and mallet might be found. We will meet before the porter's lodge as soon as may be."

The kitchen was equipped with several iron pokers. I selected the longest and hurried to the college entrance hall. I was at the door before Sir Jaket and Thomas, but did not have long to wait. They soon appeared, Thomas carrying the mallet and Sir Jaket a spade, which he held at arm's length. When he came near I learned why this was so. The porter had indeed known where a spade might be had. His brother, he said, had several. The brother was a gongfermour, which explained why Sir Jaket had not swung the tool over his shoulder. The spade was wooden, and had absorbed the fragrance of the substance to which it had been applied.

We immediately set off for the East Bridge, and shortly came to the wood where some man had laid me low. Without thinking, my hand went to the knot on the back of my skull. 'Twas smaller than a few days past, and not so tender. A man's body has a remarkable ability to heal itself, so long as its mending is not interfered with overmuch. Broken bones must be set, surely, and cuts sewn together, but surgeons and physicians must know their limits. Especially those who brew up cures for the pestilence, which they sell for much profit and no good purpose.

We wandered through the forest for half an hour seeking the tumbledown swineherd's hut. I knew where it was, yet it was only with diligent searching that we finally came upon it, so well did it blend with the surrounding vegetation. We split our party, and with each taking a segment we began to search the forest near the hut for some sign that would tell of a thing which needed to be located for some future discovery.

I had mentioned that the felon might choose a rotting stump as a marker, and there were several within twenty or so paces of the hut. Sir Jaket drove the poker into the ground near each of these stumps. The poker went easily into the soil, except for once when it caught an unrotted root.

We temporarily gave up the search and hastened back to Queen's for our dinner. 'Twas a fast day. Dinner was stewed herring with maslin loaves.

Master John went with us to aid in the search after dinner. Our party gathered curious glances as we marched past St. John's Hospital and across East Bridge: a man garbed as a knight carrying a spade, a gentleman carrying a poker, a youth with a mallet, and a bearded scholar.

'Twas no trouble to find the swineherd's hut after having located it but a few hours past. Again we divided the forest amongst our company and surveyed the trunks and rotting stumps. Branches fallen in winter storms would tell us nothing. We ignored them. No man would use such a marker. These limbs would be gathered for winter fuel in autumn and no longer serve as an aid to memory after a few months.

Wycliffe called out that he had found a suspicious scar upon a young beech tree. The bark was smooth except for a blemish which seemed fresh, about a man's height above the ground. Sir Jaket pounded the poker into the soil in four places before the scar, but there was no resistance to the iron shaft as it penetrated the soil.

We widened our search, and Sir Jaket drove the poker into the earth at several likely looking stumps. To no effect. After an hour or so of exploring the wood we had enlarged the examined area so that the forlorn hut was barely visible through the trees. I called for the others to return to the hut. We needed to re-examine our scheme.

"If the pot is buried here in the wood, which I am beginning to doubt, it will not be so far away as we have wandered in the search. 'Twill be closer, or not here at all. If the felon did bury it he would surely not go to the bother of hauling it forty or fifty paces away from where he had put it to use. Would he?"

"The farther away, the more difficult for the rogue to find whatever sign or stump he used to indicate the pot's location," Wycliffe said. "The pot is near, or not buried at all. That scar I found seemed likely to mark the place. I am disappointed that 'twas not so."

"Aye," Sir Jaket agreed. "When I saw it I felt sure we had discovered the pot."

"If 'tis a scholar who has slain two of his companions," I said, "he will be no dolt. If he was a simpleton he'd not be admitted to the college. I wonder if he might have left that scar on the beech tree, but created it with an indication only he would recognize. Let's return to it."

I examined the torn bark closely. Where the bark was stripped away I saw what seemed a straight edge, as would be produced by a blade applied to the bark. This was at the top of the wound. The bottom seemed torn, as if the bark had been peeled downward. A limb falling from a nearby tree would not produce such an unbent slash as appeared at the top of the scar. I pushed a finger under an edge of the torn bark and found I could lift it from the wood. Sap moistened the tear and my fingers. This wound was not old. I peered under the raised bark. I cannot say why but that I had become suspicious that the torn bark was the work of a man. Just under the raised bark I saw what an observer might think a worm's path. But worms will not make the sign of an arrow.

"What have you found?" Master John asked.

I lifted the loose bark further and said, "Come and see."

They did.

"Some man has carved an arrow with the point of his dagger," Sir Jaket said.

"Indeed," Wycliffe agreed. "But what can it mean? It points up, not down or to the side. And what appears to be the number three is also engraved in the wood."

"We tested the soil before this tree," Sir Jaket said. "Mayhap the arrow points to a place beyond, opposite the torn bark."

"Aye," I agreed. "Let's step off three paces from the tree opposite the scar and see what may be found."

The matted leaves beyond the tree seemed much like those covering the forest floor everywhere else. There was no visible sign that the earth under them had been disturbed. Thomas held the poker in position a few feet beyond the tree and Sir Jaket drove it deep into the soil. It met no resistance.

Until the fourth attempt. Sir Jaket had driven the poker perhaps two feet into the ground, about three paces from the tree, when his next blow produced a muted clang of metal striking metal. The knight raised his head and grinned, and Thomas dropped the poker and shook his hands. The meeting of poker and pot had stung them.

Sir Jaket dropped the mallet and took the spade from Master John. 'Twas but a matter of minutes for the knight to push away the leaves and ply the spade to the loose forest soil. When most of the earth was cleared away Thomas dropped to his knees and lifted the pot from the hole. 'Twas somewhat discolored and corroded from its stay underground, but was certainly the pot missing from the Hospital of St. John. Of that there was no doubt. "St. J" was clearly visible engraved upon the rim.

I had found the pot in which some man had distilled the saltpeter which ended Richard Sabyn's life. What good had the discovery done? When I first set out to find the pot I assumed it would be in some man's possession, or that of some institution, and the holders could be traced back to the man who stole it from the hospital for his nefarious purpose. But the earth beneath the trees of a forest could not tell me who had possession of the pot before it was buried.

'Twas just past the ninth hour when we departed the wood. Sir Jaket and Thomas carried the pot. The weight was not great for two strong men, but its rounded form provided no good handles. Master John carried poker and mallet, and I the shovel. This tool, after its use in the wood, was not so redolent as a few hours past.

We re-crossed the East Bridge, again attracting the attention of those who found it curious to see a knight and squire carrying between them a dirty pot. A few folk working the hospital garden stared as we approached the entrance. A sharp rap upon the door brought the porter. He took a look at the pot, recognized what it must be, and when I asked for the warden hurried off. He so forgot good manners that he left us standing at the door.

De Tyve appeared a few moments later and was effusive in his appreciation for the return of the vessel. Well might he be. The pot was well made and worth at least eight shillings. I explained where it had been found, and told him of the use to which I thought it had been put.

"Who has access to your kitchen? Can anyone residing in the hospital enter?" I asked.

"Nay. The door to the kitchen has a lock, else men would enter in the night and gorge themselves from the larder."

"But in the day the kitchen is open to any?"

"Aye."

"How many are employed in the kitchen?"

"The cook and two assistants. And a scullery maid."

"Do all of these have a key to the kitchen lock?"

"Nay. The cook only... and me, of course."

"Is your cook in his kitchen?"

"Now? Probably. Preparing tomorrow's dinner."

The hospital, I knew, provided no supper. Its residents, like monks, were supplied one meal each day. Which is why some appear before the door to Queen's College awaiting a helping of pease pottage for their supper.

"I would like to speak to the man."

"Follow me," the warden said.

The cook was a slovenly man. We found him ladling some unrecognizable gruel into two small pots set over glowing embers in a fireplace. Here was tomorrow's dinner slowly congealing. The cook's eyes fell upon his missing pot. He recognized it and his fleshy face split into a wide smile. Sir Jaket and Thomas set the vessel down before him, pleased to be relieved of their burden.

"The warden," I said, "has told me that you and he have the only keys to the kitchen and larder. Did this pot disappear whilst the door was locked?"

The cook looked to the warden as if asking permission to answer. I wondered why. "Aye, sir, it did. 'Twas 'ere one day, an' next morn, when I would've prepared canabeans, 'twas not to be found."

"Where is your key kept?"

"In me chamber."

"And where is that?"

"Just beside the door to the kitchen."

"Show me."

The cook glanced to the warden, shrugged, and led the way to a narrow corridor. The door to his chamber was three paces from the kitchen door. He pushed open his chamber door, then stood aside to allow me entrance. 'Twas well he did. The room was so small it was barely larger than a closet. A narrow bed and small chest were the only furnishings.

Just inside the door was a nail, and a key hung from it. A man who knew where the key was kept would need to open the door only wide enough to admit his hand. And there was no lock upon the cook's chamber door. Whilst the cook slept the key could be removed, the kitchen door unlocked, and the key replaced. And this might be done in little more time than it has taken me to write of the possibility.

When the cook inserted the key next morning and found his great pot gone, would he have noticed that the kitchen door was already unlocked? Mayhap not, unless he was an observant fellow. His manner and appearance did not say as much. Of course, the thief might have thought to relock the kitchen door after he removed the pot.

Could a scholar of Queen's College gain entrance to the hospital of St. John in the night? Not likely. And where would the pot be carried once it had been taken from the kitchen? I had convinced myself that Richard and Simon were slain by some man or men of Queen's College. I began to question that assumption.

Or did two men – or more – connive in the murders? If so, what connection could a scholar of Queen's College have with a resident of St. John's Hospital? A scholar would be more familiar with Bacon's writing which told of the explosive mixture than would a poor man dwelling in the hospital of St. John. Could such a pauper read Latin? Or English, for that matter? But could a scholar of Queen's gain entry to the hospital in the night and make off with a valuable pot? More questions. Few answers.

As we departed the kitchen I heard the warden berate his cook for leaving the kitchen key where it might be easily found. I suspected the great pot – and other kitchen utensils – would be more closely guarded in the future.

Supper at Queen's College was pease pottage flavored with a bit of onion. On a fast day one should expect nothing better – although Queen's cook occasionally found stockfish for his kettle. I thought our numbers at supper were reduced, and when the meal was finished discovered that this was so.

I saw Wycliffe in a brief conversation with the provost and shortly thereafter Master John approached me. "William Sleyt has taken to his bed," he said. "Whitfield fears plague. Will you see the lad? I know you are a surgeon, not a physician, but your remedies are as effectual as those of any doctor."

"Damned with faint praise," I replied. "My remedies save no man."

"Nor do those of the physicians," Wycliffe countered. "But your physics bring some relief to the dying. We all will someday perish. So God wills it. But He does not require that we die in pain. So if William has indeed fallen to plague, 'twould be a mercy if you could ease his distress as you did for Henry atte Brooke."

I followed Wycliffe to William's chamber. 'Twas as Whitfield had feared. Plague had once again visited Queen's College. The lad lay curled upon his bed, blanket drawn up to his chin as if he was chilled, yet his face was red and feverish. His neck, such as was visible, was swollen and already become dark.

"There will yet be some pottage," Wycliffe said. "I will get a bowl and see if the lad will eat."

I thought this a useless errand, for if Master John could get the lad to swallow a few spoonfuls he would likely spew them up a short time later. And this indeed was what happened.

"Perhaps he will take some ale," Wycliffe said, "with those seeds you crush and mix with the brew."

"He might. I have nothing else with which to relieve him."

I mixed a thimbleful of crushed hemp seeds and a small measure of dried lettuce sap into half a cup of ale, then helped Master John to prop the lad to an elbow so he could drink. Sir Jaket and Thomas had learned what we were about and peered through the open door.

Two things pleased me: William did not retch after swallowing the ale, nor did he cough. Had he done so 'twould be a sign the pestilence was in his lungs, and Master John and I would be in mortal danger if we continued to minister to the lad. He suffered from plague. Of that there could be no doubt.

Before I left his chamber I told William I would call upon him in the morning. Whether or not he would be alive then was another matter. The young and strong may fight the pestilence and linger many days before they perish. A few may even survive the fight. But only a few.

As I passed through the door I heard William call to Master John. Wycliffe looked to me, suggested that I and Sir Jaket and Thomas await him in his chamber, then turned back to the afflicted scholar.

A few moments after we entered Wycliffe's chamber he followed. "William wishes to be shriven," he said.

"I will wait here," I replied. "There are matters for which I desire your opinion."

The mended shoe, the missing awl, the found pot – none of these had provided information which could bring a felon to justice. If these did not, what could? Was I on a fool's errand, with only a slowly shrinking knot at the back of my skull by which to measure my failure?

I missed my Kate and Bessie and John, the more so because the pestilence had returned. Was it even now afflicting my family? If I gave up the search for a murderer and returned to Bampton could I protect them from disease? Nay. I prayed for them daily, but are prayers more effective if the subject is nearby rather than fifteen miles distant? What do a few miles matter to the Lord Christ?

Chapter 11

'Twas near dark when Wycliffe returned from his unhappy task. He lit a cresset, then sat heavily, as if the weight of William's agony rested upon his shoulders. He did this silently, then after a sigh he spoke. "You may return to Bampton and your family when it suits you," he said softly.

"Why so?" I said with a good deal of surprise.

"I cannot say. It is forbidden."

What had Master John heard in the last few minutes which he could not tell me, but which would allow me to quit the search for a felon? Did William know whom we sought? Did he tell Wycliffe? I understood why Wycliffe could not give me the name, but why tell me I need no longer seek the murderer? Unless William had confessed to the crime. Or crimes. Why else would the felon no longer be sought?

If the man who slew Richard Sabyn and Simon Duby now lay upon his death bed I could understand Wycliffe releasing me from the search. But if William had named some other, why should the quest be ended? Wycliffe might believe he could no longer take part, but would he not want the felon found out? It must be that William confessed to the villainy and sought absolution.

How could this be? William could have placed the explosive compound under Richard's bed and set it off, and he might have pierced Simon with a bodkin, but how would he steal a pot from St. John's Hospital, haul foul water to a wood, and boil away several hundred gallons of the water? The fish trapper had seen two men upon East Bridge. Was one of these William, the other Simon? Or did William have an accomplice who helped toss Simon into the Cherwell? And William's chamber was searched not many days past. The awl taken from my chamber was not within. There were surely many places where he might have disposed of it, but why take it? It could not speak his name and there was nothing about it which would suggest he had employed it to slay another. Or so I thought.

Mayhap William Sleyt was the felon who slew Richard and Simon, but I returned to my chamber unconvinced that, if so, he had acted alone. So as before I moved table and bench before my door when I took to my bed. Few men suffer harm from an excess of caution. Unless he be a swain who would wed a fair maid.

I awoke with the dawn, splashed water from a ewer upon my face, and was in the act of withdrawing table and bench from my door when I heard knuckles applied to it. 'Twas Master Wycliffe.

"William yet lives," he said, "but is in much distress. Have you more of the herbs you provided last night?"

"Aye. If you will seek ale I will crush some hemp seeds and meet you at William's chamber."

My supply of dried lettuce sap was nearly exhausted, so I added less of that herb and more of the hemp than I otherwise would to the ale Wycliffe brought. As before we raised the lad as much as we could to help him drink. But unlike a few hours past he was not able to retain the draft. He had no sooner rested his head upon his pillow than he spewed up what he had consumed.

Master John said nothing. He did not need to. His doleful expression spoke his thoughts. He nodded toward the chamber door, then stepped from the room. I followed.

In the corridor Wycliffe turned to me and spoke

softly, so the sufferer would not hear. "He is near death, I fear."

"Aye. Did you see the stain on his kirtle when we lifted him to drink? A buboe in his armpit has ruptured. When such a thing happens the afflicted will soon perish."

"Will you return to Bampton today?"

"Nay. I have promised to discover a felon and have not yet done so."

"But William..." Master John fell silent. He was about to say "confessed", I think, but caught himself.

"I pondered in the night over what you said last evening when you returned from hearing William's confession. You faced a quandary. If you sent me home to Bampton you would have as much as admitted to what William told you when he was shriven. But if you said nothing you believed I would waste time and effort seeking a murderer already in his grave."

Wycliffe turned away, as if he saw something worth examining on the opposite wall. "The seal of the confessional," he said, "does not permit even an implication of what the penitent said."

"You may trust me to remain silent, but I must tell you I do not believe William did these felonies. I thought on his guilt as I lay abed, and I believe he may be proclaiming himself a malefactor to protect another. Or several others. Mayhap he is in part responsible for the deaths of Richard and Simon. Mayhap not. But if not, he likely knows who is."

"So he has asserted his guilt to protect his fellows?" Wycliffe said. "He knows he is to die, whereas those who did murder may live if he takes their blame?"

"Mayhap."

"But to lie in confession is a mortal sin. Will a man send his soul to hell to save another?"

"Did William say he acted alone? Ah... you cannot say.

I suspect he did not. If he had even some small part in the felonies then his confession would be no invention."

Wycliffe did not respond. He did not want to betray the slightest confidence placed in him – although he had already done so, to his consternation, seeing no other way. Whether William Sleyt's confession was true or not, neither of us could say. Master John was willing to accept it. I was not, although I was tempted. To approve William's confession would mean I could go home. Where I would for the next fortnight or more fret that a felon had escaped the consequences of his wickedness.

"You cannot betray the seal of confession—"

"What? More than I already have?"

"Allow me to continue. If I speak to William alone and ask him what he knows, if anything, of the deaths of Richard and Simon, he may reply. If he is yet rational he will understand that speaking the truth will not bring him now to the attention of bishop or sheriff. If he is complicit in murder as he evidently claims, he will know that he will perish of plague before he could face an archdeacon's court. If he did not do murder, but is claiming guilt so as to free some others of due punishment, I will remind him that he should not approach the Lord Christ with a falsehood upon his lips. Wait here," I said, and re-entered William's chamber.

My logic might have persuaded the lad to speak truth had he been alive to hear it. When I approached his bed I saw no rise or fall of the blanket and thought immediately that he had died. A closer examination – but not too close – told me this was so. His mouth hung open, and a buboe upon his neck had ruptured, gushing pus and blood upon the blanket. I backed from the chamber. Wycliffe did not need to be told. I had entered prepared to reason with the dying youth. Master John had heard no conversation.

"Dead?" he said, and then crossed himself.

I nodded. The chance of discovering a felon was lost. Along with a mended shoe, a stolen awl, and a bronze pot shorn of its history, whenever I thought I had found a clue to the evils done in Queen's College the hint was snatched from me.

I sent Thomas to Father Hubert with instructions to sound the passing bell, then hurried to Henry Whitfield's chamber to tell him that he had lost another scholar. The provost heard the sad tidings, sighed, but gathered himself and when I left him was calling for the porter's assistant. No doubt he intended to assign the man the task of wrapping William in a shroud and finding bearers who would carry the corpse across the lane to St. Peter-in-the-East.

The passing bell echoed from the stones of church and college as I hurried to Master Wycliffe's chamber. My stomach growled in protest of its empty state, but I had no desire to break my fast. A cup of ale would be welcome, however, and when I arrived at Master John's chamber I found him pouring ale from a ewer into a cup. He saw the appeal in my eyes, for he produced another cup, and moments later a third. Sir Jaket had followed me through the door.

We sat upon benches and drank our ale silently, each of us seeking solace in our private thoughts. Until Thomas entered. As with most youths, for Thomas silence was an emptiness which begged to be filled. Even death could not still his tongue, although had he seen William's oozing sores from closer than the door the sight might have quieted his prattle. The lad chattered on about Father Hubert's concern that another Queen's scholar had died, and of the priest's preparation for William's funeral and burial. He had assured Father Hubert, he said, that William had been shriven.

Shadows passed Master John's door and Thomas fell silent. Finally. 'Twas the assistant porter and three others carrying the shrouded corpse of William Sleyt. We four rose and followed. We made a small cortège as we departed Queen's College and crossed the lane, and the bearers set William's corpse under the lychgate, where Father Hubert and a clerk were waiting.

As the priest spoke the funeral mass I heard from beyond the church the sound of spades applied to sod. Father Hubert did not tarry over the corpse, nor did any of the mourners want him to do so. He spoke no homily, and within a few minutes directed the bearers to lift the litter and follow.

The sexton and a servant were completing the grave as we rounded the corner of the church. William would await the return of the Lord Christ beside Henry atte Brooke, whose fresh grave adjoined the place selected for William. Father Hubert sprinkled holy water into the pit, William in his shroud was lowered to his resting place, and we of Queen's departed. I was troubled that the provost had not seen fit to honor his deceased scholar. But men worried about the pestilence will often think first of self. Of course, other than those willing – or coerced – to carry William to the churchyard, none of his friends at Queen's accompanied his corpse to the grave either.

Amongst those friends, I thought, there may be a felon. Or two. And did one of these find a way to enter St. John's Hospital unseen and make off with a heavy pot?

Thomas Rous, along with William, had been sent by Wycliffe to Bampton to ask my aid. I thought he might have known William well enough to know who the lad's friends were. If I questioned any he named I would be unlikely to hear a confession, but a bailiff learns to hear words unspoken and to read that which may be written upon a man's face. I resolved to seek the scholar.

There was yet an hour before the trumpet would sound for dinner, so we four sat in Wycliffe's chamber and discussed the role William Sleyt might have played in two murders. Master Wycliffe would not speak of William's confession even though he knew that cat was out of the bag. And if Sir Jaket and Thomas did not know this when the conversation began, they soon did.

The problem was that William had many friends. He was liked by all. Even Richard Sabyn, as caustic as he was with others, seemed well disposed toward William. So Master John said. Or as well disposed as Richard was toward any, other than himself.

A shout and thump and clatter of one object striking another interrupted our musing. Two men were arguing fiercely and blows quickly displaced words. I looked to Wycliffe and before I could speak he leaped to his feet and bounded to the door. Sir Jaket followed, with Thomas and myself a step behind as we raced up the stairs from whence came the racket.

Several doors to scholars' chambers were open, and wide-eyed faces peered from doorways toward the source of the uproar. The din came from William's chamber. Two scholars rolled about the floor, pummeling each other and upsetting bench, table, and bed. William's blanket, with caked blood and pus upon it, lay askew upon the overturned bed. William's chest, the lid raised, lay beside the upended table.

Wycliffe shouted for the combatants to desist. He might as well have commanded the sun to stand still in the sky. Come to think of it, the sun did stand still once many years past, although I suspect it will not do so again. Without just cause.

Master John cried out a second time for the combatants to cease the brawl. He stood directly over them so they could not ignore his words, and when they realized who it was who ordered them to halt, they reluctantly did so. Scholars do not study combat, so the antagonists had done each other little harm. One had suffered a split lip which showed a trace of blood; the other displayed a reddened cheek which, in a day or two, would probably turn purple.

The tumult had attracted Henry Whitfield. The provost stormed into the chamber just as Wycliffe had succeeded in ending the contest. One glance told him that two of his scholars had been at each other's throats. They were yet upon their knees and Whitfield commanded them to rise and explain their unseemly conduct. This they were quite willing to do. Both at the same time, as small children attempting to blame each other for some misdemeanor before an unhappy parent.

The provost, his rage barely under control, shouted for silence. Perhaps it crossed his mind that word of the fracas would eventually escape Queen's College, and those who heard of it would shake their heads that a provost governed his hall so loosely that his scholars would attack one another.

I had, of course, seen the combatants before, and heard their names. They were two of the secretive translators who, with Simon Duby and Richard Sabyn, had been setting down the gospels to English: Gospatric Map and Robert Talley. Here were two scholars who had been comrades at the same illicit business now exchanging blows. What had caused them to turn against each other? I was about to learn, but as with all such confessions much was omitted. When the pugilists fell silent, Whitfield spoke first to Robert and asked his version of the disagreement. He was eager to answer.

"When William took sick he feared pestilence, so told me that if he perished I might have his books and all else in his chest."

"Not so," Gospatric interrupted. "He'd not do so. We had an agreement that did one of us succumb to plague the other would have what the dead man possessed."

"When did you make this agreement with William?" Whitfield asked.

"When Henry atte Brooke died," Gospatric said indignantly. "Long before William fell ill." He scowled at Robert and folded his arms as if in triumph, the matter now settled in his favor.

The chest containing William's possessions lay open on the floor, between Robert and Gospatric. It was not overturned, in spite of the struggle which had upset other furnishings.

"We will empty the chest," Whitfield said, "and learn the value of William's bequest. Mayhap we will come to a compromise."

A compromise would please neither Robert nor Gospatric and the provost would, rather than solve this dilemma, add two more names to those hostile to his governance. I was only an interested observer to this squabble but was suddenly thrust into it.

"Sir Hugh," Whitfield said. "Empty the chest and I will make a division of William's goods."

I did so. The contents were what would be expected in any scholar's chest: extra kirtle and braes, a tunic and chauces which he wore before entering Queen's College, three goose quills ready to be sharpened, a small knife with which to do so, and a gathering of parchment of middling quality. A small leather pouch contained two groats, nine pennies, four ha'pennies, and six farthings. Resting upon the bottom of the chest were two books: *Elements* by Euclid, and *Perspectiva* by Witelo. I transferred each item to the table, which Sir Jaket had set aright. I assumed the books would complete the emptying of the chest, but as I set *Perspectiva* upon the table I glanced into the dark interior of the box and saw there a scrap of dark wool. The fabric was of little value, but the provost had requested I empty the chest, so I bent to withdraw it.

A patch of threadbare wool is soft to the touch. Not this wool. 'Twas wrapped about some firm but slender object. I set the cloth upon the desk and unwrapped the article within. An awl. I raised it for a closer examination, but already I was convinced it was the awl with which some man intended to pierce me, and which had been removed from my chamber. All in the room knew of the attempt against me, knew of the awl gone missing, and most knew I suspected it to be the weapon used to dispatch Simon Duby. Eyes widened and mouths dropped open. Those old enough to grow a beard stroked their whiskers thoughtfully. Wycliffe spoke first.

"'Tis the awl gone missing from your chamber, is it not? I'd never have suspected William of taking it, or of having a reason to do so. I fear I misjudged the lad."

When the awl was in my possession, before it was removed from my chamber, I had examined it closely. There was little to distinguish it from other such implements, no scars upon handle or shaft, but I had seen what appeared to be a stain where the metal entered the wood of the grip, and this, I thought, might be a bloodstain. Simon Duby's blood. The same stain was visible upon the awl I now held before me. Would two similar tools have matching stains? Not likely.

The provost divided William Sleyt's possessions equally between Robert and Gospatric, thereby earning the enmity of both. I did not place the awl upon the table and Whitfield seemed to forget about it as he apportioned William's goods. Gospatric and Robert exchanged foul glances as each gathered his share of the dead scholar's belongings.

The combative scholars made to leave William's chamber, but I stepped before them. Would friends become such serious enemies over a few pence worth of goods? I invited Gospatric and Robert to accompany me to my chamber, where I might speak privily to each. They seemed reluctant to do this, but Sir Jaket scowled and placed a hand upon his dagger and they were persuaded to accept my invitation.

If Gospatric and Robert disliked each other they would be willing, perhaps even eager, to accuse the other of malfeasance and felony. But neither did. This was a disappointment. Either they knew nothing of the other's activities, or they were indeed friends who had had but a brief falling out. Their responses to my questions did not make either option clear, but the latter option seemed to me most likely.

Queen's cook had no part in the business, indeed likely knew nothing of it, so the trumpet called scholars to their dinner shortly after this. I placed the awl in my pouch as we departed my chamber. 'Twas too long to fit entirely within the pouch, so the point extended past a corner flap which closed the purse. As I sat for my dinner the point rose and scratched my forearm.

Dinner this day was roasted capons, disjointed, and maslin loaves. Most of the conversation at table had to do with the morning brawl and I saw that scholars were beginning to take sides, some supporting Gospatric's claims, some Robert's. Of course this meant that the partisans of both blamed Whitfield for considering the claims of the scholar they opposed. The Lord Christ said that peacemakers are blessed. Perhaps in the next life. The provost was condemned by nearly all for his compromise.

Master Wycliffe spoke softly to me as we departed the refectory. "Attend me in my chamber."

I assumed he meant immediately, so followed him. Sir Jaket and Thomas had not heard this request, I think, but followed me. They probably wondered what was now to be done to seek a felon.

Wycliffe closed the door to his chamber behind us, sat upon a bench and motioned us to do likewise. "It is a violation," he began, "to break the seal of confession and speak of a man's sins to another. But I've not heard that to speak of what a man did not confess is also a transgression. William said nothing about taking the awl from your chamber, nor did he confess to attempting to use it against you in the night, or to piercing Simon Duby with it. William was, to my knowledge, a devout lad. He would not wish to meet the Lord Christ with sins unconfessed and unpardoned."

"If he did indeed slay Richard Sabyn," I said, "then some other is responsible for the death of Simon and the attempt on me. And if he did not take the awl from my chamber, someone else did and either gave it to him for safekeeping or placed it in his chest to implicate him. But why do so? There is nothing about it which will lead to a felon." As I said this I drew the tool from my pouch and held it before me. All present had seen it several times. It held no secrets from us. Or did it, and I was too simple to understand?

"When you asked to explore the scholars' rooms," Thomas said, "I was assigned William's chamber along with two others. I emptied the chest. The awl was not within, nor was the scrap of dark wool it was wrapped in."

"You are certain?"

"Aye. I even felt about in the bottom of the chest to learn if the maker had fashioned a hidden compartment. The odd thing about the chest, though, is that one thing I found within was not there today."

"What was that?" I asked.

"A sheaf of parchments, about two gatherings; not bound, but tied. Someone – William, I suppose – had covered each leaf with a small script."

"What was written?"

"Don't know. 'Twas Latin. I'm no scholar. I can read and write English, and make my way in French, but I have no Latin."

"And this bundle of parchments was not there today," Wycliffe said. "Are you sure it was William's chest where you saw them? Mayhap you have confused his chest with some other."

"Nay." Thomas seemed peeved that his report would be questioned. "'Twas William's."

"I wonder," Wycliffe mused, "if Gospatric or Robert entered the chamber and took the gatherings before the other arrived?"

"Why do so?" I said. "What could make two unbound gatherings of greater value than books or a purse full of coins?"

"What, indeed?" Wycliffe replied.

"And how did this," I lifted the awl, "come to replace the parchments?"

At its thickest, where the grip was affixed, the awl was about the diameter of my little finger. From there it tapered to a point nearly as sharp as one of the needles I use to suture wounds. If there had been at one time blood upon the iron it had been wiped clean, but the handle had absorbed some gore and the stain remained. The grip and bodkin were of simple assembly. A hole had been bored into the wooden handle and the shaft forced into the hole. What, I wondered, might I find if I separated the two parts? Nothing, most likely, but who could know?

I gripped the iron shaft in one hand, the wooden grip in the other, and twisted until I felt the iron come free of the wood. The portion of the bodkin enclosed within the wooden handle was lightly rusted. I scraped the corrosion with a thumbnail and was surprised to see letters materialize: an "M" and a "C".

Wycliffe saw me examine the haft and asked what

I had found. I showed him. "Hmmm. The initials, perhaps, of the man who owns this? Odd. Why hide the information where it might not be seen? And how did some man engrave the letters into the iron?"

"'Twould not be difficult," Sir Jaket said. "A smith could fix the shaft in his vise, then carve the letters into the bodkin with a point of hardened steel and a hammer. I've seen it done."

"When this was first made," I said, "it was not supplied with a wooden handle. If it had been, the owner's initials would have been engraved somewhere else, I think. A more visible location, where a thief might see and reconsider his intent."

"Of what good would it be without the wooden handle?" Thomas said. "A man could not force the point through leather or hempen cloth without doing injury to his hand."

"'Twas not made for such use," Wycliffe said. "My belief is that it was intended for a copyist, who used it to prick out the lines on his parchment. Only later was it modified for nefarious purposes, and the wooden handle contrived."

"Is there a scholar at Queen's whose initials are MC?" I asked.

"I've been scratching my head about that. No one that I know of. And I'm sure I know of all who reside and study here."

"What might have been written on those gatherings Thomas saw?" I said. "William was not one of those translating the gospels into English. Had he been, Thomas could have read what he found. Why would he keep something written in Latin hidden away?"

"Mayhap," Master John said, "'twas not in the chest to be hid away. Mayhap that was simply the best place to keep whatever it was. I suspect he had copied some work, or a part of some book he could not afford to purchase."

This was a common practice. Most scholars are too poor to afford more than a few books. So they rent the tomes they wish to own and copy them. When they have a few coins saved they may then see a bookbinder and have their work bound. Likely that was what Thomas discovered. But where was the work now? Had William taken the gatherings to a bookbinder, then fallen ill before he could retrieve the volume? Or had he given the pages to some other? Or did someone steal his effort whilst he lay ill? If so, 'twould be someone who knew what the gatherings contained and thought the knowledge valuable.

"Might the 'MC' refer not to a man," Wycliffe said, "but to Merton College? Perhaps the college possesses such things so that scholars and copyists will not need to purchase their own."

"How could we know?" I asked.

"The warden at Merton, John Bloxham, is a friend." Wycliffe does have a few friends in Oxford. "Shall we seek him?" he continued.

The shortest way from Queen's College to Merton College would take us down Grope Lane. This was a path neither Wycliffe nor I wished to follow, although I cannot speak for Sir Jaket or Thomas. The longer way around took but a few extra minutes, and along that route there were no serpents to whisper in a man's ear, nor tempting forbidden fruit to beguile a man's eyes. When we reached Merton College the porter recognized Master Wycliffe and was quick to send his assistant to seek the warden.

Bloxham greeted Wycliffe and asked how he might be of service. Master John told him, and I produced the bodkin for the warden's inspection.

"I've not seen this before," he said, "but if, as you suggest, 'twas used by a copyist I'd not be likely to. Our librarian would be the man to seek."

Only two years earlier Merton College had become the first of Oxford's colleges and halls to create a library, where its scholars might borrow books. Other colleges were now considering doing the same, if they could afford it. The stationers of the town would not approve, for then scholars would not need to rent set books from them.

"Come," the warden said. "I will take you there."

The room used for Merton's library was well lit, with four glass windows facing the south. Immediately under two of the windows two men bent over their work, copying pages of some text. When we entered, a third man rose from behind a table to greet us. The librarian. Opposite the windows the inner wall of the library was lined with books. More than a hundred, I thought, although there was no time nor reason to count. Here indeed was a boon to scholars and their learning.

"You will remember Master Wycliffe," Bloxham said by way of greeting as the portly librarian approached. The fellow did not seem as pleased to see Wycliffe as the warden had been. "This fellow," Bloxham pointed to me, "has a tool which may be ours. What say you?"

I held the bodkin before the librarian. He took it, saw the letters engraved on it, and spoke. "Wondered where this went. We had two, and one went missing more than a fortnight past. Giles and Henry have to pass the other back and forth. Where did you find this?"

I told him.

"Used to slay a man, you say, and would have been turned against a second?" The librarian seemed to move the bodkin away from him, at arm's length.

"You have no thought as to how this tool made its way from Merton College to Queen's?" I said. "Do others use such implements, or only these two?" I nodded toward the copyists, who had straightened from their labor and were listening to the conversation.

"All scholars of Merton have access to the library and may use its facilities," the librarian replied. "Some who borrow books take them to their chamber to copy. Mayhap the bodkin was removed for this purpose."

"Then how did it find its way to Queen's College?" I said.

The librarian's reply was to shrug and lift his palms. This was not an unexpected response.

Chapter 12

W e departed Merton College, leaving the bodkin but not the wooden handle. Both warden and librarian promised that they would seek the Merton scholar who had made off with the bodkin, but I had small hope of their success.

We were nearly back to Queen's when a past remark of Master John's came to my mind. He had said there was no rule to silence a priest from speaking about what a man did not confess. I reminded him of the observation.

"What is it that William did not confess which interests you?" he replied.

"Did he confess to bringing an oak limb down upon my head six days past, or knowing who did and protecting them?" If Wycliffe did not answer, the silence would be answer enough.

He did not respond for a moment, considering, I think, how close he might come to breaking the seal of confession without doing so. Then he spoke, and smacked himself aside his head. "I am an oaf," he exclaimed. "He could not have attacked you in the wood. He attended the disputation. You remember I could not search the forest last Friday afternoon as I was to lead a disputation. William was present. If any part of his confession was true it means he acted in concert with another."

"Or several others," I said.

A bodkin from Merton College, a bronze pot from the hospital of St. John, an explosive blast at Queen's

College, a blow delivered to the back of my head by a man wearing a mended shoe; one man could not be the source of all these, although one man might coordinate a conspiracy. Did William Sleyt assemble a company of men who despised Richard Sabyn? From what I had learned of Richard this would not be difficult. But what of Simon Duby? Might he have been a part of the plot against Richard? If so, why was he slain? And what had Richard's association with three others in translating the gospels to English have to do with this business?

Whilst studying surgery at the university in Paris for a year I saw a portrait done in small pieces of colored glass, cunningly arranged so that the lady was wondrously rendered. If I stood too close to the likeness I saw only the fragments of glass which seemed assembled in a random pattern. Only by standing away from the work could I see the lady's face. Was I studying each of the incidents too closely? Did I need to somehow back away, to more clearly see the whole?

The conversation continued when we entered Queen's College, but without my participation. I considered how I might step back from the scattered portions of the riddles before me, the better to see the entirety. But first I would consume my supper. The trumpet sounded as we four entered Master John's chamber.

The pottage this day was of peas and beans, flavored with bacon, and wheaten loaves with parsley butter. The cook had also found a wheel of hard cheese. We all enjoyed a fragment. I suspect the poor who waited at the gate did not.

The early summer evening was long and warm. I wished to be alone with my thoughts, so when supper was done I told Wycliffe, Sir Jaket, and Thomas that I intended to stroll Oxford's streets and try to make sense of the disjointed discoveries we had made.

"Try to avoid cutpurses," Sir Jaket grinned, "and louts who might aim a blow at your skull. You do not complain of a sore head, but I imagine it is. Your injury was less than a week past."

I promised to avoid shadows and the unsavory parts of town, then passed the porter's chamber and set off down the High Street. But rather than considering felonious events my mind traveled to Bampton and Kate and Bessie and John. Thoughts of my family crowded out Oxford's bustle. The spires, the colleges, the scholars hurrying to and fro – all these I saw but did not see. Walking Oxford's streets saw me as bereft of solutions when I returned to Queen's as when I had departed.

There was yet light entering my chamber window when I entered. On this Midsummer's Eve a man could seek his bed and rise from it whilst the sky was bright at both ends of his slumber. As darkness slowly settled over Oxford, bonfires began to appear in fields and streets. Youths tempted harm by leaping over the flames. Many wore garlands of rue, roses, St. John's wort, and trefoil, as these are thought to have wondrous properties, even allowing the wearer to see the fairies. When I had last seen Thomas he was chasing a laughing lass around a bonfire.

I sought my bed whilst the celebrations noisily continued. As with the past few nights I pushed bench and table before my chamber door, although I thought as I did so 'twas unnecessary. Unless some assailant had acquired a weapon to replace the awl. A club would serve. The thought caused me to reach to the shrinking lump behind my ear. As I did so my lowered eyes fell to the planks of the floor and I saw a small dark spot where a moment before the table had been. At first I thought it a stain, as if some man with a nosebleed had dripped his blood there. But under a table?

I bent to see the speck more closely and saw 'twas no stain but a hole, about as large as my smallest finger. I had seen such an opening not many days before. In Richard Sabyn's chamber. Under his blasted bed.

I put my eye to the hole, but whatever was beneath was dark. I had paid little attention to what might be under my chamber upon the college ground floor, but guessed it might be the refectory. There was a way to determine if this was so. I lit the cresset and moved it from table to floor, so that the flame was directly above the hole. I then moved bench and table from my door, went quietly to the stairs, and descended to the ground floor.

The corridors were quiet. Scholars had sought their beds even though the northwest horizon glowed with a soft pink light. I entered the dark, empty refectory and walked past tables and benches to the place I thought might be under my chamber.

My supposition was correct. I saw above me a dot of light from the cresset flame. Whoso had bored a hole here thought, I believed, that the opening would be under my bed, as with Richard Sabyn's chamber. They were wrong. The hole was more than a yard from the middle of my bed. But how would some man know even the possible location of the bed, unless he had knowledge of my chamber and its furnishings?

I returned to my chamber with a degree of apprehension. Some man with knowledge of Richard Sabyn's death now plotted the same for me. So I thought. This must mean that somewhere near was a store of saltpeter, sulfur, and charcoal. Unless the felon who slew Richard was now boiling away more of the water leeched through the droppings taken from Father Hubert's dovecote.

Would the malefactor wait for a thunderstorm as he had before slaying Richard? He might then wait many weeks. What if he thought I was near to discovering his perfidy? Would he try to blast me through the gates of pearl without waiting for a storm to disguise his deed? Why not? All associated with Queen's College knew that Richard's death was thought to be murder. A similar death would bring nothing new to that assumption.

Before I could be slain in such a manner the felon would need to enter my chamber and secrete within it a pouch of the explosive mixture. And he would need to insert a match of hempen cord infused with saltpeter through the hole in my floor. I could make certain that would not happen.

With my dagger I carved a small length of wood from the door jamb, then fashioned from the splinter a round section about the size of the hole. With the pommel of my dagger I pounded the dowel into the hole. This made some considerable noise and I thought it might bring Sir Jaket from his adjacent chamber. It did not, and the insert was so tight I was sure that to remove it a man would need to make as much noise as I had in banging the dowel in place.

"There is a conspiracy," Wycliffe said early Friday morning when I told him of the hole bored between my chamber and the refectory. "We must be cautious to whom we speak. Who knows how deep this swamp may be?"

"'Tis sure that there was more than one hand against Richard Sabyn," I agreed. "But was one of those also against Simon Duby? You said Simon was a quiet lad and well liked. Did some man use the death of Richard as a cover to slay Simon, I wonder, assuming all might believe the same malefactor did both murders? Or did Simon know something of the conspiracy against Richard, so was slain to silence him? The more who share a secret, the more likely one will say something which will lead to the felons. Mayhap Simon heard some words before Richard's death which caused him, after Richard was slain, to realize who the guilty were. One of them, perhaps."

"Simon was made to appear drowned," Master John said. "Do you suppose he was about to come to you with his suspicion?"

"Perhaps his slayer thought so. Whether or not he was, who can know? The bronze pot troubles me," I continued.

"Why so?" Wycliffe asked.

"How did some man remove it from the hospital of St. John without anyone seeing him do so? The cook, the warden, the porter... all claim they know not how the thief could do this."

"Claim? You sound skeptical."

"Bailiffs are always skeptical. Lord Gilbert did not hire me to be credulous."

"Well, at least no man will run a length of hempen cord through that hole in your floor," Wycliffe said. "You are sure the piece of wood you inserted fit snugly enough that it cannot be removed?"

"Aye, but the more I think on it, the more I believe plugging the hole may be a mistake."

"How so?"

"When the miscreant sees that his work is undone he will know I am forewarned that he may try to deal with me as he did Richard Sabyn. Mayhap 'twould be best to allow the felon to believe he has not been found out, so as to trap him when he attempts to destroy me as he did Richard."

"Such a scheme could be dangerous. Would you really use yourself as bait?"

"I see no other clear way to discover who slew Richard. At least one other was in league with William Sleyt, and mayhap slew Simon if William did not. I will be cautious, but for now I will return to my chamber and dig out the obstruction before dinner. The man who drilled the hole may look up to see his handiwork while he consumes his meal, and if he does I do not want him to see anything amiss."

"We must keep a sharp eye upon all in the refectory," Master John said, "to learn if any man spends time gazing at the ceiling."

"Indeed."

I used the point of my dagger to chisel away the wooden plug. I was somewhat concerned that there might be a scholar in the refectory seeking a loaf and ale with which to break his fast, so worked as silently as I could. A last splinter fell through the hole to the refectory, but 'twas small and I doubted it would be heard or seen.

Was more saltpeter being distilled? I sought Sir Jaket and Thomas, told them to seek a loaf with which to break their fast had they not already done so, then join me in Master Wycliffe's chamber. When they arrived, cheeks bulging with bread, I told them of the hole in my floor.

"You're sure 'tis not a knot hole," Sir Jaket said.

"Come and see," I said. Sir Jaket, Thomas, and Master John followed me to my chamber. I moved the table so that they might see the hole clearly.

"'Tis no knot hole," the knight said. "Now that you have opened it again how will you prevent some man from pushing a cord infused with saltpeter through it?"

"I will move the table each night so a leg is over the hole. But if there is no store of explosive powder hid in my chamber, placing a match cord through the hole will do the felon no good. For now, I'd like to explore the swineherd's hut where some man boiled away foul water to distill saltpeter. It may be that he is at it again, although he will know that I know where he has done so in the past, so 'tis not likely he will use the same location. If he is wise. But there may be some other place near the hut where he is collecting more saltpeter. If he needs more. I suppose it may be that he has enough remaining from slaying Richard that he can make another blast without a pot and fire."

Wycliffe was unable to search the forest that morning as he had arranged a tutorial with three students who sought aid in comprehending Boethius. I could sympathize with their puzzlement.

A light mist dampened our cloaks as Sir Jaket, Thomas, and I departed Queen's, passed the hospital of St. John, and crossed East Bridge. The unseasonably cool drizzle kept sensible folk inside, so we saw no man after we departed Queen's College. We went first to the decayed hut where a batch of saltpeter had been distilled in the pot stolen from the hospital. I did not expect to find evidence of the same process occurring again in that place, and did not. Even a simpleton would not return there knowing his method was discovered. But one must never disregard the possibility that a felon may also be less than wise.

I suggested that we walk the forest to the east about five or so paces apart. Close enough that if a man had been about some industry we would notice it. And close enough that a call for help from one would bring the others to his speedy aid. I wished for no more blows, to my skull or any other portion of my anatomy.

We walked silently to the verge of the forest, where the wood ended at Temple Cowley. We saw no sign of human activity. We reversed our travel and returned toward Oxford farther to the south, away from the road. All we accomplished was to become wet and chilled. I found no ashes, nothing of man's making. If the man who intended to place an explosive in my chamber was making more saltpeter it was being done far from his first location. And there was always the chance that he had produced more than he needed to slay Richard Sabyn.

'Twas near time for dinner when we crossed East Bridge and hurried past the hospital. My cloak was drawn up to my chin and as I glanced to the hospital I saw a man peering at our passage through the gatehouse door. When he saw me looking his way he ducked within the gatehouse. Why would he do so, I wondered? Who was he that he did not wish to be seen there? Did he know me? Did I know him? Is that why he disappeared so suddenly?

Across the road from the hospital was a grove of oaks, some of which were large enough that a man might hide behind them. I told Sir Jaket and Thomas to proceed without me – that I would explain why later – then left the road and concealed myself behind one of the larger oaks.

My intent was to watch and see if the man observing our passage would reappear at the entrance to the hospital, and if he did, could I identify the watcher and divine his interest? And mayhap learn why he did not wish to be observed peering at we who passed the hospital. I suppose most men would see nothing suspicious about some other viewing their passage, but bailiffs learn to be mistrustful.

I had not long to wait. Sir Jaket and Thomas had scarcely vanished past the East Gate when the secretive fellow reappeared. He glanced in both directions from the open door of the gatehouse, then studied the road between hospital and East Gate. He was evidently satisfied with what he saw, or did not see, for he left the gatehouse and strode off toward the East Gate.

The man wore a scholar's gown – black, not red as those of Queen's. Of course, a Queen's scholar may don a black gown when he departs his college. He must wear red only when within its halls. The fellow was tall and slender, and was attempting to grow a beard but with small success. Once he decided upon his course he walked quickly, turning neither to the dexter nor the sinister. I left the shelter of the oak and followed, curious as to where the young scholar might go and if his destination would tell me why he had not wished to be seen poking his nose out of the hospital of St. John's gatehouse.

There were others walking the High Street, so I slowed my pace to allow those to come between me and my quarry. When the fellow came to Queen's Lane he slowed his steps and glanced toward the college. Evidently he saw nothing of interest – Sir Jaket and Thomas had disappeared – so quickened his pace again.

At Grope Lane the youth left the High Street and sauntered past the tarts who called out to him. I did not follow, preferring to avoid the inconvenience required to fend off the strumpets who reside in that neighborhood. I watched the scholar turn to his left at Merton Street and thence disappear. Did he travel to Merton College? Why else go in that direction? But if the college was his goal, why not leave the High Street sooner rather than go a longer way around? Was he but tickling his fancy as the trollops sought his custom?

I turned on my heels and hurried back to Rose Lane, thence south to Merton Street. When I came to that thoroughfare I searched for my lanky quarry, but he had disappeared. Black-gowned forms hurried hither and yon, and mayhap one of these was the youth I had followed from the hospital. One tall scholar is difficult to identify from another, and half a dozen or so scholars who fit the description were about their business upon Merton Street.

A scholar from Merton College – so I supposed – from which the bodkin used against Simon Duby had come, had been skulking about the hospital of St. John, whence the bronze pot used to brew saltpeter had come. Was this but coincidence? Bailiffs do not trust coincidence.

From Merton Street I circled back to the High Street and Queen's Lane, hoping to arrive at the college in time for dinner. I did not, but as 'twas a fast day the cook had prepared a pease and bean pottage, and there was plenty remaining when I entered the refectory. Most were pushing back their benches, ready to leave. I had hoped to consume my dinner in company with those who regularly dined at Queen's, so as to watch for any man whose eyes might go to the tiny hole in the refectory ceiling which opened to my chamber. Master John knew of this intent, as did Sir Jaket and Thomas. I hoped that in my absence they might have observed some scholar or fellow or chaplain cast his eyes toward the hole. They watched, they told me later, when I had finished my dinner, but saw no man give evidence of interest in the refectory ceiling.

Sir Jaket was curious as to why I had sent him and Thomas ahead when returning to Queen's from fruitlessly searching the forest. I told him of the secretive face observing us passing the hospital, and of following the slender scholar to Merton Street. Master Wycliffe was present, and when I had related the event, spoke what I thought.

"The bodkin which may have been used against Simon Duby came from Merton's library. And the pot in which saltpeter was distilled came from the hospital of St. John. When the stink of a dead mackerel comes to my nose I know the fish cannot be far away. And the odor of something rotten is now strong."

"Aye," Sir Jaket said. "But does the stink come from Queen's, or the hospital, or from Merton College? Or all three?"

"You did not recognize the slender scholar you followed from the hospital?" Wycliffe asked.

"Nay. But if the scholars of Merton College were marched past me I might remember the face, though I saw it but briefly."

"That can be arranged, I think. We will seek John Bloxham and ask his cooperation. Today, while the face you seek is fresh in your mind."

The Merton College warden was amenable to our request and took us first to a chamber where many Merton scholars were attending a tutorial. There were nearly a dozen scholars present, but none wore a face I remembered. The warden took us next to the library, where four scholars pored over books and one worked at a copyist's table. I recognized none of the five.

"Are there scholars absent from the college today?" Master John asked. He saw from my blank expression that none of the fellows I had seen could I recognize.

"There are always a few about Oxford on matters of their own," Bloxham said.

"When these return," Wycliffe said, "send them to me at Queen's."

"I have complied with your request, Master John," the warden said, "because I know you and know you would not ask frivolously. But I believe I have cause to know why you seek a scholar of Merton College."

Wycliffe looked to me, but did not speak. Not with his mouth. But with his eyes and expression he told me the reply to Bloxham's appeal was up to me. The warden knew already of my suspicion regarding the bodkin from his library, so I kept this explanation brief, telling the man only that I sought a man whose behavior caused me to believe he might know of felonious deeds, and that some hours past I had followed the scholar from the hospital of St. John to Merton Street, where I had then lost the pursuit.

"The hospital of St. John, you say? Then you seek no felon," Bloxham replied. "Stephen often visits the hospital. His uncle is warden there."

"Robert de Tyve?"

"The same. Stephen is Robert's nephew and a Merton scholar. Tall and slender, is Stephen."

I was confounded upon learning this. Had it been my imagination that the youth I saw peering guardedly at me from the hospital gatehouse seemed guilty of something and wished not to be seen? Or had he but begun to depart the hospital, then been recalled, or remembered something he wished to do or say? Such an explanation would account for his appearance at the gatehouse, his brief disappearance when he saw me look his way, and his eventual reappearance. But it would not account for his scrutiny of the road before he departed the hospital. He most certainly wished to know if he was observed, and set off on the High Street only when satisfied that he was not.

"Your suspicion of the man you followed from the hospital of St. John was, it seems, unfounded," Wycliffe said.

"I am not convinced of that. You did not see his surreptitious behavior."

"True. But I have heard you say that the post of bailiff has caused you to be skeptical of all men until they prove themselves honorable."

"I admit the fault," I said. "Nevertheless, there have been occasions when my incredulity has proven accurate."

"Will you wait here for the warden's nephew to return?" Sir Jaket asked.

"To what purpose? The scholar will claim his appearance at the hospital but a visit to a well-loved uncle. Whether or not 'tis true who could gainsay?"

We returned to Queen's as the poor were beginning

to queue for their supper. We who dined in Queen's refectory gave up flesh on fast days, but for those at Queen's gate one day was like another: pease pottage with an onion or leek for flavor, mayhap with a handful or two of beans also ladled into the pot.

The pot. What better way for a man to gain use of a large bronze pot than to be the nephew of the man to whom it belonged? But once having it, why bury it in the forest? Why not return it when it was no longer needed? Because some way must be found to account for its disappearance and recovery. I had unwittingly done that.

Chapter 13

Master John, Sir Jaket, Thomas, and I were prepared to watch for any man who studied the refectory ceiling during supper. I saw no man do so, although I glanced to the tiny hole myself a few times. The aperture drew me like iron filings to a magnet. Whenever this curiosity overcame me I next peered about the refectory to learn if my interest on things above had attracted some other man's interest.

'Twas as I emptied my bowl that my sense of place was jarred. The hole which I had been surreptitiously observing was not where it had been when I first found it. It was an arm's length from its first location. A hole cannot move. 'Twas a new hole, different from the earlier. I was sorely tempted to study the ceiling where I thought the original hole was located, but resisted for fear my interest would be seen and noted by the felon I sought.

I lingered when the meal was done so as to inspect the new hole without attracting unwanted attention. Master John saw, and then Sir Jaket and Thomas, and hesitated also, 'til we four were the only occupants of the refectory.

"What do you seek?" Wycliffe said. "I saw no man study the ceiling whilst we ate. Did you?"

"Nay, but there is something amiss. Look to the hole." I pointed above my head. "What do you see?"

"The same small hole bored through the planks of your chamber floor... hold! What is here? 'Tis moved."

At these words the knight and squire stepped directly under the hole and gazed up. Thomas spoke.

"See where the hole was. It has been plugged so craftily that a man would not know 'twas there but he'd seen it in the past."

"We must inspect your chamber," Wycliffe said, "to discover where the new hole emerges."

"I can tell you without going there," I said. "'Twill be found under my bed."

It was. Whoso had bored the first hole recognized their error and, whilst I was absent from my chamber, righted it. The original hole was cunningly filled so that unless a man knew where it was he might never notice the repair. I might not have seen the hole even before it was plugged except that I had moved the table before the door. The felon would not have known this, so now likely thought his new hole as successfully obscured as the first.

And it was placed like another hole, found beneath Richard Sabyn's bed, through which a saltpeter infused cord had set off an explosive pouch and blasted Richard through the gates of pearl. This was the destination in mind for me, I was sure. I devoutly wish to pass through those gates. But not yet. Some day, when my vision is dim and my joints ache and folk must shout in my ear to make themselves heard, then I will be content to join the Lord Christ.

"What will you do about this?" Sir Jaket said. "'Tis clear some man intends to slay you, and he is surely the man who slew that obnoxious scholar."

"You intend to offer yourself as bait?" Wycliffe said. "Is this yet your scheme?"

"If anything is done which would tell the culprit his plan is uncovered I will miss the chance to solve a murder. Perhaps two."

"You intend to sleep this night in your chamber?" Master John asked.

"No harm can come to me tonight. There is no pouch of explosive under my bed, and no way for any man to place one there so long as we are present. As before I will move bench and table before the door so no man can enter in the night and hide the powder whilst I sleep."

"You cannot remain in your chamber all of the day," Wycliffe said, "to keep the villain from hiding the explosive substance under your bed. I suppose we could create a rota, so that one of us is here in the chamber all the while."

"Nay. We would never catch the miserable fellow should we do that. We must allow him to enter and do the evil he has planned. Well, not all of what he has planned."

"To bore holes in the floor of your chamber means the miscreant is surely of Queen's College," Wycliffe said. "Yet the bodkin from Merton's library and the conveniently missing pot speak of a conspiracy which includes two colleges and mayhap the hospital of St. John."

"And," I reminded him, "Simon Duby was one of a group secretly translating the gospels to English. Would so doing get a man killed if his activity became known?"

There were yet several hours before darkness would envelop Oxford. I decided to put the daylight to good use and visit the cook at the hospital of St. John. I doubted he had knowingly provided his pot to Stephen de Tyve, but he might, if properly prodded, remember something about the day it went missing which would cast some light upon the warden's actions at the time.

I took Sir Jaket and Thomas with me. Wycliffe begged to be allowed to remain at Queen's. Who am I that Master Wycliffe would ask my sufferance to do anything? While there was yet light, he said, he wished to complete a reading of St. Paul's Epistle to the Ephesians.

"I fear," he said, "that I approach the age when candles and cressets will no longer cut the gloom enough for my eyes to read what is upon a page. But I would learn of your discovery as soon as you return from the hospital."

The poor folk who queued at Queen's College gate were gone, and the High Street was nearly bare of traffic when we set off for the hospital. The porter recognized me and before I could ask said he would seek the warden and return anon. I quickly disabused him of my intent, and told him I desired to meet with the hospital cook, in his chamber, not there at the hospital entrance.

The corridor leading to the kitchen and the cook's chamber was becoming dim as the porter's assistant showed the way. A scullery maid was completing the scrubbing of the great bronze pot as I passed the kitchen doorway. She glanced up, wiped a hank of hair back under her wimple, and continued her labor. The hospital served its inhabitants no supper. Had the lass been at the work since dinner? Mayhap. A thick gruel can be as difficult to remove as the best hide glue.

The porter's assistant pointed to the cook's chamber door, bowed, then departed. I rapped upon the door, heard from within the scraping of a bench against the flags, then saw the latch turn.

The cook was not, I believed, pleased to see me. He had the door half opened, saw who it was who stood before him, and seemed to hesitate. Why? I had returned a valuable pot to him. Although the warden had castigated him for allowing the key to the kitchen door to be so easily accessible, this was not a fault which could be assigned to me.

The door was open far enough that I could plant a foot between it and the jamb. I did so, because the cook's expression said he would rather not have discourse with me. He had not seemed so obtuse the first time we met, when his pot was returned. What had transpired since to change his demeanor?

"You be him what dug me great pot from the wood," the man finally said.

"Indeed. Do you not fear it may be stolen again?" I replied, and looked over his shoulder to where the kitchen key was yet hanging from the nail. "Did not your warden tell you to safeguard the kitchen key?"

"Aye. But no matter now me pot's returned."

"Why is it you do not fear it will be taken again? Surely if it was so easily purloined once, and no changes have been made, it may be so again."

The cook shrugged but made no reply. I wished to speak privily with him, with no danger of being interrupted or overheard by some man traveling the corridor, so told Sir Jaket and Thomas to return to the passage, close the door, and allow no man to enter the chamber.

The cook's eyes widened and he glanced to my dagger, even though I had not placed a hand near it. Why, I wondered, did he fear me? His only previous meeting with me was when I had returned his pot. Had he been in conversation with some other man about my investigation of two murders? With the warden, mayhap? Why would such a conversation cause him to fear me? He was old and fat, whereas I was young – well, not old – and armed. But that was not sufficient to cause fear. Was it? I determined to find the reason for his anxiety.

When the door was shut I motioned to the man's bench and told him to sit. I have, in similar encounters in the past, learned that when an apprehensive man must look up to me as he answers questions he is more likely to speak truthfully, or give away his deceit with unspoken signs of lies.

I missed Arthur. I could rely on him to stand behind

me when I questioned miscreants. With his brawny arms folded and a frown creasing his forehead he could persuade most men to cooperate without himself speaking a word.

"Your warden," I began, "demanded that you secure your kitchen key so that the bronze pot, nor any other utensil, would go missing from the kitchen again. Why have you not done so?"

"Uh, like I said, saw no need. An' where would I keep it?" He glanced about the tiny chamber. Where, indeed. A bed and the bench upon which the cook now sat were the chamber's only furnishings. Mayhap the key could have been secreted under the mattress, or within an open seam.

I suggested this. "And why do you say there is no need?" I added.

"I know who took the pot. He'll not do so again."

A man could leave the hospital in the night with a large pot only if he had influence over the porter, his assistant, and perhaps the warden. Or if the taker was one of the three.

"Why did your warden take the pot?" I plunged ahead. "Did he ever tell you why he had need of it?"

The cook's eyes widened. "The warden?" he exclaimed. "Why would he do so?" From the cook's response I thought this a new and unwelcome thought.

"He had need of it. Or I should say he knew a man who needed it, but he did not want any other man to know of this."

The cook shook his head in disbelief.

"This is why, now the pot is returned, de Tyve does not berate you for keeping the key where he said you must not. He knows the pot will not go missing again, for he knows why it did some months past."

"Well... he's warden. 'Tis his pot, I suppose. Do with it as 'e will."

I could have told the cook the reason for his pot's disappearance, but I thought that if I did, there was a chance he would inform the warden of my suspicions. Until I had proof of de Tyve's complicity with his nephew in the making of explosive granules I would not cause the warden alarm. If I did so both he and the nephew and their confederate in Queen's College would hide their tracks. More so than they already had. Although, when I thought about it, I realized the cook would likely tell the hospital warden of this conversation. Nonetheless, I believed my questioning of the cook vague enough to not cast suspicion that I was on a murderer's trail.

I departed the chamber, collected Sir Jaket and Thomas, and in reply to the question in their eyes told them I would tell all when we were away from the hospital.

"Why would a Merton scholar want to slay a fellow from Queen's?" Sir Jaket asked when we were clear of the hospital of St. John.

"Richard Sabyn made adversaries wherever he went, so Master John said. He was not careful to limit his foes to one college, I suspect. Few men, Wycliffe said, could best him in debate, but he was not willing only to prevail, he must tyrannize those he overwhelmed."

"A reason to do murder," Sir Jaket said.

"Aye. Tomorrow I intend once again to seek the warden of Merton College. Master John will accompany me. The warden may remember some disputation, perhaps last autumn, when Stephen de Tyve and Richard Sabyn quarreled."

Master Wycliffe and I broke our fast with maslin loaves fresh from Queen's oven and ale gone stale, then set off in the cool morning fog for Merton College. Warden Bloxham is not, I think, a man who springs from his bed the moment dawn lightens the eastern sky. Well, neither am I. He was rubbing his eyes when the college porter guided us to his chamber, and he had not yet run a comb through his thinning hair.

"Last autumn, you say?" Bloxham repeated, pulling at his beard. "Stephen de Tyve is not a gifted scholar. He is generally bested in debate, so avoids polemics. He will go far. But yes, I remember a disputation shortly after Martinmas when Stephen was made to appear a dolt. I do not recall who it was who used him so. 'Twas not a Merton scholar, I believe. The disputation followed Aristotle's *Categories* and Stephen was so vexed he turned red in the face and left the hall. Some others laughed openly at his humiliation."

"Reason enough to wish a man dead," Wycliffe said when we departed Merton College.

"Aye, reason enough to wish it, but reason enough to see the desire become reality? If I knew this Stephen de Tyve well I might better be able to judge what he is capable of."

"Or who of Queen's College might prod him to act on his hatred," Master John said.

"Or who of Queen's Stephen might prod to do murder," I added.

Dinner at Queen's this day was a simple pottage of pease and beans, flavored with leeks and onions, as 'twas another fast day. No fish. Mayhap Whitfield had commanded the cook to conserve the contents of the college strongbox. Well, the poor who came to Queen's seeking supper this day would approve of the leeks and onions.

Sir Jaket, Thomas, Master John, and I kept an eye out for any Queen's scholar whose gaze might travel upward to the small hole in the refectory ceiling. We agreed after the meal that we had observed no suspicious glances.

215

Could it be that someone not of Queen's College had bored the hole? Or mayhap the culprit was a master of self-control.

"Have you looked under your bed since you awoke this morning?" Wycliffe asked as we approached his chamber. "You did not return there before dinner. It might be wise to inspect the chamber."

I agreed. We ascended the stairs to my chamber and I immediately went to hands and knees to peer under the bed. All was as before. The hole was visible, for the light streamed through the oiled skin of my west window, but there was no pouch of explosive granules near the hole, nor could I see any change in the dusty appearance of the boards under the bed.

I scrambled to my feet and blinked at the bright golden glow of the window. The brilliance of the oiled skin cast all else on the west wall to shadows. So I nearly missed the thin crack of light barely visible under the gleaming skin and frame. The window was apparently not fully closed. I wondered how I had missed seeing that, and hadn't felt the draft on a day when cold, wet wind would pierce the chamber.

I approached the window, which hung from leather hinges at the top and was closed at the bottom by pins on either side which penetrated the skin frame and the jamb. To open, the window was pushed outward.

The closing pins were withdrawn, so a strong wind could have opened the window. I had not removed the pins. We had enjoyed some warm days in the past weeks, but not so oppressive that I had felt a need for a cooling breeze.

Wycliffe saw me examine the withdrawn holding pins and divined the importance of the unsecured window. "You would not be frowning at the window," he said, "if you had withdrawn the pins."

"Just so. Although today bids fair to be a day when

an open window would be agreeable." I nudged the window open on its leather hinges and pushed my head under the frame and through the opening. The soil under the window was soft, and in the sun-washed earth I saw two impressions in the dirt about as far apart as my forearm is long.

I stared down the side of the building and Sir Jaket realized I must have seen something which caught my eye. "What is there?" he asked.

I withdrew my head carefully – the place at the back of my skull where I had received the blow was yet tender and I had no wish to thump the sore against the window frame. "Come," I said. "There are curious dents in the soil 'neath my window."

We four clattered down the stairs, circled the building, and approached the peculiar depressions in the dirt under my window. The stone wall was warm in the sun and the glare caused me to shade my eyes.

The indentations were clear. I stopped before them and my companions did likewise. I said nothing of my suspicions regarding the marks, trusting that Master John, Sir Jaket, and Thomas would interpret the depressions in the dirt as I had. They did.

Wycliffe looked to the soil at his feet, then up to my window. "Some man," he said, "has rested a ladder here. See where the rails have made dents in the earth."

"Look there," the squire said, and pointed across the college yard to the row of mulberry bushes which marked the limit of Queen's College premises. We followed his extended finger but did not see what had caught his eye. At least, I did not, and Wycliffe and Sir Jaket were silent as well.

"A ladder," Thomas said.

"Where?" I replied.

"Hidden in the hedge of mulberries, just there."

And then I saw it. 'Twas crudely made of old grey

lumber, aged so that it blended with the shrubbery in which it was hid.

The lad trotted ahead of us to the hedge and was about to pull the ladder free when I told him to stop. "Leave it where it is. The felon who slew Richard Sabyn seeks to do the same to me. He has prepared a hole for the match, he has gained entrance to my chamber and believes he may do so again when he will, and he has concealed the tool by which he will do this."

"Your window is not large," Master John said, gazing up at it. "Could even a slender scholar slip through it?"

"There is a way to know," Sir Jaket said, "if we move the ladder. Thomas is a lean lad. What say you, Thomas? Could you scramble through yon window? We could take care to replace the ladder just as it is when the experiment is done."

"I did not replace the fastening pins," I said, "so with a gentle tug the window should open. Are you willing to do this trial? That ladder does not appear sturdy."

"I'll take care," the lad said, and with those words he and Sir Jaket drew the flimsy device from its hiding place. 'Twas a matter of ten or so steps to place the ladder at the base of the west wall of Queen's College and shortly after, it was propped against the structure. Thomas scrambled up, the ladder creaking and swaying as he rose. He pulled the window open easily, soundlessly. Had the hinge been iron rather than leather 'twould not have been so quiet.

Thomas glanced down at our upturned faces, grinned, then plunged head first through the opening. The last I saw of him was his feet as he disappeared into my chamber. A moment later Thomas's beaming face appeared at the window. He seemed about to retrace his steps down the ladder. I told the squire he should return by way of the stairs within the building, rather than use the frail ladder. The lad is speedy. He trotted around the corner in little more time than it has taken to write of it.

"Would a man entering your chamber in such a way be able to do so quietly?" Wycliffe said. "If he tumbled head first to the floor after crawling through the window the thump might rouse you from the deepest slumber."

"He might, I suppose. But I do not intend to risk the discovery. I am willing to become bait to catch a felon, but not at such great risk. I intend to replace the fastening pins, and inspect them each night before I seek my bed."

"A wise decision," Wycliffe agreed. "I think no man will attempt to enter your chamber using this ladder during the day. He would likely be seen, and how would he explain his actions? All he need do in the day is prowl the corridor when he knows you are away. He may then gain access to your chamber unseen."

"Then so long as I keep a close watch under my bed each night, and make certain the fastening pins are secure in the window frame, I will be safe. Probably."

"Aye," Master John said. "Probably."

"But safety will not snare a felon. He will not know that we have discovered his plot, unless someone has seen us with this ladder, and I think not. Whitfield scheduled a disputation for this afternoon. Queen's scholars would attend, so mayhap no man has seen us investigating the ladder. So we must quickly replace it in the hedge, as it was, and watch in the night for a man who comes for it."

"The man may not come for a fortnight or more," Sir Jaket said.

"He might wait for another thunderstorm," Wycliffe added. "Although I see little reason why he would. All of Queen's know by now that Richard was slain. No bolt of lightning did away with him."

We replaced the ladder and retired to Master

Wycliffe's chamber. There we designed a rota to watch in the night for a man who might approach the hedge to withdraw the ladder. I desired to be part of the watch, but Wycliffe dissuaded me.

"You must take to your bed as usual. If some man is observing your activities they must appear normal."

"I am under scrutiny, you think?"

"No doubt. Mayhap we all are."

"I've not seen a man following me, or who seems interested in my actions."

"Have you been alert to such men?" Wycliffe asked. "You have been so intent upon discovering felons that you may not have perceived that the felons have discovered much about you."

"We are about to learn more of these felons than they will wish," Sir Jaket said.

"Felons, we say," Master Wycliffe observed. "We are agreed that a cabal slew Richard Sabyn, I think."

"And mayhap Simon Duby," I said, "but why they did so I cannot guess."

Thomas, being but a lad and likely less able to force himself awake in the night, was assigned the first watch. Master John provided him and Sir Jaket with old, threadbare scholar's gowns so they would blend with the night. A waning moon would not rise till well past midnight. Sir Jaket volunteered for the second watch, as Master Wycliffe said that he always awakened well before dawn, so the last watch of the night would suit him.

To disguise the fact that some man had departed Queen's in the night, Wycliffe would replace the bar to the door after Thomas went to his post. Then, when Sir Jaket relieved Thomas, the squire would replace the bar upon entering the building. Sir Jaket would do likewise when Master John took his place. If the felon put his scheme to practice he would thus find the bar in place when he crept from the building and not be alarmed that his plot was discovered. If either Thomas or Sir Jaket saw a man collecting the ladder he was to open Wycliffe's window upon the ground floor and seek his assistance in rousing the rest of us.

The porter might be troublesome. If he was yet awake when Thomas lifted the bar to leave Queen's, he would surely hear. We would have to trust that he and his assistant would, one or the other, be snoring loudly and muffle the scrape as the bar was raised.

This night would be one of the shortest of the year. This was good. Watch over the ladder would require no more than six hours, from dark till dawn. And the night would be balmy, so with Wycliffe's discarded gowns covering their cotehardies Thomas and Sir Jaket would be warm. Not too warm, I hoped, for Morpheus is more likely to seek out folk who are comfortable.

I was tempted to walk after supper to the hospital of St. John and hide in the copse across from the entrance. What was I seeking? I could not say, so gave up the idea and remained at Queen's as the sky turned from patchy clouds of gray amongst the blue to orange and pink and then a dull amber.

When my chamber grew dark I drew the fastening pegs from the window frame and quietly pushed the window free of the jamb. Thomas, Sir Jaket, and Master John had agreed that they would conceal themselves at the east end of the mulberry hedge, perhaps six paces from the hidden ladder. I peered under the upraised sash and stared intently at the place where I knew Thomas should be. I could not see him. If he was invisible to me, who knew where to look, I was confident he would be unseen by the felon I sought.

I lit a cresset, took one last glance under my bed – just in case – then reinserted the window closing pins, extinguished the flame, and slept soundly, bench and table shoved against the door.

This was a disappointment. When I rested my head upon the pillow I had hoped to hear a rapping upon my chamber door sometime in the night, and when I moved table and bench and opened the door, there would be one of my companions to tell me that some miscreant had dragged the ladder under my window and was even now mounting the creaky device.

But not so. We four gathered in Wycliffe's chamber at the first hour and the three watchers reported that the night had been undisturbed. The ladder was yet concealed in the hedge. How many nights would we have to wait for the villain to try his scheme? Would we wait for a thunderstorm? We might spend the summer waiting for the felon to set about his plot. What of Kate and Bessie and John? Should I take Wycliffe's advice and admit defeat? It seemed likely that William Sleyt was indeed guilty of participating in Richard Sabyn's murder, although he could not have acted alone. Was the discovery of one guilty man enough to satisfy justice?

We broke our fast with loaves, and ale which for once was fresh, then again met in Wycliffe's chamber before mass to examine our choices. We decided that we would continue the watch for a week, no more, and to provoke the felon Master John would draw the provost aside after dinner and tell him that we were near to discovering who had slain Richard Sabyn. 'Twould be no lie. We were surely nearer than a fortnight past. Near is a relative term. Mayhap the provost would let slip the news.

We attracted many sideways glances at mass that morning. Most parishioners at St. Peter-in-the-East knew why I had come to Queen's College, and assumed that, as I was yet present, I had been unsuccessful. There were whispers behind raised hands.

As before, while at dinner we four watched to see if any Queen's scholar raised his eyes to the refectory ceiling. And as before, none did. If the man furtively entered the refectory at some time in the day he could assure himself that the hole under my bed was yet there and thus might not be seen looking to it when others were present.

We enjoyed roasted mutton with barley loaves for our dinner, and when all were departing the refectory Master John touched Henry Whitfield upon his elbow. When he had the provost's attention he led him to a corner of the refectory and spoke quietly to him. Whitfield raised his eyebrows and whispered something, and Wycliffe responded with a shake of his head.

I departed the refectory before Master John and awaited him at his chamber door. I did not need to ask of his conversation with Whitfield. As soon as we four were in his chamber he closed the door and spoke.

"When I told the provost we were about to name the felon who slew Richard he asked why he had not been kept better informed. I told him we feared the felon might learn of our progress and slip the noose, so had spoken to no man, not even him. He then asked for a name. I told him he would learn of the man as soon as our proof was ready to take to the bishop. In the meanwhile he must not, I said, speak of this to any man."

"Which, of course, he will do," Sir Jaket said.

"I'm counting on it," I replied. "Mayhap not tonight, but soon the villain will seek to do away with me."

"Or give up his place and flee," Wycliffe said.

"He will believe he has two choices," Sir Jaket said. "Slay you, and mayhap me and Thomas also, or take flight."

"'Twould be easier to abscond," Master John said, "rather than to slay three more men."

"Not if he had assistance," I said. "And if he leaves Oxford under such a cloud he will know he can never return. The prosperous life he envisions will be ruined beyond remedy should he prove his guilt by fleeing the town."

"He might claim that he fled because the pestilence has returned," Wycliffe said. "I heard the passing bell toll from St. Mildred's Church this morning a few moments before the dawn Angelus. Of course, men die of many afflictions, but plague has returned, no doubt of that, and would be a good excuse for a man who desires a reason to withdraw from Oxford."

No man came for the ladder Sunday night, nor Monday night. I intentionally absented myself for much of the day Monday, unsure whether the felon would attempt to place a pouch of blasting granules under my bed in the day, whilst I was away, or use the ladder and enter my chamber while I slept. He had provided himself with two options.

Sir Jaket, Thomas, and I did our best to appear busy both Monday and Tuesday, even to walking casually past the hospital of St. John. I hoped to be seen studying the place, thinking that to do so might prod a worried man to action. A few days past I had wished not to be noticed. That was now changed. If I was to return to my wife and babes I must force the issue, or yield, admit failure, and return to Bampton under the cloud of defeat. I would then have to swallow my pride. This is not a tasty dish, but will not cause a man indigestion for long.

Tuesday evening became chill and wet. Rain fell so heavily that the queue of hospital residents seeking a pease pottage supper was half the usual number. Some folk would rather be warm and dry than have a full belly.

The storm provided no lightning or thunder, but because of the low clouds darkness came early. Thomas reported to my chamber that he was ready for the first watch and I nearly absolved him of the duty, so wretched was the weather.

A few moments later, whilst I was pulling my blanket up to my chin, I heard a soft rapping sound on my door, then Thomas whispered that I must come with him. I drew on my cotehardie and opened to the lad.

"What troubles you?" I asked.

"I went past the porter's chamber silently as could be, as in past evenings, and listened at his door. There was no sound, so I went to unbar the door, which I can now do in the dark, and found the bar already raised. Some man has departed the college in the night."

"'Tis not likely Sir Jaket or Master Wycliffe did," I said. "We have not changed the rota. But we should seek them and discover if one misunderstood some word of mine or yours."

They had not. Both were abed and had to be roused. I knew then who had departed Queen's College and what he intended to do. Wycliffe and Sir Jaket also understood immediately the implication of the unsecured door. They hurriedly dressed and we four made our way past the porter's chamber and through the unbarred entrance door. I gave thanks again that some man had smeared lard upon the hinges not many weeks past.

The night was cold, and rain soaked us before we had walked three paces. The downpour would mask our approach to the hedge, but would also deaden any sound the rogue might make as he dragged the ladder from its hiding place.

I stopped at the northwest corner of the building and held up a hand to signal to my companions. I doubt they could see it, so dark was the night, but they somehow detected that I had stopped and did likewise. I peered around the corner and held my breath so as to better hear the slightest sound. I neither saw nor heard anything. One of my companions stepped past me. I could not tell which. From their new position they had a perspective which would show the west wall of the college, had there been enough light to do so.

I felt a tug upon my sleeve, and then beside my head I saw the white of a hand. A finger extended toward the wall of the college. Then, from within inches of my ear, I heard Thomas whisper, "A man is about to climb the ladder." The squire's eyes, he being youthful, are better than my own. I followed the pointed finger but saw only darkness.

My vision may not be what it once was, but my ears function well. I heard, above the rain, a faint thud. I felt another form move past me. 'Twas Sir Jaket, although I did not know this at that moment. The black shape was instantly lost in the gloom.

A sudden shout shattered the silence, then a scream and the sound of a body meeting the earth. I rushed toward the sound, with Thomas and Master Wycliffe close behind – although at that moment I did not know who accompanied me. About five strides into the darkness I tripped upon some object and fell headlong. But not to the mud of the yard.

I stumbled to hands and knees upon two shouting, brawling men. I knew not who they might be, but thought it likely one was Sir Jaket or Master John. Likely Sir Jaket, as Wycliffe was not of an age to initiate combat with another. The second man under me must then be the felon I sought, but I dared not strike out for fear of hitting Sir Jaket or Thomas, whichever had entered the fray. Nor could I draw my dagger. I'd be as likely to pierce friend as foe.

Then, through the din, as I scrambled to my feet, I heard Sir Jaket shout, "I have the knave!"

I stumbled again, this time as the fallen ladder became entangled in my feet. I finally steadied myself and looked in the direction of the fight, which now, but for an occasional gasp, seemed over. I again heard

Sir Jaket. "We'll take this fellow to Master Wycliffe's chamber and light a cresset. We'll soon learn who we have caught trying to ascend to the window."

We stumbled to the entrance of Queen's, our captive silent in Sir Jaket's tight embrace. I thought he might protest innocence, but he was likely busy thinking to invent some excuse for setting a ladder against Queen's College under my window.

We came around the corner and heard running footsteps. "See there," Thomas said. "A man is running down Queen's Lane to the High Street."

"After him," Sir Jaket shouted.

A waning moon was rising, providing Thomas with some light. He darted off and I also gave chase. I did not see the man Thomas pursued, but I could see Thomas. 'Twas not easy to stay close to the fleet squire. Kate's cookery has slowed my pace.

The black scholar's gown flapping at his ankles did not slow Thomas. He tackled the fleeing fellow as we reached the church of St. Mary the Virgin. There followed a tussle in the mud, which I entered, and together Thomas and I subdued the rogue. I did not know who this captive was, but if he was escaping Queen's College just moments after we had snared a probable felon he was surely up to no good.

We returned, wet and muddy, to Queen's Lane and at the college entrance we found the porter and his assistant tending the unbarred door. Wycliffe, Sir Jaket, and their prisoner had roused them from their beds. They took a look at our bedraggled company and the porter said, "Master Wycliffe awaits in his chamber."

The porter had lit a candle and in its glow I saw that Thomas and I had Stephen de Tyve in hand. He was not eager to enter Queen's, but Thomas and I convinced him 'twas in his interest to do so. Thomas is not so proficient at such persuasion as was Arthur, but clever enough.

Master John had lit two cressets and he and Sir Jaket stood over a sodden figure seated upon a bench. I could not at first identify the man, but he turned to see who had entered and I recognized Gospatric Map. Here was the Queen's scholar who had intended to slay me.

The capture of Stephen de Tyve did not surprise me. The bodkin missing from Merton College library, his relationship to the hospital of St. John's warden, and the pot missing, then conveniently found, all pointed to his participation in Richard Sabyn's death. I could guess too what he was doing inside Queen's College in the night whilst Gospatric was placing a ladder under my window.

"Take a cresset to my chamber," I told Thomas, "and see if a match cord has been pushed through the hole under my bed."

The lad hurried away.

"Where is the explosive powder you planned to place under my bed this night?" I asked Gospatric. "'Tis a wet night. Where did you put it to keep it dry?"

"What explosive powder?" Map protested.

"That which remains since you slew Richard Sabyn."

"Richard died of a lightning bolt," he protested. "All know this."

"Nay. All know he was slain in a blast of the granules Roger Bacon wrote of nearly a century past. You intended to enter my chamber this night with another pouch of the stuff. Nay… do not trouble yourself to deny it."

I heard rapid footsteps approach and a moment later Thomas appeared at the door, a length of stiff hempen twine as long as my arm dangling from his hand.

"You," I looked at Stephen, "entered Queen's after Gospatric raised the bar, and inserted this match into the hole which enters my chamber from the refectory. What was the signal to strike flint and steel and set it alight?"

Stephen looked to Gospatric, shrugged, then said, "He was to tap twice upon the floor above the refectory."

"And then?"

"Gospatric would leave your chamber as he entered, through the window. The match cord was long enough he would have time to withdraw. We were to meet at the lychgate to the churchyard of St. Peter-in-the-East and wait in the church porch to keep dry. When the blast awakened everyone, Gospatric would mingle with the crowd whilst I went to the hospital and waited there in a shed for dawn."

"When you slew Richard Sabyn you were three," I said. "William Sleyt was the third. Did you," I turned to Gospatric, "convince the dying scholar to confess to slaying Richard, or did William do this on his own?"

"Don't know what you speak of. Mayhap William and this fellow were plotting together against Richard."

"Why do you dissemble so?" Wycliffe said sharply. "You were caught attempting to enter Sir Hugh's chamber in the night. Where is the explosive stuff you intended to place there? In a waxen pouch, I'd guess."

"I'll find it," Sir Jaket said. "He'd not be mounting the ladder without it." The knight jerked Gospatric to his feet and ran his hands over the scholar's chest and back. A moment later he drew a cord from about Map's neck and lifted a pouch which was suspended under the scholar's gown. He handed the pouch to me. Carefully. A flame is required to cause the granules to explode. There were two lighted cressets in the chamber.

I opened the flap of the pouch and found within a bundle wrapped in waxed parchment. I knew what I would find when I opened the sealed edges. The packet contained enough of the dark powder to fill my palm thrice over. Would this be enough to slay a man if it was detonated under his bed whilst he slept? 'Twas much more than I had set off in the college yard some while past, and that had left a cavity in the dirt more than an inch deep and larger around than my hands together.

Master John sought the porter and explained that we had apprehended two villains and required cords with which to bind them until the new day. Shortly after Wycliffe returned to his chamber the porter appeared with a length of hempen cord with which Sir Jaket bound the wrists of Stephen and Gospatric behind their backs. The knight then shoved them to a corner of the chamber where they sat disconsolately upon the floor. We watched over the captives for the remainder of the night, no one desiring sleep after all the success and excitement.

When dawn touched the tower of St. Peter-in-the-East Master John went to Henry Whitfield's chamber to tell him of the resolution of Richard Sabyn's death. I was yet troubled, for there was another death still unaccounted for. How had Simon Duby become involved in this matter? And did the scholars translating the gospels to English know of or have a part in either death? Nay, as I eventually discovered. Although bound together in a secret scholarly task, the instigation of Richard's murder came from another quarter. Gospatric's hatred of his fellow translator had nothing to do with their mutual endeavor of inscribing Holy Writ into the common tongue. But what of Simon Duby?

I decided to pretend more knowledge than I possessed and addressed Stephen de Tyve. I viewed him as the most yielding of our captives, and he had had access to the awl which pierced Simon. Neither Stephen nor Gospatric could have taken time from their studies to keep a pot of foul water boiling in a wood, but I had an idea of how 'twas done.

"When you stole the pot from the hospital of St. John how much did you pay the men you hired to boil water down to saltpeter?"

De Tyve looked to Map, sighed, then said, "Tuppence each week."

"And when you saw me pass the hospital you followed and laid a blow across my skull. Nay, do not deny it. I see your shoe." 'Twas the mended shoe I had seen before all became blackness. "But why did you slay Simon Duby? What had he to do with the three of you who connived at Richard Sabyn's murder?"

Before replying, Stephen glanced again to Gospatric as if seeking advice. He received none. Map looked away. "Simon overheard us speaking of our design. We did not know this 'til after we'd slain the scoundrel Richard Sabyn. He went to Gospatric and said we must confess our deed or he would go to the provost. We did not wish to slay Simon. He gave us no choice. This world is a better place now that Richard Sabyn is in the next."

"Did William Sleyt have a part in slaying Simon?" I asked. The fisherman had seen two men upon the East Bridge.

"Nay. We told him nothing of Simon. He did not know Simon had threatened to seek the provost."

"So you and Gospatric slew Simon and never told William?"

"Aye. No reason to. Thought all who learned of Simon's death would think he'd drowned. Didn't think any man would see such a small hole as the bodkin made. A man dead in the river has drowned. That's what all would believe."

"Many did."

Master Wycliffe returned with Henry Whitfield. The provost was not a happy man. The felons were his responsibility until the Bishop of Lincoln could send men to take them to an archdeacon's court. They would not hang for their crimes, but what remained of their lives, and that might be many years, would likely be unpleasant and remind them daily of their felonies.

My business in Oxford was done. I had no wish to stay in the town an hour longer. Master Wycliffe was quite able and willing to give evidence against Map and de Tyve in an archdeacon's court. My witness would be unnecessary.

Sir Jaket, Thomas, and I broke our fast with barley loaves and ale, set off for the Green Dragon, retrieved our beasts, and crossed Bookbinders Bridge before the third hour. Our palfreys and Sir Jaket's ambler were well rested, so we spurred them to an occasional trot and saw the spire of St. Beornwald's Church rise above Lord Gilbert's forest as the sun stood overhead.

I unfastened my instruments bag from the saddle and dismounted where Church View Street meets Bridge Street. I sent Sir Jaket and the squire on to the castle whilst I hurried to Galen House. Worry for my family had nagged me since leaving Oxford and I feared what I might find when entering my house.

I was relieved to find a loving wife and two healthy children. My Kate was pleased that I had returned, but unhappy that I had neglected her and Bessie and John for so long. I might have reminded her that, nearly a month past, she had urged me to accept Master Wycliffe's summons. But I did not. I know when to remain silent.

Before I departed Queen's College I had asked Master John to send word of the fate of Gospatric Map and Stephen de Tyve. Not long after my return to Bampton two scholars rapped upon Galen House door with information regarding the felons.

The archdeacon's court required the malefactors to stand at the porch of St. Peter-in-the-East for two consecutive Sundays and confess their sins to all who entered. Now they were walking barefoot to Lincoln. When they arrived they would be sent to a house of Carmelite friars in Scotland. Banff. There they would serve the friars as lay brothers. Winter nights there are long and cold and they will awaken in the dark with aching bones. Holy Mother Church hangs no man, but after a few winters purging themselves of sin Gospatric and Stephen may be agreeable to meeting St. Peter at the gates of pearl.

William Waraunt, one of Lord Gilbert's tenants, had died of plague six days before I returned to Bampton. I could have done nothing for the man had I been present to treat him. He was the third man of Bampton and the Weald to die of the pestilence, Arthur being the first, along with one woman.

Four days after Wycliffe's messengers returned to Oxford I was called to Father Simon's vicarage. His clerk told me the priest was ill and could not leave his bed. I took some pouches of herbs to the vicarage, but their purpose was to abate, not cure. Only one thing can remedy plague. Death is a hash physic, but never fails.

Mel Starr

WHAT'S YOUR NEXT
HUGH DE SINGLETON NOVEL?

The chronicles
of Hugh de Singleton,
surgeon

MEL STARR

Author of *The Unquiet Bones*

ISBN: 978 1 7826 4306 7

e-ISBN: 978 1 7826 4307 4

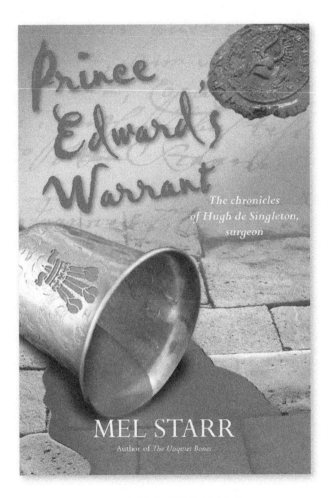

Prince Edward's Warrant

The chronicles
of Hugh de Singleton,
surgeon

MEL STARR

Author of *The Unquiet Bones*

ISBN: 978 1 7826 4262 6
e-ISBN: 978 1 7826 4263 3

Without a Trace

The chronicles
of Hugh de Singleton,
surgeon

MEL STARR

Author of *The Unquiet Bones*

ISBN: 978 1 7826 4267 1

e-ISBN: 978 1 7826 4268 8